I0763518

The Virtuous Feats of the Indomitable Miss Trafalgar and the Erudite Lady Boone

Geonn Cannon

Supposed Crimes LLC • Matthews, North Carolina

This book is a work of fiction. Names, characters, places, and incidents are products of the author's imagination or are used fictitiously. Any resemblance to actual events or locales or persons, living or dead, is entirely coincidental.

Published in the United States.

First Edition

ISBN: 978-1-938108-78-5

www.supposedcrimes.com

This book is typeset in Goudy Old Style, licensed by Ascender Corporation.

For once, an author has an answer to the question "Where do you get your ideas?" In this case, I had a dream about two treasure hunters stepping into an elevator with a bearded man. All three were weary, but as the doors closed the women looked at each other and started to laugh. The man just rolled his eyes. That was all I knew, beyond the added information that the characters were named Trafalgar & Boone. The image was intriguing enough that I took it to Twitter. Three of my followers picked up on it and, the rest of that morning, we tossed around ideas until I had the whole backstory ready to go. Without them, who knows if I would have stuck with it and created these characters and their world? So this book (and the series) is dedicated to them!

Alix Comeau
AJ Cousins
Melissa Scott

DRAMATIS PERSONAE

Lady Dorothy Boone....................an adventuress
Miss Trafalgar of Abyssinia...........scholar, explorer
Beatrice Sek..........................attendant to Lady Boone
Leola Kidane..........................assistant to Miss Trafalgar
Desmond Tindall.......................professor, suitor to Lady Boone
Ivy Sever.............................private investigator, thief
Threnody the Crafter..................designer of weapons
Araminta "Minty" Crook................captain of Skylarker
Felix Quintel.........................the enemy

Prologue

1899

Two boys sat on the divan in the Boone family parlor, spines straight and hats resting properly underneath folded hands. Theodore Weeks, Esquire, and William Anderson the Second smiled politely and nodded as they waited for the girls they had called upon to arrive. Mary and Olive, the eldest of the Boone girls, were upstairs preparing for their dates that evening. Elmer, the family's footman, waited by the door to chaperone the happy couples. Clara Boone, matriarch, smiled as she interrogated the boys, never giving them cause to believe she was seeking a reason to send them away. It appeared that they were 'suitable suitors', as her husband Bernard was wont to say, and she was extraordinarily pleased at the prospect of their girls finding happiness.

The calm of the moment was shattered by a sudden clamoring on the front porch. Clara Boone started at the ruckus but she composed herself before leveling a cool look at the footman. The set of his lips revealed he shared her irritation, and that he knew as well as she did who was responsible. He reached for the door handle to step outside, but the door flew open and the perpetrator swept inside like a small and surefooted wild animal. He was forced to take a step back so as not to get tail over teakettle as the ruffian dashed to the stairs.

Clara shot to her feet and bellowed, "Dorothy Boone!"

The whippet thin child froze where she stood. Her shirt, an inheritance from her older brother Bernard, was untucked and smeared with dirt and grass stains. The bright red hair their maid had spent so long braiding that morning was a maelstrom around her head. She had a smattering of freckles across her brow and the bridge of her nose, but a stranger would never be able to tell due to the mud smeared there. Most offensive, however, was the girl's lack of shoes and the trousers - also Bernie's - that were rolled up tight above her bare knees.

"What..." Clara looked her youngest child up and down. It seemed to be the only word she was capable of producing, so she repeated it. "What..."

Dorothy drew herself up to her full height, shoulders back and chin up. "Fierce creatures, mum. I've dispatched 'um."

Her mother bristled, her eyes flashing anger at the improper speech. "Young lady..."

She was cut off by a second rude arrival, a small orange creature that bumped the ajar door and flashed up the stairs almost too quickly to see. Dorothy twisted to watch the cat and already forgetting her mother's ire - or more likely deducing that she couldn't get into deeper trouble than she was already in - and pounded barefoot up the stairs in hot pursuit. There was a screech and a yowl from the second floor, a flurry of screams from the older girls who had apparently gotten in the way, and then a door slammed.

Clara, flustered, watched as the maid hurried upstairs to try and put a lid on the tempest in their teapot. The footman straightened his vest and looked at her, and then they both looked at the smears of mud that now marred their fine entryway. Crimson flooded Clara's cheeks as she turned back to the boys and forced a smile.

"That... was... our youngest daughter. Dorothy." She smoothed her hands over the front of her dress and took a seat. "I assure you, Mary and Olive are quite docile in comparison to her."

The boys smiled, but shared a sidelong glance with one another. Both were wise enough to leave their mutual thought unspoken, that sometimes docile was nowhere near as fun as unpredictable.

Dorothy's erstwhile nemesis, an orange shorthair named Jasper, was curled at the foot of her bed fast asleep by the time Grandmother Eula arrived that evening. Dorothy had been scrubbed clean and banished to her attic bedroom to await her punishment. She didn't mind missing dinner as she'd stashed a loaf of bread in her toy chest a few days earlier, and she welcomed the reprieve from socialization to spend more time with her books. She was dressed for bed when Eula knocked on the door and slipped inside. The older woman was Dorothy's hero. Mysterious and jovial, quick with a smile or a quip. She lived in London and seemed more amused by Dorothy's antics than most adults were.

"I hear someone was a bit rambunctious today," the older woman said with a conspiratorial smile. "Your mother said something about fierce creatures?"

Dorothy was seated on the floor in front of her bed, legs folded in front of her. She closed the book and puffed out her bottom lip. "I didn't mean to cause a fuss."

Eula walked to the window seat and eased herself down. She patted the cushion and Dorothy got up to join her. Jasper opened his eyes to see what all the movement was about, then twisted his head upside down and went back to sleep. Dorothy put her elbows on her knees and pushed at her cheeks with both fists. Her grandmother patted the top of her head and smiled down at her.

"I see you're still reading the books I got you."

Dorothy immediately perked up. "They're amazing. I can't believe all the other worlds buried under this one. Thousands and thousands of years of history and we're just looking at one tiny sliver of it. All these people who ruled the entire world and we don't know any of them. Ozymandias."

Eula and Dorothy intoned together: "'Look on my works, ye Mighty, and despair!'"

Eula laughed. "And one day our world will be dust, and some rowdy little girl will read about it when she's supposed to be getting punished. There are whole worlds out there waiting to be uncovered. Forgotten worlds to be dug up. Treasures to be gained, monsters to be vanquished. They'll wait until you're old enough to go find them yourself. Don't be in such a hurry to grow up, dear, and don't antagonize your parents with your pretendings. You'll need mummy and daddy to finance your real adventures." She tapped the side of her nose and winked.

Dorothy smiled. She threw her arms around her grandmother in a tight hug. "Thank you, Grandmother Eula."

"Of course, dear. Now your mother told me you were sent to bed without supper. That is only fair, I suppose. I hope you can survive your hunger until breakfast. Your mother made me promise I would not undercut her punishment." She reached into her bag and produced an apple, a banana, and a block of cheese. She tucked them under a pillow and shared a secret smile with her granddaughter. She kissed Dorothy on the forehead and patted her arm.

"Be good, Dorothy. For your mother's sake. And if you can't, be bad cleverly."

"I'll try, Grandmother."

When the older woman was gone, Dorothy retrieved the cheese and went to her bed to share some of it with Jasper.

Dorothy found balance on the top strut of the fence, barefooted so her toes could curl around the wood as she brought up her sword. The weapon was thick at the bottom to afford her a grip but tapered near the end to cause maximum damage. She thrust it at an invisible enemy and carefully advanced, sneering as she swayed back and forth to keep from falling. Below her Jasper hunted small creatures in the tall grass that marked the edge of their property. When he caught something, she congratulated him with a bellowing, "Well done, Sancho!" and declared a victory for their quest.

Out in the fields she recreated stories she read in books. Her parents had bought dozens of volumes to make the library look impressive for guests. As far as Dorothy knew she was the only one who bothered reading any of them. Once she had exhausted their shelves, her grandmother began bringing her new volumes from London. Her sisters rolled their eyes at her whenever they spotted a book tucked under her arm, Dorothy found comfort hunting giants with Don Quixote or exploring distant lands with Lemuel Gulliver. When she discussed the books with her grandmother, she complained that only the men got to go out and have adventures while the women were stuck at home.

"That's because the men do all the writing and make themselves the heroes," Eula said. "While the women are out having real-life adventures."

She showed Eula her sword-fighting skills, and the older woman surprised her by offering pointers. Dorothy watched with wide eyes and smiled when the demonstration was over.

"Where did you learn that?"

"I had a life before I settled down and started my family, you know."

Dorothy grew into a lanky and awkward young woman while her grandmother trained her to be more poised and graceful. They told Dorothy's parents they were meeting for dancing lessons, and Dorothy was surprised how similar dancing was to swordplay. She found that she could now hold her own at the balls her mother insisted she attend, and she found herself becoming stronger as an added incentive.

Time marched on. Bernard, the eldest child, began training to follow in his father's footsteps and learn the family business. A banker proposed to Mary and they vanished to start their own family. Olive soon followed, and her mother's matchmaking attention focused on Hilda. Dorothy, meanwhile, fast growing into a young woman herself, insisted on spending her time exploring the grounds. She drew maps of their acres, transforming the apple tree at one corner into a pirate cove. The cottontail rabbit's hole was the entrance to a den of thieves. She began wandering further, strapping an old broom handle to her belt to act as a sword, with Jasper trailing along to destroy any mice or insects that might attack her.

When she was fifteen her grandmother gave her an archery set. Dorothy kept Jasper far away from the range until she was confident with her skills, then she trained him to retrieve the arrows from the target. The feathered tips seemed to make him feel as if he was dismembering some sort of beast, and the arrows were always triumphantly left at her feet with fresh chew marks on their shafts. She alternated between training with her sword and her arrows until the muscles in her arms and back ached so badly she could barely get home.

One afternoon she was returning from her target practice with sweat dripping from her brow and grass stains on her bare feet. She trekked around to the back door in the hopes of avoiding her mother before she had a chance to wash up. If she could get into some clean clothes before their paths crossed she could avoid the lecture about how important it was to be ladylike. She was crossing the back porch when she passed the study window. She could heard her father's voice muffled by the glass but still loud enough to be heard. She slowed, then stopped completely when she heard what was being said.

"Hilda should have known better. We raised her better than that."

"There's no point in arguing about it now," her mother replied. "We'll send her to stay with my cousin Rebecca for a few months, and then the child can be placed with a good family. Have you spoken to the boy's parents?"

"I'm certain they'll convince him to do the right thing. It's unfortunate. He's hardly the sort we would have chosen."

Her mother snorted quietly. "He would never even have been in the running if I had my druthers. Honestly, what was the girl thinking? Sabotaging her future this way?"

Dorothy's skin had grown clammy. Hilda was pregnant. As bad as that might be for Hilda, it was even worse for Dorothy. If Hilda was going to be sent away then nothing stood between her and the matchmaking her mother certainly had in store. There would be boys, dinners, courtship. She felt her bile rising in her throat and dropped the quiver she had forgotten was in her hand. The noise startled Jasper and he leapt up onto the windowsill.

"What in blazes? Jasper?"

She turned and ran before her parents could make the connection between the cat's appearance and her eavesdropping. She ran, certain they were pursuing her with a veil in one hand and a ring in the other. She didn't even know why the thought of marriage worried her so, only that it brought to mind images of shackles and iron bars. The independence she enjoyed, currently tolerated by her parents, would be quickly snuffed by a husband who no doubt would have thoughts of an obedient chef and baby-making machine. As she ran, she wept hard enough that she couldn't see the road. Eventually she realized she would never be able to run all the way to her grandmother's house, so she turned back and walked slowly home as if it was a death march.

Her parents were waiting for her when she returned. "Look at you," her mother said as soon as the door closed behind her. Dorothy stood in the foyer, hands behind her back, waiting out the perusal and awaiting the sure to be harsh judgment. "I can't imagine the size of the dowry we'll have to offer to get a man to agree to marry such a mess."

Dorothy, who thought she'd emptied her eyes at the thought of marriage, felt fresh tears popping up at the implication she was unwanted.

"May I go upstairs?"

"By all means. Take a bath and put on proper clothes."

Dorothy went upstairs and stripped out of her clothes. She filled the bath and sunk down in the water until it was lapping at her lips. Her books remained untouched next to the tub untouched because she couldn't bear to be with her true friends at the moment. She stared unseeing at the tile wall in front of her, letting her hands float weightlessly in the water. She brought them up above the surface and looked at the small scrapes and callouses she'd formed while learning how to swordfight, and a smile spread across her face as she formed an idea.

One week later, her first suitor arrived. The footman announced Frederick Carney and Dorothy surprised the entire household by eagerly accepting his visit. He waited in the parlor with Carla while Dorothy did her hair and makeup, dressed in her finest outfit, and pranced downstairs to greet him. Carla smiled with genuine relief when she saw her youngest daughter dressed properly for the occasion. Her father was also present, and he smiled as Dorothy entered the room looking like a young lady for a change.

Frederick was tall and ginger, with a weak chin and a bulbous nose that made him look like a weathervane wrapped in a tailored suit.

"Good morning, Lady Boone." The tremor in his voice was almost adorable. "With your mother's permission, I would like to take you out to a picnic. Then perhaps a stroll on my parents' estate."

Dorothy had her hands clasped behind her back and spoke in her most placating tone. "Why, that sounds like a lovely plan to while away an afternoon, Mr. Carney."

Carla's eyes sparkled with surprise. She was no doubt wondering who this delicate flower was and what she'd done with her hellion. "Fantastic! If you'd like to leave at once--"

Dorothy held up a hand. "On one provision, of course. I won't be courted by any man who fails to meet one requirement." Her parents exchanged worried looks before she continued. "I will not agree to any excursion with a man who cannot best me in a duel."

Her father snapped, "For heaven's sake, Dorothy!"

She looked at him without emotion. "Papa, would you marry me to a man who couldn't defeat a woman in a test of strength?"

He started to respond but then realized the trap she had set. He clamped his jaw shut and stared at her with barely disguised fury. Frederick Carney, on the other hand, looked as if he was about to soil his trousers.

The poor boy looked at the elder Boones for assistance. "I can't... I can't fight a woman."

Dorothy smiled. "Ah, well. A forfeit, then. A shame. Elmer will show you out."

Frederick quickly retreated from the parlor. Dorothy watched him go, unable to resist a soft chuckle at her victory. She turned forward just before her mother's hand smacked her in the cheek. She recoiled in shock and took a step back. Her right hand balled into a fist but she fortunately managed to stop her initial reflex to strike back.

"I hope you are very satisfied." Her chin trembled, her eyes wide and wet with tears. "Do you believe this is a game, Dorothy? We are only trying to arrange for your future, and your attempts at self-sabotage have me at wits end."

"Then stop," Dorothy said. "Stop trying to arrange my life for me. I'm not Mary or Olive or Hilda. I will find my own way."

"Then you will not find it here. One way or another, you are leaving this house." She turned and walked away. After locking eyes with his youngest daughter for a moment, her father sighed heavily and followed his wife out.

Dorothy watched them go, then sank onto the divan to try to enjoy her victory.

The moment Eula heard about the eviction, she set out for the Boone estate. Dorothy could hear the argument echoing up the stairs. Several times her father shouted, "But mother–" only to have her shut him down before he could get another word out. Dorothy packed her bags, along with essential books from the library that she knew her parents would never miss, and waited. She would have been willing to leave Jasper behind - he was a mouser and needed the acres of the estate to roam, after all, but he climbed into her bag thrice despite her attempts to keep him away. She sighed and scratched between his ears.

"Fine. I suppose I shall leave this house tied to a man after all."

She was standing at the head of the stairs when she heard her grandmother storm out. Dorothy placed a wide-brimmed hat on her head, her brother's, but one he would never miss - and marched down the stairs after her. She knew her parents were watching from the parlor but she refused to give them the satisfaction of a final glance. They wanted her gone, and they were prepared to ignore her wishes to make it happen. She was simply granting their wish.

Eula didn't react when Dorothy loaded her bags onto the carriage and then climbed inside next to her. She settled in the seat and faced forward with both hands folded in her lap.

"You can still turn back, you know. It's not going to be easy and it isn't going to be fun and games all the time. I have rules of my own. Rules you may not agree with."

Dorothy said nothing. Finally Eula nodded and continued to the car. Dorothy followed, looking back at the estate only when they were far enough away she wouldn't feel its pull.

After the initial shock wore off, Dorothy discovered that living with her grandmother was the best thing that could have happened to her. Dance lessons officially became self-defense classes, and Dorothy didn't have to worry about explaining away bruises on her arms and legs. Most importantly she could now read whenever she desired, and her grandmother could retrieve books from the library for her. She had to adjust to living in town as opposed to their country estate, but Jasper still had three stories to explore. She often took him to a field outside of town where he could chase vermin to his heart's content. While she and her grandmother went for runs.

Seven months after Dorothy moved in, Eula started spending more time upstairs in her bedroom. She slept most of the day and was often too weak to make the trek downstairs. Dorothy would take her food and read to her until Eula said it was time to sleep again. One evening when Dorothy bent down to kiss her grandmother goodnight, Eula grabbed her arm with surprising strength.

"Go away, Dorothy."

"I... I thought you wanted me here, Grandmother."

Eula smiled. "I do. My only regret is not getting you out of that house sooner. Your sisters are discovering the mysteries of men, but you'll have your own mysteries to unravel. There are far stranger mysteries out there than any man could offer. Civilizations underfoot, wonders that you must see to believe... I saw them for myself, before I fell victim to..." She sighed and rolled her eyes. "Love and family and romance." She squeezed Dorothy's hand. "I don't regret my family. Not for an instant. But I do wonder what I left out there waiting to be found. And when I saw you, Dot, covered in mud and swinging an old broomstick like it was a broadsword..."

Dorothy laughed at the memory. "I still have that broomstick."

"I know. But you're a woman now. It's time to trade the worlds in your imagination for the real thing. Trust me, Dorothy. Oh, trust me, the real thing will be more amazing than you'd ever dreamt."

Dorothy blinked away her tears; it was obvious what her grandmother was preparing her for but she didn't want to face it. "Don't leave me, Grandmother. I'm not ready."

Eula patted Dorothy's hand. "What makes you think I am? That's the thing about our lives, Dot. We don't get to choose the most important parts of it. They just happen to us when they happen and we try to cope as best we can. When I'm gone..."

"No."

"When I'm gone," Eula repeated with more force, "I'm leaving you quite a portion of my estate. Some will go to your father, of course, but I've earmarked a certain amount that will be yours and yours alone. I'm leaving you a few other items as well, just to help ease you on your way, and all I ask in return is one promise from you. Don't get married before you're ready. Love is something that needs to happen gradually or not at all. You can be twenty, thirty-three, or forty-five. It can be forced and finessed, but it shouldn't be. Focus on knowing who you are before you find a man to write the definition for you. Be Dorothy Boone, not Mrs. Whomever of Wherever."

"I promise, Grandmother."

"Good girl."

Eula didn't live to see another month. The rest of the Boone family gathered at the funeral, together in one place for the first time in years. Her brother was a dashing man now, and all three of her sisters looked content in their lives. Hilda was toting around a fat baby, her second or third, and she smiled as it pulled her hair from under her bonnet. Happy, Dorothy thought with wonder. How could they be happy, keeping a home for their men, cooking dinners and hosting guests? Churning out fat little children who pulled hair and wept at the slightest provocation seemed to be the worst fate Dorothy could have imagined. She caught her mother watching her during the service and Dorothy nodded to her. Clara tightened her lips and turned away.

After the funeral the family met with the executor of Eula's will. All three of her sisters scoffed and tutted when they heard how much money Eula had left to Dorothy, but they weren't being left out in the cold. Everyone got a share, but Dorothy knew that her share was large enough to start a whole new life. She would be able to buy her own home, as it would be far too painful to remain in Eula's house. After that, she had no idea where she would go or what she would do, but the money provided her all sorts of options.

She was also given a key to a safe-deposit box at a London bank, and she set out immediately to see what her first real treasure would be. The corridor to the safe deposit boxes was narrow and high-ceilinged, and the thick carpet seemed to absorb every stray sound. It seemed to be a place of quiet power, the place where wealth was distributed and doled out to those lucky enough to be deemed rich. She wondered if she counted as one of their number. Lady Dorothy Boone of the elites. Imagine.

Her grandmother's key opened one of the largest boxes in the quiet room. She opened it to find stacks of foolscap bound together to form journals, each page filled with her grandmother's tight handwriting. Underneath the journals were larger sheets of vellum, and she chose one at random to unfold on the table.

It was a map. It took her a moment to orient herself, but the language and the sliver of water marked MEDITE RANEO indicated it was a map of southern France. The rest of the safe deposit box was filled with other maps in a variety of languages, and her hands trembled at the thought of exploring them all.

Clipped to the top journal was an envelope with her name on it. She removed it carefully and teared up as she recognized her grandmother's handwriting on the note within.

"I spent my youth collecting these maps. Some of them I edited myself. They will take you to remarkable places, and show you remarkable things, but my path is not yours. Don't echo my footsteps but use them as a starting point for your own trail. Go beyond the edges of the maps and forge your own trail. The world will never give up all of her mysteries, but it falls to women like us to do our part. I saw myself in you from the moment you escaped your crib and went exploring through the manor (though oh! How your parents fretted you falling down the stairs!)" Dorothy didn't remember that, but it certainly sounded like her. She laughed in the small room, and it sounded like a hollow bark as it echoed off the tall walls. "Take up where I left off, brave girl, and unveil the world's mysteries."

Dorothy carefully transferred everything to her bag. She paused to smell the maps, smiling when she caught a whiff of her grandmother's perfume. She imagined Eula packing these treasures away, could almost see her running unwrinkled hands over each journal before consigning it to storage, and she felt the torch being passed to her. She had no clue what work her grandmother had left undone and even less of an idea how she would ever follow in such grand footsteps. But thanks to her grandmother's legacy she had the means, and she would be damned if she let her grandmother down.

Ethiopia
1899

The tall girl was told she would be a nurse, an occupation that didn't excite her but was nonetheless respectable. It meant training and education that would be impossible to achieve in her home. She was the only child of a woman who had died giving birth to her, and whoever fathered her took the opportunity to escape responsibility by becoming invisible. She was an orphan, and any name she might have been given was quickly forgotten. There was every chance she was never named; girls in her village weren't given the luxury of names until they were older and it was clear they would live long enough to require an identity. Due to her height she was simply referred to as the tall girl, and she soon accepted it as a title.

When pale men arrived seeking volunteers, Tall Girl was one of the first in line. She had nothing tying her to the small village, and going out into the world would be a dream come true. The men were frightening strangers armed with weapons, but she suspected they threatened nothing worse than she feared from the men of her village. She was ten years old and the men were beginning to take note of her womanly shape in ways that made her run whenever she was out after dark.

The men chose her and a handful of other girls to be loaded onto a cart strapped to three lumbering camels. The men referred to her and the other children as Abyssinians. She didn't know what it meant, had never heard the word Ethiopia, and in her mind their word became hers. The men spoke English and she listened to them as they traveled through vast grasslands toward their destination. She tried to keep track of how far they traveled but she knew it was a pointless endeavor. Sometimes they tracked around foothills or lakes. Sometimes they would go north for five days to cross a river, then travel south for five more days to get back to their eastward track.

The other girls on the cart passed the time by chattering about the lives they were going to have in the new world. They would be nurses or governesses, things they had heard about in stories but never seen. They would be respectable ladies. Tall Girl didn't understand why they were so certain they would be chosen; they were unfamiliar with big cities like London and Paris. What respectable family would entrust their children to such blank slates? Who would pay for them to be educated as nurses or taught how to take care of a child?

When the caravan stopped for the night the girls would practice dancing for all the government dinners they would be attending. Only Tall Girl remained suspicious of the truth. She sat apart from the rest, tuning out their blabber and focusing on the guards. None of the girls could speak English so the men spoke freely. Tall Girl listened and soon she could work out their meaning from context or body language. Soon she could understand their meaning if not the full content of their conversation.

She watched the men standing on the perimeter of their camp. They carried guns ostensibly to protect from wolves and leopards, but she saw that they mostly kept their eyes on the caravan instead of the wilderness. They were preventing the girls from running away. If what they offered was so great, why would they worry about runaways? One man named Clayton Lee noticed she was attempting to learn their language, and some nights he gave her short lessons. She was worried he would want something nasty in return, but he never forced himself on her.

"Where do we go?" she asked one night.

"A place called Djibouti. It's about two hundred more miles that way." He pointed off into the darkness. Tall Girl couldn't even comprehend two hundred miles as a real distance, let alone one she would have to cross. "Two hundred miles is what we've already crossed. This spot of land is as far from your home as our destination is. Once we get there, we're getting on a boat."

She furrowed her brow and he mimed water with one hand. He used the other hand to cut across it. "A boat, to cross a great body of water. As much water as there is land around us right now."

Tall Girl knew he was lying. There was nowhere with that much water. She decided not to press the issue. "And then?"

He chewed carefully, thoughtfully, and kept his eyes on the fire rather than looking at her.

"Not nurses," she said.

"No. Probably not."

Once they crossed the border into Djibouti, their escorts relaxed the pretense of being kindly guides. They were rougher, meaner, cruder, and they gave the girls less food at their increasingly rare rest stops. The laughing chatter ceased, and the girls became quietly frightened. Tall Girl sat with her back against the wall just behind the drivers so she could listen to their conversations. Clayton hadn't told anyone about their lessons and she never spoke English where anyone but him could hear. She quickly learned what was in store for them, and she hugged herself against the chill that settled over her.

When they arrived at the docks their fright faded at the magnificent revelation of Arabian Sea. Tall Girl had never seen so much water in her entire life. For a moment she believed some seam had been ripped open and a flood had poured forth from the belly of the earth. The men herded her and the girls she now considered sisters out of the cart and into a long line. Tall Girl's entire body ached from the cramped conditions. She was hungry and sore, so when a guard passed her it wasn't difficult to fake a collapse. She slumped against him like a rag doll, her cheek flattened against the chest of his uniform. One button pressed against her cheek before he yanked her back by twisting a handful of her long, thick hair. He called her a word that she'd heard many times on their cross-country trek but that Clayton would never translate for her.

She smiled and winked, pursing her lips in a lazy kiss.

He sneered at her. "Save it for your new master. They like to break in the new ones themselves."

As he shoved her away, she folded one hand around his gun and the other around the hilt of his knife. His push was all the force she needed to free the weapons. His eyes widened when he realized he'd been disarmed. He reached for her and she swung the knife. A fan of blood spilled from his palm and he shrieked in pain and shock. Someone else tried to grab her and Tall Girl's finger tightened on the trigger. She only intended to shoot at the ground but one man's boot erupted in a smoky red bloom. The girls around her scattered like a murder of ravens, shrieking at the sudden twig-snap sound of the gunpowder. Tall Girl slashed with the knife and cut the throat of the man she had disarmed; she told herself it was a kindness when compared to what his employers would have done in the face of his failure.

Other men converged on the troublemaker. She fired at one while slashing in the other's direction. The one dodged her knife and wrapped his arms around her, so she jammed the blade up into his bicep. The man howled in her ear like a stuck pig, and in his pain she became the stronger of the two. She twisted the knife as she freed it and bent her knees. She dropped into a crouch and bowled him over her back, standing suddenly to make him fall backward. He grabbed for her foot but she slammed her heel down on the back of his hand with a satisfying crunch.

Three other guards grabbed hold of her. One closed his hand around hers in an attempt to pull the gun away, but Tall Girl's grip was too strong. She pulled the trigger and the bullet entered the soft flesh just below the man's arm. She used the man's grip to spin him around into one of his friends, knocking them both down. She stooped and stole the other man's gun since she feared hers was nearing empty, and she pulled her hand free as the boss barreled toward her.

She turned and brought the gun up, closing one eye to get a bead on his forehead. She had never aimed a gun before but it seemed fairly straightforward: trigger, sight, arms braced against the force of the tiny explosion that would propel the bullet.

She was about to fire when she was tackled from behind. She twisted to retaliate but saw that her attacker was one of the other girls. More piled on top of the pile, holding her down and shouting horrible names as the weapons she'd stolen were wrenched out of her hands to leave her defenseless once more. The boss ordered the girls up with harsh words barked as he shoved them out of his way, kicking a few in the rear ends when they didn't move fast enough.

He grabbed Tall Girl by the hair and lifted her onto her feet as she squirmed desperately to get free. She bared her teeth at him despite the pain in her scalp. He drew his knife and held the blade against her throat, and Tall Girl knew she would be used as an example as to what happened to troublemakers. The bleeding men lying on the ground around them would be more than enough to justify her death. But then someone shouted from near the ramp and hurried over.

Her salvation came from a bald man wearing a cream suit under a long brown coat. "This is the perfect opportunity. Don't waste her."

The pressure of the blade lessened and she could swallow without fear of being decapitated. He sneered at her. "You are very lucky. You are very, very lucky."

He tossed her away and Tall Girl fell. The girls gave her a wide breadth when they boarded the ship. Tall Girl didn't blame them for attacking her. They didn't know where the men were taking them, but the world they knew was four hundred miles behind them. They would never find their way back. They could never go home and being alone in this strange place was more frightening than anything the men could do to them. They had no choice but to go forward.

She saw the bald man in the brown coat after boarding, and he singled her out of the crowd. Two crewmen carried her below-decks on the strange swaying maze of iron, and they locked her in a cramped closet. She was terrified by the sway under her feet, as if the world was no longer locked into position, and the metal of the walls was cold to the touch. She cowered in her cell, chewing her thumbnail and crying silently as she waited for whatever came next. She thought of the other girls on the ship and, in the dark, became resentful of them. She had tried to save them all, so why had none of them tried to save her?

Hours passed before the door to her prison opened again. She blinked against the light of the man's lantern as he bound her wrists with a thick rope. The hemp bit into her wrists when he checked to make sure everything was secure, and then he ordered her to "get up and move, now!" She wondered why these men who didn't know she spoke English insisted on using that language to issue their orders. Three more men stood in the corridor with weapons in hand. She deduced news of her actions had spread across the ship, and they were responding to her reputation.

They were scared of her. At this realization, Tall Girl smiled.

She was led up, out of the ship and into a freezing and windy night. Over the railing of the ship she could see water. It was black as ink and reflected the night sky perfectly. The waters were still as glass and her jaw dropped at the thought of being on such a massive sea on such a tiny vessel. Her chest clenched in terror as she was dragged closer to the railing and for a moment she was certain they intended to toss her over the side.

"No, no. Please. No!"

The bald man in the brown coat was standing by the railing with a book in his hand. Despite the darkness he was still wearing the same round-lensed sunglasses she'd seen at the docks. He looked back at the sound of her voice and straightened as he closed the book on his thumb to mark his place.

"She speaks English?"

"A bit," Tall Girl said. "Please, do not throw me overboard."

The man smiled, but she was not comforted by that flash of pearl. "My name is Solomon. Do you know Solomon? From the Bible? Have they brought the Bible to this hellish place yet? Solomon was a very wise king, a very long time ago. Do you have a name? Something we can call you?"

She stared at him and shivered in the cold, and from fear. She hadn't gotten a good look at him on the dock, but now she was able to take note of the man's unusual features. He had a small chin and widely flared cheekbones, the combination making him look like a cobra. His eyebrows were arched with a tuft of longer hair at the apex. After waiting for her to answer, he waved his hand dismissively as if to erase the question from the air.

"No matter. We don't need to know your name. Untie her arms, please."

The ropes were loosened, but the men gripped her arms hard enough to hurt. Did they expect she would run? Where did they think she could have fled? The man Solomon handed his book to one of the men and reached into the pocket of his overcoat. He withdrew a small glass jar and unscrewed the top.

"If you have a name now, soon it will be nothing but a meaningless word to you. That fight on the dock was impressive. You were clever, and you were fast. These men are trained killers and yet you managed to take several of them out before they subdued you. I knew when I saw you fight that you were the perfect choice for host. Soon you will be the commander of me, of these men, of this entire vessel. We are going to give you a gift as a reward for the fire in your heart. We are going to give you Power."

"You wish to steal my body. Hollow me out like a shell."

He fished into the jar. "We are giving you the chance to become something much more than you could ever have dreamed. You got onto the caravan to be a nurse, a chambermaid, a house girl. I'm giving you the opportunity to be a god."

"At the expense of my soul."

Solomon laughed. "Such a trifling thing. People trade money, lives, other people in pursuit of power. What is one soul?"

"A precious thing. I do not accept."

"That's the glorious thing about this." He removed his fingers from the jar to reveal they were coated with black ink. "You don't have to consent. Hold her head."

The wind picked up off the water as he began to trace designs on her forehead and cheeks with the ink. From his expression she gathered that the designs he was making were complex and had importance, but they felt utterly alien to her. She tried to imagine what they were by picturing the movement of his fingers in her mind but they made no sense. He ripped open the front of her dress and drew another hieroglyph on her chest, making her shudder as his finger traced over her sternum. The ink dripped down the curve of her cheeks, off her chin, and it felt like snails slithering over her skin.

From his other pocket, he withdrew an egg-shaped stone. He pinched her chin and pulled down until she was forced to open her mouth, and she grimaced as the stone was placed on her tongue. It was small enough not to gag her, but it felt wrong in her mouth, and it tasted strongly of sand and dust. One of the men clapped his hand over her mouth. She thought of how Solomon had said the word 'Power,' as if it were a tangible entity. If that was how English worked, then the stone in her mouth could only be called Wrong or Evil.

Solomon wiped his fingers when he was done, then retrieved the book from the man who had been holding it. Tall Girl watched the men, watched how they all adjusted their weight with the sway of the vessel underneath them, and she mimicked them to regain some of her balance. They could not plant themselves to the deck under their feet, and that made them vulnerable. Solomon flipped through the book until he found the proper page, all while the black ink slithered over Tall Girl's skin. She shuddered in the cold and blinked the salt air out of her eyes. The stone felt as if it was gaining weight on her tongue.

Solomon began to read from the book, and Tall Girl thought she saw something spark out over the water behind him. He continued reading and fear shot through her as if she'd been struck by lightning. She tensed her arms against her captors but they head fast. As Solomon droned, the waves beneath the ship turned calm as glass while waves on the horizon churned. They rose and fell on the current. She continued to move her body in rhythm with her captors.

She felt a tingle in the stone, as if she really had been hit by lightning and it was being conducted through the strange object.

Solomon raised his voice against the howls of wind, and Tall Girl begin to kick and fight against the men holding her. She could feel something dark and evil crowding in on her consciousness, a creature of some sort, from the depths of the darkness. She didn't know how she knew, but she could feel the presence as surely as if a door had been opened. She was terrified in a way she'd never been before as Solomon continued to read. The ink on her face began to burn.

The ship creaked under the assault of the wind. The man covering her mouth turned to look behind them. The ship rose on another wave and his weight went onto his back foot. He was leaning away from her with a fractionally weaker grip... weak enough for her to pull away. Tall Girl twisted from him and lunged forward. The man released her mouth to grab at her collar, but he was already tumbling backward due to his unstable position.

She opened her mouth and spit out the stone.

Though the stone hit him in the chest, she was unable to propel it with enough force to cause any harm. He dropped the book in a desperate attempt to grab the stone before it hit the ground. The becalmed sea suddenly burst back into life, and Tall Girl was thrown to the deck with her captors. Solomon shouted in his own language as the stone hit the ground and rolled toward the rail. Lightning flashed overhead as storm clouds seemed to spontaneously blossom above the ship's position.

The cant and roll of the sea caused the stone to move erratically so that Solomon couldn't get hold of it. He let out a shrill cry as the stone went over the edge into the water. Tall Girl watched as he reacted without thought, tearing off his overcoat so it wouldn't weigh him down. He put a foot on the railing and used it to push himself off, arms stretched out as he followed the stone into the wild sea. There was a boom that echoed so loudly she was certain it had been heard in Addis Ababa, and then quiet descended once more.

The men holding her were so shaken by what had just happened that she pulled away from them without effort. She walked to Solomon's discarded coat and picked it up, wrapping the heavy leather around herself. Instantly she was warm, and she tucked her arms up into the sleeves to thaw out her fingers. The men looked at her and she remembered what Solomon had promised. Power.

"Your work is done. Leave now."

They fled. She turned and walked away from them, stumbling on the uneven deck of the ship. She felt sick, and her mouth was dry where the stone had sat. Her mouth felt rotten, and she smacked her lips as she searched the vessel. Soon she found a flight of metal steps leading up to the shining beacon of the bridge, and she ascended with purpose. She set her jaw and held her head high. The darkness she'd felt descending upon her dissipated as soon as she spit out the stone, but she felt there was still a trace of the power Solomon had promised.

The captain, navigator, and the man who was in charge of the girls all looked at her, fearful but wary. "Did it work?" the captain asked in English. Her hair had come loose in the maelstrom and she knew she must look like a wild beast wrapped in a man's coat. Due to her height, the coat fit rather well, but the sleeves were too long for her. The tail dragged on the ground behind her feet. She hoped she didn't sound like a frightened girl when she spoke.

"Solomon told you to expect this?" Her tongue was numbed by the stone, turning her sibilant letters into lisps. The men nodded, and she could see their terror. "He told you my final destination?"

"Yes. Cairo."

"Then do not make me wait. I have been patient for far too long."

"Yes, mistress."

She turned to leave, but one of the men said, "What do we call you?"

"I am called Tall Girl."

Her heavy tongue coated with dust and dirt, combined with her lack of fluency in the language, slurred the words together. When later the crew began referring to her as Trafalgar, she didn't question it for fear of drawing their ire. Besides, there was something about the sobriquet that appealed to her.

She left them to their navigation and went down to stand on the railing. The tails of the coat flapped against her thighs as she stood on the upper deck and watched the coast of Africa roll by. She kept Solomon's coat because it was warm, and because she had never had anything with material quite so fine. She went through his pockets and found all sorts of trinkets, bizarre items that she couldn't pretend to understand. She knew when she arrived in Cairo she would demand all the girls in the hold be set free. As for Solomon's men, she hadn't a clue. She would kill if she had to, but the men seemed too frightened of her to put up much of a fight.

She had no idea what awaited her in Egypt, but it had to be better than what was in store for her back home. She'd escaped her stepfather, she had survived the attempt on her life, and now every day ahead of her was a gift. She stuffed her hands in the pockets of her new coat and clung to her new name, repeating it in her head until it was a word of Power.

When she arrived in Egypt, she was Trafalgar even in her own mind. She strode down the gangplank with her head held high as she headed out to discover what exactly that meant.

Chapter One

1919

THE SIX weeks Dorothy Boone spent in Mexico exploring the ruins underneath Teotihuacan didn't afford her more than two or three hours of sleep per night, and the long journey back to London was spent transcribing all of her quickly-scribbled notes into a proper notebook. When she set out on her latest journey the idea of traveling by steamer was akin to suicide, but the war had ended and the waters around England were no longer being patrolled by those atrocious U-boats. Still, her journey had been restless and full of work. When she did stretch out on the cot it was purely biological need rather than a rest.

Once she was back on solid ground her fatigue caught up to her, and she dozed off moments after relaying her address to the cab driver. The sounds of London were a lullaby to her after so long away, and the familiar smell of the Thames made her feel comfortable for the first time since leaving. She lived to explore, but there were times she wondered if she only traveled so she could truly appreciate coming home. London, the cluttered metro so different from the countryside in which she grew up, but now she couldn't think of anywhere she felt safer.

She could also hear laughter, voices raised in celebration. When she had left there'd been a veil over the entire world as 'a war to end all wars' waged all across the continent. It had stymied countless expeditions, and for the first few years of the conflict her main concern had been wondering how many artifacts and tombs were being trampled underfoot by the soldiers. Then in 1916, they received word that her brother Bernie and twenty thousand other soldiers were killed by a river called the Somme. There were nights Dorothy woke to find tears on her pillow or drying on her face, and she knew she'd been visited by a dream of her lost brother. They'd never been close, but the thought of him dying in some French field...

But now the war was over. They could process their grief and begin healing along with the rest of the world. The British sun shone through the clouds, through the window of her cab, and she smiled as it warmed her face as if to welcome her home.

The cab made the familiar turn onto Threadneedle Street and she opened her eyes to watch her home come into view. The building was white stone flanked by dull brown buildings on either side. The front door was painted red and set back slightly so as not to draw attention to her callers.

Threadneedle was a place of commerce, of bankers and stockbrokers, but it suited her needs perfectly. Her grandmother's inheritance had allowed her to buy the townhouse, and a series of wise investments over the years had brought in enough extra money for her to purchase the property on either side for added protection. The entire street was zoned for banking, which meant the walls were reinforced in advance. Instead of money she used the vaults to store the items she brought back from her expeditions.

She paid the cab driver and accepted his help unloading her bags. The front door opened and Beatrice Sek stepped out. Dorothy smiled a greeting to her majordomo, paid the driver, and let Beatrice help her carry everything inside. She paused on the checkerboard tile of the foyer and took a deep breath of her home's air. To her left, a staircase led up to the second and third levels of her home. To the right, Beatrice had opened the parlor doors in anticipation of her return.

Dorothy smiled and released a satisfied sigh. The house was dark and cozy, a welcome retreat from the clamor and glare of the city. Just stepping inside was like wrapping herself in a thick blanket and drawing it up over her head.

Beatrice was dressed in her work uniform; a white dress shirt with a sharp collar under a charcoal gray vest, black trousers, and shoes so shined that Dorothy could see her reflection in them. She was of mixed heritage, Chinese and French, and she could speak both languages fluently. Her hair was short enough that she couldn't braid it, but one wave of finger curls fell across her right eye. Dorothy kept her spine straight as she scanned the house for any obvious signs of damage.

"I trust everything went well in my absence."

"As well as it ever does, mum. You were greatly missed."

"Was I?"

"Professor Tindall stopped by several times inquiring as to when you would return. Threnody also left word, but I believe she is only concerned with an outstanding payment you owe."

Dorothy clucked her tongue. "I do so hate leaving debts. I'll settle with her at once." She faced Beatrice. "Anyone else pained by my absence?"

Beatrice considered for a moment and then shook her head. "No one I recall."

"You are impossible." Dorothy put her arm around Beatrice's waist and pulled her close. Beatrice leaned back with a smile, forcing Dorothy to come to her for a proper greeting after nearly two months apart. When they parted she smiled. "If you will not say it, then I shall. I missed you terribly, Trix."

Beatrice smiled and smoothed down the front of Dorothy's blouse. "You're tired from your journey. Go upstairs and draw a bath, take a nap, and I shall put away your things. I'll wake you for dinner and then we can discuss your homecoming celebration."

"Splendid."

She went upstairs to the familiar comfort of her bedchambers, pausing once more on the threshold to breathe in the scents and cast her eyes over the environs. Beatrice had been made aware of her impending return and the curtains were open to air out the staleness.

Dorothy unbuttoned her blouse as she crossed to her en suite. Her clothes were clean as she had put them on only that morning, but the last time they'd been laundered was in Mexico City. In her periphery she could see her reflection in the mirror but she refused to give herself a thorough examination. She knew her skin was reddened from exposure to the sun, her freckles standing out proudly across the bridge of her nose, and her hair without a doubt resembled a fright wig. It hadn't been properly tended in two months.

Dorothy drew a bath as she undressed, scrubbing what grime she could from her hands and face so she wouldn't soil the water. She wet a razor and shaved her legs, applied cream to the cracked skin of her feet and hands, and finally sank down into the water feeling more human than she had in ages. She soaked with her eyes closed, letting the warm water draw the dirt of another country from her pores. She was close to drifting off when the air was disturbed by Beatrice joining her in the bathroom. She brought her hand up out of the water and Beatrice placed a sponge against her palm.

Dorothy curled her fingers around it and finally opened her eyes to look at her majordomo, her representative, her driver, her closest and possibly only friend.

"Say that you missed me, Trix."

"I missed you."

"How much did you miss me?"

"Terribly, Lady Boone." She lightly grazed her lips over Dorothy's before kissing her properly. Beatrice teased Dorothy's bottom lip with her tongue until Dorothy took it into her mouth. She tasted something sweet on Beatrice's tongue and realized the younger woman had been downstairs eating a scone. The honey taste lingered and transferred from Beatrice's mouth to hers, a subtle hint of sweetness. Dorothy moaned softly into the kiss; now she felt as if she had truly returned home. She reached up and trailed her wet fingers through Beatrice's hair before opening her eyes.

Beatrice moved to sit between the edge of the tub and the wall, and Dorothy obediently leaned forward and drew her legs up so she could rest her head on her knees. Beatrice put her hand in the water next to Dorothy's hip and drew the water up over the curve of her flanks, letting it trickle down her back. Her strong and sure hands paused on a crescent arch of pink skin where a wound was almost completely healed over.

"This is new," Beatrice said. "An arrow?"

"Just glanced off me," Dorothy said dismissively.

Beatrice bent down to kiss the injury before continuing. Dorothy closed her eyes and sighed her contentment. The purpose of her trip to Mexico was to explore the hidden catacombs beneath Teotihuacan to determine if they held any clues to the city's sudden and complete destruction. It had once been a culture and social mecca, but in a handful of years it had been completely abandoned. Within a few centuries the same fate befell three other large social centers in the same area. Signs pointed toward some sort of civil unrest, an uprising against the wealthy, but if that was true then where were the victors?

The expedition she was with hoped to find answers in a honeycomb of tunnels underneath the city. Professor Watkins of Oxford believed they were escape tunnels used by the city's elites to escape when their people rose up against them, but the network they found was much more complex than that. There was an entire city hidden underneath Teotihuacan, and they'd explored only a fraction of it when their funds dried up and they were forced to withdraw.

Beatrice's strong fingers drew her back to the present. The remaining grime had been sluiced off her skin, leaving it pink and red, and Beatrice had moved on to a massage. Dorothy grunted as a particularly stubborn knot in her shoulder was deftly unwound. She lifted her head and wrinkled her brow as she moved her neck without limitation for the first time in three weeks. Beatrice squeezed with her fingertips while her thumbs dug deep into the tissue to work out long-neglected aches. Dorothy gasped and arched her back at the slight pain followed by sweet relief.

She sighed blissfully. "Goodness. That feels wonderful. You truly are a miracle worker."

She could hear the smile in Beatrice's voice when she responded. "Anything for my mistress, Lady Boone."

"Hm. And did you take any other mistress while I was away?"

Beatrice hummed. "There may have been dalliances."

"I wish to hear all the sordid details. But perhaps later. I am exhausted, and your ministrations have made me believe I could actually succeed at taking a nap."

Beatrice slid one hand down Dorothy's front. She circled a nipple with her thumb and then continued lower. She drew Dorothy back against the curve of the tub and Dorothy allowed herself to be guided, moving her legs apart to press them against the walls of the tub. Beatrice's hand moved under the water without regard for the cuff of her blouse, and Dorothy bit her lip in anticipation. Beatrix twisted the hair between Dorothy's legs with her fingers, stroking it before extending her middle finger to seek out the slick, pink flesh hidden by the dark red tangles.

"Who touched you here while you were away, Lady Boone?" Beatrice asked against the shell of Dorothy's ear. "Whose fingers ventured where mine are about to?"

"Only myself."

Beatrice's other hand stroked Dorothy's neck. "Then I am jealous of you twice over. Both for feeling and being felt. I wish I could have been there to enjoy either."

Dorothy's lips curled in a lazy smile. "As do I."

"Let me make up for it now." She dropped her hand to cup Dorothy's breast and she used her middle two fingers to press against the hidden folds. Dorothy arched her back with a gasp, bringing one hand up out of the water and reaching back to touch Beatrice's face. Beatrice turned her head and sucked Dorothy's finger into her mouth. She used two fingers to spread Dorothy wide as her middle finger unfurled and ventured forth.

"Trix," Dorothy whimpered, biting her lip, squirming so much that the water threatened to overflow the edges of her tub. "Please."

"I have missed you so terribly," Beatrice murmured. "It's time for your homecoming."

Dorothy came with a trembling sigh, lifting one foot out of the bath and curling her toes as water rolled down her leg in sheets. She sank down lower, and Beatrice rested both hands between Dorothy's breasts. When Dorothy stopped shivering and the flush had faded from her throat and upper chest, Beatrice retrieved the sponge and finished bathing her. Dorothy's skin was once again pink and pristine like every other high society ladies one might encounter on the streets of London.

"You are once again cultured."

"Bully for me," Dorothy said.

"Up."

Dorothy rose out of the water and allowed Beatrice to towel her off and wrap her in a thick robe. She dressed in her softest nightgown, kissed Beatrice once more, and crawled into the blissful luxury of her own bed. It had been one of her first extravagant purchases after the house. She wanted a proper place to lay her head after an arduous journey, and the Elizabethan four-poster bed was exactly what she had in mind. The posts were thick and ornately carved and supported a sheer curtain that could be drawn to completely enclose her.

She chose to leave the curtain open slightly. She wanted the light and sounds of the city to be with her while she slept as a reminder of where she was. Too many nights in tents, too much sleep lost to the sound of jungle birds and threatening beasts that she never saw in daylight. In the ten years since striking out on her own she had yet to grow tired of the expeditions, but the politics of setting them up made her weary. Though she could afford to fund the occasional solo expedition, she would quickly go broke paying for every member, for their travel and their bribes to the locals to act as chaperones. It was easier to find a patron willing to pay their way so she and her fellows could focus entirely on the exploration and discovery aspect of their journey.

Her eyelids became heavy as her body accepted the fact she was actually going to let it sleep. Weeks of exhaustion and deprivation closed around her like a shadow, and Dorothy surrendered to it even as a part of her mind considered what her next excursion would be.

Beatrice checked fifteen minutes later to confirm Dorothy was indeed asleep, then went about unpacking the bags she had taken to Mexico. The mundane reference books were returned to their proper places in the library on the second floor, while the more esoteric volumes were taken next door to the vaults. Dorothy hadn't returned from this particular journey with any new artifacts, but the weapons she had taken - a dirk, a quarterstaff, and the Colt M1909 - went back into the armory on the other side of the house. Beatrice made sure the gun was unloaded and clean before putting it away. Dorothy was always careful with her weapons, but double-checking never hurt anything.

Once everything was sorted, Beatrice returned to the kitchen. Dorothy would no doubt be famished when she woke up. Expeditions fed Dorothy's spirit but all too often she neglected to properly feed her body. Beatrice started a beef roast, with carrots, peas, and potatoes. There was a lot of food for two people, but Dorothy could be quite voracious. Anything left over would be donated to the urchins who often loitered in the alleys around Threadneedle Street. Dorothy had no problem being charitable, but Beatrice gave them food for another reason; until she met Lady Boone she had been one of their number.

The idea of preparing a fine meal in a fortressed home on Threadneedle Street, and the idea of being entrusted with everything within the home while her mistress was on another continent, was quite the adjustment for her. Her earliest memory was cowering in the cargo hold of a steamer ship, clinging to the ratty and moth-eaten sweater of an old man she assumed was her grandfather. He was constantly in pain, grimacing and clutching at his bulbous gut as he tried to fight the sway of the ship. She had no memory of where they'd come from, or where they were going. Her life was the ship.

When they arrived in Paris she clung to the same disgusting sweater as the man shuffled through the narrow and winding streets. Each step seemed to be agony for him and he put a heavy hand on her shoulder for balance. The hand was as much acknowledgement as she got from him, as he never spoke and half-dragged her through the city like she was luggage. She stumbled and lurched on legs unaccustomed to solid land. Occasionally the old man would let go of her long enough to clutch his side or to clap her on the side of the head.

Eventually they reached a small house with a soft yellow glow coming through the windows. Beatrice huddled against the wall while the old man pounded on the door and shouted in Mandarin until someone opened the door. The man was Chinese, like her, but his wife was French. They tried to push the old man away until the woman spotted Beatrice shivering behind him. She was the only reason they allowed him to come inside. The woman took her into the kitchen while the old man went into the living room with the husband. The woman gave Beatrice a warm meal and tucked her into the first real bed she'd ever had before going downstairs to join the argument.

The old man vanished while she was sleeping. Over the years she managed to dig up only bits and pieces of information about him. His name was Shen, he claimed to be her grandfather, and he said that he had fled with her to protect her from an evil mage. He never said why the mage wanted her dead, or who the mage was, but he claimed Beatrice would be safe if she was kept far away.

Her new parents were Lin and Cosette Sek. They named her Bao Tai, but she anglicized it to Beatrice when she ran away from home. She feared her parents or the people her 'grandfather' had been running from would find her in Paris, so she fled to London. One city's streets were the same as another, she decided.

In London's alleys and byways she learned how to steal, how to fight, how to use magic, and how to avoid being detected by the police. Her hands were quick, her mind quicker, and she quickly started earning her keep with the other thieves and hoodlums occupying London's demimonde.

Her life changed the day she noticed Dorothy Boone out for a stroll. She was walking briskly, her clothes indicating a modest salary but there was no denying she was wealthy. Her shabbiness was far too contrived to be real, and she wore a pocket watch that anyone truly destitute would have pawned ages ago. Beatrice followed at a safe distance until she discovered the woman's residence. She waited until Dorothy left again, then found a way inside.

It was the mother lode. Even before she discovered the armory, before she even knew there was a second or third wing to the home, she was trying to figure out which antiques she could carry away and which she would have to come back for later. She sincerely hoped there would be a later. Artifacts, artwork, an array of gewgaws she couldn't begin to identify... Part of her feared that the things she saw were invaluable, which would be useless if she couldn't find someone willing to buy them from her.

She was still doing reconnaissance when she picked up what looked like an ordinary stone tablet to see what was inscribed on the face of it. Her lips formed the unusual words carved on the face of it as she tried to make sense of it. It was a moment before she realized her arms had become unusually stiff, and her body had acquired a new weight that made her feel anchored to the floor. She managed to unfold her arms to put the tablet down, but the damage had already been done. Her legs wouldn't move her farther than a few steps, and her hands froze on the way up so she could see the gray stone spreading across her flesh.

There were no windows in the room so she had no idea how long she stood there. Her confusion wasn't helped by the fact she was forced to sleep with her eyes open and had no idea how much time passed before she woke. It might have been eons, but she never became hungry or thirsty. At first she thought that was a mercy, but the longer she remained entombed she realized it was part of the punishment. She would not die of natural causes, but she would pray for death long before her wish was granted.

She was asleep, or more accurately unconscious, when she finally heard movement elsewhere in the house. A woman humming softly, the steady drum of footsteps on the stairs. The owner of the home went into her bedroom for a time, then finally came into the room where Beatrice stood frozen. The redhead stopped dead in her tracks and stared at the intruder as if she was nothing more alarming than a misplaced shoe.

"Crumbs," Dorothy Boone muttered. "Where in the blazes did you come from?"

She stepped in front of Beatrice and looked into her eyes. Beatrice had no choice but to stare back. After a moment Dorothy nodded and began searching the nearby tables. Finally she found the tablet. "The Medusa Tablet... bloody hell. When did I leave that lying about?" She looked at Beatrice again. "Hell of a security system, however. Hello? Are you still conscious in there?" Dorothy stroked Beatrice's cheek with the back of her hand. "Warm. Hm. Okay. Remain calm. My name is Dorothy. I'll see what I can do to help you."

Dorothy left. If Beatrice had been able to move her lips she would have called out to her to stay. It didn't matter that even if Dorothy could save her, she would in all likelihood call the police to cart her off immediately afterward. The mere presence of another person, and a touch even of flesh on stone, had been enough to overjoy her. She felt as if she was crying even though she knew that was preposterous. But Dorothy was already gone, and Beatrice could only remain standing as she had stood for untold days while her erstwhile victim sought ways to save her life.

She returned an hour later with a shallow dish filled with a viscous fluid. "I had to cobble this unguent together from things I had lying about. Hopefully it will do the trick." She brushed her sponge over Beatrice's cheeks and brow. The ointment was thick, and stung like beestings where it coated her cheeks and chin. She was certain it wasn't working, already convinced that even the homeowner's knowledge wouldn't be able to save her. The thought distressed her to the point that a single tear fell from the corner of her eye. It was only after it fell from her lashes that she realized it was proof the ointment was indeed working.

"It's all right," Dorothy said softly. "It's a slow process, but it will work. Just relax."

It took the better part of an hour for Dorothy to sponge the unguent over Beatrice's entire body. Her clothes resisted the treatment, leaving them stiff and uncomfortable, so Dorothy retrieved a robe for her to change into. "The ointment won't harm your skin, but it would probably be best not to let it dry. Come with me. I've prepared a bath."

Beatrice soaked in Dorothy's bathtub, taking her time to enjoy the simple pleasure of clenching and stretching out her fist. She watched her muscles move under the skin, rolled her head forward and back, and listened to the crackle and pop of her bones as they moved for the first time in days, perhaps weeks. The movement of air on her flesh was almost sexual, almost too much for her to bear, but sitting in the water was something she could tolerate.

Finally she put on the robe and went downstairs to face her punishment. Dorothy was sitting in the parlor with a book open on her lap, but she closed it on her finger when Beatrice appeared. She had changed out of her traveling clothes and wore a simple burgundy blouse over a dark purple skirt.

"How long after my departure were you ensnared?"

"A few hours."

Dorothy stood up and returned the book to its shelf. "Three weeks, six days, eight hours. Give or take a few minutes, of course." She turned to face Beatrice. "I can't imagine what an ordeal that was, but I'm certain it was..." She scoffed at herself. "I was going to say 'unpleasant,' but the truth of the matter is that it must have been a literal hell. I apologize."

Beatrice furrowed her brow. "I w-was trying to rob you." Her voice was little more than a croak, and the air felt unbelievable cold on her skin. She realized she was swaying, shifting her weight from the balls of her feet to the heels. She felt as if a strong breeze would topple her. "I broke into your home and rifled your things."

"The punishment hardly fits the crime. That tablet was found on a small island in the Cyclades. There were men and women in the cavern who had been trapped in stone for centuries. Our expedition attempted to free them but... the damage to their minds was too great. They had become deranged. More animal than people. We were forced to do the merciful thing and kill them. One of our own men was afflicted, but we freed him after a few hours. Even so he required a great deal of recuperation time. Four weeks..." She shook her head. "If you would like a proper rest, I have a spare bedroom. There is food in the kitchen as I'm sure you must be famished."

"Why are you being kind?" Tears rolled down her cheeks. "You should be alerting the constables, you should be..."

Dorothy crossed the room. "You're not well, dear. The trauma you've gone through has left you weak in mind and spirit. I was careless with a dangerous artifact and you suffered the consequences. Shall we call it a draw?" She took Beatrice's hands in hers. "I am Lady Boone. Dorothy. And what is your name, dear?"

"Beatrice Sek."

"It's a pleasure to make your acquaintance, Beatrice Sek." Beatrice stared at her in disbelief and Dorothy rolled her eyes. "Oh, please. I've made friends under circumstances far stranger than these. Come now. I'll show you to your room."

Beatrice sagged against Dorothy's side as she was escorted up the stairs. She was overwhelmed by Dorothy's kindness, and she spent the rest of the evening trying to think of the last time someone had offered to help her without expecting anything in return. It made her determined to repay her however she could in order to wipe out the debt. When she discovered Dorothy needed help around the house, Beatrice offered her services. When Dorothy offhandedly mentioned she only took cabs because she didn't know how to drive, Beatrice offered those services as well. She wasn't sure when her favors became a permanent occupation, but she knew her days of thieving were in her past.

Dorothy gave her more than a job, more than a place to sleep. Dorothy gave her somewhere she could feel not only safe but welcomed. And she was needed. Dorothy could be scatterbrained and neglectful when it came to household chores. She would leave her bags beside the door from the end of one expedition to the beginning of the next. Beatrice didn't realize how much she needed to be needed until she met Dorothy.

She also didn't realize her feelings for Dorothy were anything but friendship until the night the very proper Lady Boone came home three sheets to the wind and clinging to the arm of a similarly soused woman dressed like a barmaid. Dorothy feigned sobriety when she saw Beatrice watching them but her giggling gave her away. She patted her "guest" on the shoulder and said, "No need to make up the spare room, Trix. Elsie shall be spending the evening in my room. The bed is certainly large enough and there's no need to make more laundry for yourself."

Beatrice tried to stay away from the third floor, but curiosity got the better of her. The sounds she heard from the other side of Dorothy's rooms made her blush and retreat downstairs as quickly as stealth allowed. She spent the rest of the night staring at the ceiling, covering her ears with the pillow to prevent even the slightest of sounds from reaching her.

In the morning Dorothy was hungover and slow. She came downstairs in her underclothes, her hair a rat's nest atop her head, and groggily inquired as to breakfast. Beatrice quietly complied while Dorothy slumped on the dining room table with a napkin draped over her face. Beatrice knew then that instead of being offended by Dorothy's behavior or scandalized by the fact she'd spent the evening with another woman, she was jealous of the barmaid.

When Dorothy was once again capable of sitting up under her own power Beatrice admitted her feelings. Dorothy listened politely and then tilted her head to one side.

"Have you ever had predilections in that arena before?"

Beatrice smirked. "I've not really had predilections in any arena before."

Dorothy raised an eyebrow. "Interesting." She sipped her tea, pressed her lips together to spread the moisture across them, and nodded slowly. "Well. If you would like to explore it further, you know where to find me."

Beatrice spent three days debating the invitation before she took Dorothy up on it. She went to Dorothy's room after closing up the house for the evening, knocked quietly, and nervously went inside. Dorothy sat in bed wearing a simple nightgown, her hair down in thick waves of golden and red. In daylight she seemed so formidable and larger than life, but here dwarfed by her bed and the grandeur of her room, she was almost mortal. Beatrice lingered in the doorway, wearing a nightshirt that reached her knees. She curled her toes in the carpet and tried to think of something to say.

"I've been waiting for you, Trix." Dorothy held out her hand and curled two fingers in a subtle summons. "Come here."

Beatrice spent the night with Dorothy, who was tender and attentive with her. She whispered assurances into Beatrice's ear when her lips weren't otherwise engaged, fingers trailing feather-light across her stomach and down between her thighs. At one point Dorothy whispered, "If at any point you want me to stop..." but Beatrice silenced her with a desperate groan. Dorothy laughed throatily and went back to what she had been doing.

They fell asleep before they could talk, but in the morning Dorothy asked Beatrice what she wanted. "We can be lovers. We can be friends who occasionally provide each other comfort. We can move on from this and go back to the way things were before. I'm comfortable with any of these options. I leave it up to you." She kissed Beatrice's lips. "For what it's worth, I enjoyed myself very much."

Beatrice chose the option that left them both free to pursue other interests, and she had yet to regret it. Dorothy occasionally returned home with someone and whiled away the evening with them in her room. Some nights Dorothy would come home alone and appear at Beatrice's bedroom door with a bottle of wine and two glasses. Their physical relationship wasn't a duty or commitment. It was a form of bonding and a show of companionship.

She closed the armory and smoothed her hands over the locks. For years she considered the only way to live was breaking locks just like this. But one woman's trust had changed everything. Now Dorothy left her in charge of the house when she was on expeditions. Weeks, months, one time half a year, Beatrice had basically lived alone in the house while Dorothy was in some tomb or another. No matter how long she was gone, no matter what treasures she left behind, she knew it would be there when she came back. Beatrice wouldn't trade that faith for the biggest score in London.

Smiling at the memories she had unlocked, Beatrice went downstairs to check on dinner.

Chapter Two

The Pierce-Arrow landau turned off the main drag not far from Threadneedle and onto the narrow streets of Spitalfields, narrowly avoiding the debris littering either side of the lane. Trafalgar sat in the backseat next to Leola and wondered if she could brush her fingers along the brick buildings by stretching her arm out the window. The streets of London were poorly designed to handle modern automobiles, and she feared what would happen to her adopted city if they were forced to make adjustments. Then again, if the march of progress meant slums like this one were eliminated, perhaps it would be for the best.

"And then where would the residents go?" Adeline asked from the front seat. "The undesirables, those who live here because they have no other choice?"

"I didn't speak my thought aloud, Adeline," Trafalgar politely scolded. "I've told you how disconcerting that is."

"You're avoiding the question."

"Yes. I am." Trafalgar sighed.

Adeline was a precognitive telepath, a gift that made her exceptionally skilled behind the wheel but an awkward compatriot. She received a constant barrage of what people intended to say, often whether they eventually spoke them aloud or not. She said it was like trying to watch a play while the people behind her constantly whispered amongst themselves. She saw aspects of the future including whether an intersection would be clear or congested in thirty or fifty seconds' time.

Trafalgar thought about Adeline's argument. She knew that ignoring the plight of the people forced to live in these slums made her a hypocrite. She had made her home in far less desirable neighborhoods over the past twenty years.

When she first arrived in Cairo she dismissed the crew who still believed she was possessed by some sort of demonic entity. She couldn't very well quiz them about who she was supposed to be, so she kept her distance and tried to appear consumed by her thoughts. Her first order upon dry land was for the crew to take care of the other children. She didn't want them sold or bartered away into a life of slavery, so she ordered them to be taken to the police at once. The men balked, but she threatened them with "all the power I can muster" if they failed her.

She set off alone with only the items in Solomon's pockets to guide her. She sold the items she couldn't identify but kept the obvious weapons just to be on the safe side. She found maps and journals, the latter of which had pages listing Solomon's allies with their contact information. She knew it was risky trying to track them down. If they somehow got word that she was the one chosen for his ritual, they might have ways to finish what he started. She couldn't allow herself to worry about the danger; if Solomon was associated with people who were kidnapping children then they must be stopped.

She had no idea how much it would cost to travel from Cairo to London, but she had overheard enough on the boat to know that was where she had to go. London, England, the capital of the world. She had no life back home, no one to give her shelter in this loud and unruly new world she found herself a citizen of, and London seemed like it would allow her the possibility to find a new path.

When she found the men Solomon intended to meet in Egypt, she was forced to make the first compromise of many: instead of bringing them to task for their human trafficking, she sold them several items she found in Solomon's coat to fund her journey to the world's capital. She consoled herself with the knowledge that she could always come back with more resources, but she could accomplish nothing if she was stranded in an alien port-of-call.

The only thing Trafalgar kept was Solomon's coat. It was far too big for her but she had faith she would grow into it. Years passed before she was able to wear it without trailing the hem along the ground behind her. She still had it, the cavernous pockets now filled with her own tools of the trade. She kept her journal in a pocket of her suit jacket underneath, however. She figured it would be much harder to lose if she kept it close to her body.

She spent the intervening years chipping away at Solomon's organization. She soon learned he was in charge of one small aspect of a much larger entity. His friends and closest allies were the first people she targeted upon arrival in London in the hopes of working her way up to the actual leader of the group. Her first attacks were sloppy and unsophisticated, but she learned from her mistakes and grew more formidable.

She traveled back to Cairo on a handful of occasions to rescue other transports of children being brought back from Africa. Once she met a young girl named Leola who helped her fight off the guards and free the children being kept in the hold. When Trafalgar asked where she wanted to go, Leola said, "You seem like you could use some muscle. How about I stay with you?"

The children were too numerous to be dumped in an orphanage, so she found other homes for them. Some believed the lies they've been told about becoming nurses, so Trafalgar took them to hospices in need of extra hands. Others earned their keep at hospitals or maternity wards where simply holding a newborn could mean the difference between the baby living or dying. She soon became well-known in Cairo and its environs, and one nurse would greet Trafalgar every time she arrived.

"You have brought me more angels?" she would ask, and Trafalgar would introduce the newest refugee. "More lives saved by Miss Trafalgar!"

On one of these journeys, a frail girl with a shaved head broke away from the group and followed Trafalgar when she tried to leave.

"You need to stay here," Trafalgar told the girl.

"I'm supposed to go with you, Trafalgar."

"Supposed to?"

"I've seen it. You and me, riding in a car together. I smelled sea air. I've never been to London, but it looks marvelous."

Trafalgar said, "Where have you seen London?"

The girl touched her temple with two fingers. "What is the building with the big golden dome? Sand Paul?"

"St Paul's," Trafalgar corrected. "My name wasn't originally Trafalgar. Do you know what I was called first?"

"Tall Girl."

"What's your name?"

"You will call me Adeline." She picked up Trafalgar's bags, giving her no choice but to follow the headstrong young woman.

"But is that your name?"

"It's what you'll call me. I've heard it."

Trafalgar said, "But do I call you that because it's your name, or because your visions say it's the name I'll give you?"

"Yes."

Trafalgar grimaced but knew the girl would prove useful. She also knew someone who could see future events would quickly be discovered at an orphanage and would no doubt find herself snatched up by any manner of unscrupulous folk. She would keep Adeline with her as a precaution, just to make sure she didn't end up in the wrong hands.

"I knew you'd like me," Adeline said.

Trafalgar twisted to look at her. "You can hear thoughts, too?"

Adeline shrugged, still smiling.

"We'll have to work on that."

"Can't wait, Miss Trafalgar. Can I have the bedroom at the top by the stairs? It gets the most light in the morning."

Trafalgar smiled now to remember. When she looked forward she saw Adeline was smiling as well, reliving it right along with her. As annoying as it could be to have her mind be an open book, there was something very nice about sharing a memory with a very dear friend. And since there was hardly any way to keep a secret from the girl, Trafalgar ended up having a more honest relationship with Adeline than anyone else in her life.

Adeline parked in front of a dilapidated building and put an end to Trafalgar's reverie. It was flanked on either side by trash-strewn alleyways where there lurked vermin of both the rodent and human variety. The front steps were cracked and weed-choked, but the front door was an impressive barrier of thick oak with shining new fixtures. Trafalgar knew from experience that the building was nigh impenetrable, knew the crumbling facade hid a steel box full of traps set to dissuade the curious, and she knew its owner did everything possible to dissuade curiosity.

Trafalgar climbed out of the backseat and took a moment to adjust her goggles. They had brass frames and the leather strap rested snugly against her temples. Her silk-smooth black hair fell straight down her back to rest on the mantle of her coat. She tugged her gloves on more securely and stretched out her fingers to make sure she had freedom of movement. The real reason for her dawdling was so she could scan the street for anyone who might be watching the building.

Confident that she could approach unseen, she tugged the lapels of her coat and continued up the fractured stairs. Adeline and Leola would remain behind to watch the car, as the neighborhood was rough and their host didn't particularly like multiple guests. Trafalgar gave the prescribed knock and stepped back to count off thirty-three seconds. Then she knocked once more, went back down the steps, and entered the alley. A rust-devoured fencing protected a staircase leading down to a basement entrance. The gate opened with a screech of protest. She descended, knocked once again on this hidden door, and twisted the knob to find it was unlocked.

She removed her goggles as she entered the darkened room. She gave her eyes a moment to adjust before she ventured deeper. Shapes took form in the shadows to either side of her; dust cloths and tarps creating unusual landscapes and vistas in the cluttered basement. The entire space was filled with row upon row of shelving with extremely little room left to serve as aisles. Trafalgar was forced to turn sideways so her jacket didn't snag on anything. After a few yards the aisle widened to reveal a staircase leading back up to the ground floor.

This entire level had been cleared of furniture or trappings of home, save for a few columns left to bear the load of the upper floors. Though the windows had been covered by several layers of curtain, there was enough early-afternoon light filtering through the seams that Trafalgar no longer had to strain her eyes to see. The home looked abandoned, but she knew the truth. She went past the vacated front rooms to the next highest level, the place where lay the house's true purpose.

No matter how many times she visited the Crafter's workshop she was always in awe of its inventory. The walls were lined with bookshelves that overflowed with calipers, micrometers, shears, clamps, gauges, tap and die sets, hammers, mandrels, and any number of other tools she couldn't hope to identify. Half-formed objects in the vague shape of arms, legs, torsos, and faces lined the many tables of the room. Tools and parts orbited these incomplete items, sometimes draped with oily rags or wrinkled sheets of paper with blueprints scrawled on them.

Threnody emerged from the back of the house with a wooden case cradled under her right arm. She wore a collarless blue mandarin vest and a flowing dress that looked like an inverted black tulip as it swayed with her movement. Her hands were hidden by kid gloves, but the most remarkable aspect of her ensemble was the plague doctor's mask, its avian beak extending out like a dark brown hook made of oiled canvas. The two round eyepieces were filled with opaque lenses to prevent anyone from seeing even a glimpse of her face. Trafalgar had once seen what the Crafter was hiding beneath the mask, and it was an experience she wasn't soon to forget.

"You're early." Threnody's voice was filtered through her mask and came out muffled, hollow, as if she was speaking through a radio. "I don't like early."

"I overestimated the travel time. It won't happen again."

"Hm." Threnody cleared a space on her worktable and put down the case. She opened it and withdrew a pair of long slender blades connected at their base by a thin golden ring. At first glance they looked like the hands off a clock face. Threnody adjusted the blades until they lined up against each other, then she turned and held the item out to Trafalgar. "Your emei piercers. Traditionally the blades are fixed in place, but this allows you to collapse and conceal the blades up your sleeve until you are ready to use them. Be careful; the ends are very sharp."

"Interesting." Trafalgar slipped the ring over her middle finger and flicked her wrist. The blades snapped into place extending out several inches from either side of her hand. She closed her fingers around the blades and gave a few twists of her wrist. The blades would slice both on approach and retreat so that no motion was wasted. She released the blades and pushed down with her index and little finger to snap the blades back down. They slid along their axis so she could push the blades up into her sleeve where they couldn't be seen.

"Marvelous."

"I thought so. It should do nicely for your close-quarter purposes."

"Yes, quite. Thank you, Threnody." She withdrew a small pouch of money from her coat pocket and handed it to the Crafter. "How are you progressing on the electrical weapon I inquired about?"

"Ah, slowly. Slowly. I am consumed with work for other clients."

Trafalgar sneered. "Lady Boone, no doubt."

Threnody chuckled. "No jealousy, Miss Trafalgar. I can't play favorites with my clients. Besides, if I did, you would be the one left out in the cold. Lady Boone was referred to me by her grandmother. If I was the sort to let petty rivalries dictate my business, her business would take preference and you would be forced to find a new Crafter. I wouldn't want that, and I'm sure you wouldn't either."

"Heaven forfend," Trafalgar said. "Very well. I shall be in touch."

Threnody folded her hands in front of her chest and bowed slightly before she turned back to her work table. Trafalgar practiced with the emei piercers a bit more as she left the building, determining how best to manipulate her wrist and the movement of her hand to get the most out of the weapon. Leola pushed away from the car and straightened her jacket when Trafalgar emerged from the alleyway.

"Did you get your new toy, Miss Trafalgar?"

Trafalgar smiled and replaced the goggles over her eyes as she climbed back into the car. "When has Threnody ever disappointed us? Take us home, Adeline, and when we arrive I will show you how to use our new weapon."

A handful of airships buzzed above the Thames as they crossed London Bridge, like fat bumblebees scooting from one side of the river to the other. Some of them were taking longer journeys and used the river as a shortcut to avoid the uneven skyline. The gondola of one low-hanging ship buzzed them, its gondola swaying like a metallic dragonfly. Once off the bridge they turned right into Bankside, past the brothels and workhouses to the tenement they called home. The windows were barred and the brick was crumbling. It looked like any number of buildings in London, and a fair sight better than some that had suffered from night raids during the war.

Like Threnody's workshop the decay of their tenement was a carefully orchestrated deception. The spoils of her career were stored in the reinforced basement of the home. The items she brought home were too dangerous to leave where they were found, and she shuddered what would happen if some grave-robber happened to get his hands on some of them. So she brought them back and kept them safe with a double layer of protection: a vault and an appearance of deterioration. She lived with Adeline and Leola lived in a proper home that was surrounded by the shell of the crumbling brick. They had all the amenities of those who lived in the more elite parts of the city without drawing attention to themselves. She often thought of Lady Boone and her extravagant townhouse, the sprawling three-property fortress which all but beckoned thieves to try their luck.

Adeline parked the car in the only alley on the street wide enough to accommodate it, then Trafalgar and Leola helped conceal it using bins and empty wooden crates. Most people in the neighborhood knew Trafalgar, knew to trust her and that she was willing to fight for them as tirelessly as she fought for herself. They left her things alone for the most part but there was no sense in tempting fate. Adeline led them back to the street, and Leola took the rear for the walk back to their building.

Adeline started up the front steps but froze halfway up. She turned and scanned the street with an odd expression on her face.

"Is everything all right?" Trafalgar asked.

Adeline nodded slowly and allowed her expression to break into a full smile. "It's quiet. All the noise. The chatter? It's stopped. For the first time, I can't hear anything. The future has finally gone quiet."

Trafalgar had a moment of intense fear for what that meant before a bullet caught Adeline just above her left eyebrow. Her blood sprayed across the front of the building and drops of it landed on Trafalgar's face as her friend fell back onto the stone steps. Leola grabbed Trafalgar's shoulders and hauled her to the side as another bullet chipped the masonry of their building. Leola pushed Trafalgar into the shadows next to the stairs and draw her own revolver. Trafalgar started to lean forward but Leola pushed her back.

"Where is it coming from?"

"I can't see," Leola said. Another bullet sank into Adeline's body with a sickeningly flat sound, like a blackjack thudding against a speed bag. Tears burned the corners of Trafalgar's eyes, a mixture of anger and grief at the thought of her friend being violated in that manner. Leola straightened slightly and fired at a window across the street.

"The butcher's," she said. "The second floor of the butcher's. On the north side."

Trafalgar pushed away from the wall and remained crouched as she moved to the kerb. She doubted a shooter from the vantage point Leola had given her would be able to hit a target at that angle, and she risked a quick dash across the street without cover. Bullets chipped the brickwork of the road but not even the chips got close enough to harm her. The alley door was locked, a fact she only discovered after she had used her shoulder as a battering ram to shove it open. The shrapnel from the destroyed lock pelted harmlessly off her coat as she took a moment to get her bearings. Large industrial sinks to the right, with grisly cuts of meat hanging from hooks just beyond. To the left a wooden cage that constituted the manager's office and a staircase leading up.

She flicked her wrist as Threnody had demonstrated and the emei piercers fell into her hand. She pounded up the stairs, her coat flaring behind her as she reached the second floor landing and nearly collided with someone attempting to escape. He was a small man wearing a balaclava and dark clothing. She grabbed the shooter's arms and used her forward momentum to swing the shooter like a dumbbell, letting herself fall and hurling her opponent back the way he had come from. He dropped his weapon and it clattered out of reach across the floor as Trafalgar got to her feet and advanced on him.

"You killed my friend," she hissed through clenched teeth.

"I was aiming for you."

"You'll die slowly, wishing you had better aim."

He threw himself at her and Trafalgar spun her piercers. The motion made him believe she'd thrown something and he ducked to one side to avoid a projectile. His attempt to evade threw him off balance, and Trafalgar caught his shoulder with the edge of one blade. He cried out and reared back to free himself, tearing flesh and muscle in the process. He stumbled from the pain and Trafalgar withdrew a quarterstaff from a deep inner pocket of her coat. She swung it underhand, catching the man on his chin and lifting him off his feet.

When he fell, Trafalgar pounced on him. He fought to get free but she pinned his arms to his sides and placed one blade against his throat.

"You will never know what a precious life you extinguished today." She felt tears on her cheeks but refused to acknowledge them. "Adeline Okoro. Say it."

He stared at her through the opening in his mask and she applied pressure to his throat.

"Adeline Okoro." The lower half of the mask moved with his lips.

"Who sent you to kill me?"

"Dorothy Boone."

Trafalgar set her lips in a firm line and pulled her arm to the side. The blade slit the sniper's throat, and she held him down until every twitch of life was gone from his body. His blood pooled around her on the floor and, when she stood, she saw it had stained the tail of her coat. It wouldn't be the first blood she had washed from the leather, and it certainly wouldn't be the last. She touched the sleeve to her cheek and smeared Adeline's blood with her tears, then began searching the assassin for clues as to his identity. She found nothing but a few pounds, some extra ammunition, and a dangerous looking blade. Whoever he was, he was smart enough not to carry anything that would identify him. She took off his mask and made note of his features, then left him to finish bleeding out in the abattoir.

Her feet were heavy as she returned to the ground floor, her hands shaking as she collapsed the emei piercers and concealed them back up her sleeve. She crossed the street and saw that Leola, rather than coming to her aid to capture the sniper, had taken the time to retrieve Adeline's body and carry it into the house. Trafalgar looked at the blood that had been spilled all over the entry of their home and stared. Adeline, the scared girl who heard voices in her head, who spoke to ghosts and frightened the other children by answering questions they hadn't asked. Adeline who had been quickly pushed out of three foster homes by asking about her new parents' deepest and darkest secrets. Eventually Trafalgar gave up trying to find a home for her and invited her to stay with her permanently. The girl was a treasure, and her mind had been opened to the world on a level others couldn't hope to achieve. The bastard across the street had silenced her voice with a single stupid bullet.

Inside, Leola was already sitting vigil over their fallen friend. She had stretched Adeline out on the parlor table, a piece of cloth wrapped around her head to keep the blood from spilling out onto the floor. The stomach of her blouse was also torn open by the postmortem bullets. Leola looked up, her face streaked with dark tracks of her tears, and her lower lip trembled.

"He's dead."

"Did he suffer?"

"Not enough." Trafalgar slipped off her jacket and let it fall to the floor. She knelt at the end of the table and framed Adeline's head with her hands. She bent forward and placed a tender kiss between her eyebrows. "I am sorry for doing this to you, Adeline. I... I am glad you heard the silence for once before you went. I know you dreamed of what it would be like to hear only the now. I am grateful you were given that small blessing."

Leola, a woman Trafalgar had once seen take a nail through her hand without making a sound, choked back a sob.

"We will punish the one who did this to you."

"Who?" Leola asked. "Who hired the shooter?"

Trafalgar's lip curled, her eyes darkening as she forced her lips to frame the disgusting words. "Lady Dorothy Boone. The man across the street died swiftly, and rightly so. He was only a tool. But Lady Boone shall suffer for the life she took today. I shall see to it personally."

Chapter Three

THE PATHS of Dorothy Boone and Trafalgar of Abyssinia first crossed six years earlier, in Istanbul. Reports of a stone road spotted underwater led many experts to believe they had found remnants of a buried city. It was common knowledge that Istanbul had been built and destroyed several times over, always a large and strategic port city in ancient times. If the stone road led to the ruins of a forgotten past version of the great city, untold treasures could be waiting to be discovered. Dorothy immediately began planning an expedition to Turkey, while trying to ignore rumors of another team setting out immediately.

Once she gained funding, Dorothy set off with a small group of researchers, archaeologists, and professors. They arrived to find the area was already sealed off by a group which had arrived three days earlier and declared the area for themselves. Dorothy ignored the restrictions and crossed the line under cover of darkness. The rest of her team refused to trespass, but Dorothy considered all fair in the pursuit of knowledge. She discovered a submersible hoisted by a metallic cage over the still waters of Lake Kucukcekmece. The expedition members seemed to be out for the night, their tents mostly dark save for one or two lanterns which still flickered.

Dorothy crossed their campsite as quietly as possible and approached the sub. She had never actually seen a submarine, let alone operated one, but it certainly couldn't be any more complicated than a car or airship. She remembered the times her friend Minty had let her steer the *Skylarker* conveniently forgetting that she had almost crashed them into the dome of St. Paul's. She put thoughts of past failures out of her mind and carefully traversed the crane holding the cage out over the water.

As she was trying to find a way into the hull, a pair of figures appeared on the shore. It was difficult to make out details in the darkness but Dorothy could tell the taller of them was carrying a weapon.

"It would be to your benefit to kindly remove yourself from our vessel."

Dorothy remained crouched but lifted her hands to show she was unarmed. "I meant no harm."

"Only to steal our tech and supplies."

"Where would I have taken it? I only have one course of retreat." She smiled and held her hands out to indicate the lake. "It's a large lake but I'm sure you would be able to track me down before long."

The tall woman on the shore raised her gun. "I won't ask you again."

Dorothy straightened and held her hands out to either side. "All right. Of course, if you were to fire that here in the dark, you would risk damaging this vessel. I doubt that's a risk you would be willing to take. In the morning you would be delayed while you searched for damage and even after a thorough inspection there would still be the chance that a seal was grazed or there's some slight hole that would affect the hull's viability. Or you could fire over my head, but then you would risk one of the brackets. I highly doubt you would be willing to plunge this thing into the depths like a stone."

"Are you willing to take that risk, madam?"

"Are you?" Dorothy dropped back down and pushed the hatch cover up so it was between her and the shore. As predicted her quarry cursed rather than firing. Dorothy dropped inside, sealed the hatch, and moved forward at a hunched shuffle to the cockpit. The seat was threadbare but surprisingly comfortable, with fat wings that extended to either side of her as if it were trying to give her a hug. A bit of fumbling revealed a gooseneck lamp attached to the control panel. She switched it on and stared at the dials and levers. A yoke steering wheel jutted out from the console in front of her, surrounded by switches and gauges marked with numbers and abbreviations she couldn't hope to decipher.

"Okay, Dorothy. You've learned more complex things under worse circumstances..." Something banged against the top of the ship. "Perhaps not with quite such a harrowing timetable, but regardless." She pressed a few likely candidates for the ignition, hoping it didn't require a key. One of the things she pressed caused a low rumble to begin somewhere behind her. The floor trembled with the force of it, and she felt the vibrations up through the seat. "Ooh." She shifted her hips slightly and smiled. "A lady could get quite accustomed to that, thank you very much."

"Lady Boone! Do not attempt to submerge this vehicle."

She smiled and shouted over her shoulder. "My reputation precedes me, I see! But you have me at a disadvantage. Should I know you?"

"I am Trafalgar of Abyssinia."

"Aha! I have heard of you. Well, Miss Trafalgar, I would suggest returning to the crane if you do not wish to get wet." She wrapped her fingers around a lever and tugged it down. The ship lurched, and the vibration in her seat increased. While appreciated she knew it must be an indication that the engine was straining. Probably not advisable. She pushed the lever back up and listened to the sound of Trafalgar and her associate speaking from atop the vessel. "Damn. Where is the release..."

Before she could finish the thought, the entire submarine plummeted down to the water. Dorothy hadn't bothered to strap herself into the seat, so she was lifted into the air and dropped back down hard. "Crumbs," she muttered, grabbing the yoke rather than rubbing her sore posterior. She assumed Trafalgar had disconnected the ship from its mooring rather than risk damage by letting Dorothy futz with the controls. Probably a wise decision.

"I appreciate the assistance. If you're still there, I should warn you I still intend to submerge."

"I won't allow you to abscond with this vessel."

Dorothy rolled her eyes. "Have it your way." She found a handle labeled BALLAST and pushed it up. The submarine groaned and its weight shifted toward the stern. Above her she heard Trafalgar and the other woman stumbling to keep their balance. She gripped the padded handles of the yoke. She wanted to reach the lake's floor, and she was confident that would happen no matter what she did to the controls. The hard part would be getting back to the surface, but she would cross that bridge when the time came.

Adeline had awoken Trafalgar with an urgent clicking of her tongue, patting Trafalgar's arm and then covering her mouth to prevent her from speaking at full voice. They had only bedded down thirty minutes earlier and Trafalgar's mind was muddied by being yanked back from the precipice of REM sleep. Adeline cut through the fog with the simple warning that someone was in their camp. Trafalgar threw on her coat, grabbed a gun, and led Adeline out into the main camp. She saw the intruder moving stealthily through the scattered tents, a shadow among shadows and almost as silent. A convenient fall of moonlight revealed the woman's features to her, and Trafalgar recognized her from the society pages as Lady Dorothy Boone. She had yet to meet the woman in person, and she felt it unfortunate they would be introduced under such inauspicious circumstances.

She and Adeline approached the shore, drawing Lady Boone's attention before they even said a word. Trafalgar squared her shoulders and raised her voice to be heard and also in the hopes of alerting the other members of their expedition about what was happening. "It would be to your benefit to kindly remove yourself from our vessel."

Trafalgar didn't believe for a moment Boone would listen to her warning, so she was unsurprised when after a brief exchange of taunts the woman lifted the hatch and jumped down inside. Trafalgar and Adeline clambered up onto the crane and made their way to the submersible. Adeline stood astride the hatch and took a deep breath. She closed her eyes and rolled her head one way, then the other. She was shutting out the present to look inward, to dig through the barrage of the possible and likely futures to find the one that was reality. Trafalgar was fascinated by the dedication it took to sift through everything so quickly, like listening to an orchestra and attempting to hear a single string of a particular violin.

As Adeline tried to focus her thoughts and visions, Trafalgar dropped to one knee and shouted to be heard inside the ship.

"Lady Boone! Do not attempt to submerge this vehicle."

The reply came from within the belly of the ship, shouted and full of echoes. "My reputation precedes me, I see! But you have me at a disadvantage. Should I know you?"

"I am Trafalgar of Abyssinia."

"Aha! I have heard of you. Well, Miss Trafalgar, I would suggest returning to the crane if you do not wish to get wet."

Trafalgar grimaced and looked up at Adeline. "Do you see anything?"

"Thick smoke. Fire. She's going to destroy the engine. We have to disconnect from the crane or she'll burn the entire works."

"Try to get that hatch open." She stood and saw a group of men gathered on the shore. She got their attention and said, "Release the ship!"

Most of them didn't move, hopefully reluctant to follow her command while she was standing on top of it, but one man moved to the console and began typing. The chain holding the submersible aloft released, and Trafalgar fell as the world seemed to drop out from under her. She grabbed hold of a curled edge in time to prevent herself from tumbling down the curved body of the vessel into the water. Adeline was flat on her stomach, clutching the hatch with both hands. Trafalgar crawled to where she was in time to hear Boone's voice echoing from within.

"--you're still there, I should warn you I still intend to submerge."

"I won't allow you to abscond with this vessel."

Boone responded, but not loud enough for Trafalgar to make out the words. Adeline grunted and started to slide.

"Can you swim?" Trafalgar asked.

"Well enough to get back to shore."

Trafalgar said, "Are you certain?"

Adeline closed her eyes. "I see myself wrapped in thick blankets and drinking something warm."

Trafalgar smiled. "Save a cup for me."

"Good luck." The water was quickly rising on all sides, the submersible turning into a rapidly-shrinking island. Adeline let herself slip toward the inky black waters, then got her feet flat on the hull and threw herself forward. She dove far enough away from the ship so that she wasn't dragged down by the undertow, and Trafalgar focused on getting the hatch open. She took a blade from the pocket of her coat, slipped it under the lip of the hatch, and broke the seal as the lake's waters finally reached her position. She pushed the hatch up and jumped inside along with a torrent of water.

Dorothy shouted something indecipherable from the front of the ship as Trafalgar tried not to drown, spluttering as she reached blindly for the hatch to pull it shut behind her. She cut off the flow of water and spun the handwheel. The water filled the cramped space of the submarine's interior, sloshing against her knees. Dorothy had stood up and was lumbering toward her. Trafalgar reached for a weapon in her jacket pocket, but Dorothy was too quick for her. She shoved Trafalgar backward, stealing her balance, and grabbing the lapels of her coat before she could fall.

"Are you completely mad?"

"Said the woman stealing my ship!" Trafalgar slapped Dorothy's arms away. When Dorothy fell back Trafalgar slumped against the wall and brought her foot up out of the water. She planted it against Dorothy's chest and pushed. Dorothy grabbed Trafalgar's ankle and pulled her into the fall as well, and both women splashed down into the water that swung back and forth through the cockpit as if it were attempting to create its own tides. Dorothy rose first, hair hanging in her face like seaweed, and watched as Trafalgar surfaced beside her.

"You have no idea what you've risked!" Trafalgar barked. She swung wildly, a telegraphed attempt which Dorothy easily blocked. "What little we've seen of the ruins below are extremely delicate. For you to blunder through with a ship you can't even hope to control... what did you hope to gain?"

"Insight, information." Dorothy wrapped her arm around Trafalgar's and forced the other woman's back against the wall. "There is power in information, and in the wrong hands that power can have unimaginable consequences."

"And when you find your answers, who will be on the receiving end? Whoever opened their pocketbooks to fund your latest expedition?" She threw her weight forward and Dorothy took a step back. The water shifted again and changed their weight just enough to make the submersible tilt underneath them. Dorothy and Trafalgar both stumbled, but this time only Dorothy sank under the water.

Trafalgar pushed her out of the way and waded up to the cockpit. She didn't bother trying to sit down, since the seat was already underwater, and she opened the ballast tanks. The console was drenched and covered with beads of water, the lower half engulfed, and she hoped the electronic components were well protected. It would take them ages to inspect everything and ensure it was safe for their descent.

She heard Dorothy getting to her feet. "I would forestall any attack you might be planning. We're close enough to the surface we may yet be able to rise again, but the damage may keep us at the bottom of the lake if we sink any deeper."

"The damage you caused by opening the hatch."

Trafalgar glared at her. "If I hadn't opened the hatch, you would have been stranded at the bottom of this lake alone and slowly asphyxiating. We would have had no way to rescue you. By being here now, I am risking my own life to save yours. I don't expect gratitude, but you could at the very least remain *quiet* and not attack me while I sort out this mess."

She heard water pouring off Dorothy, heard her catching her breath, but she refrained from attacking. Trafalgar emptied the ballast tanks, then opened the vents that would drain the contents of the passenger cabin so they wouldn't be splashing around as the ship ascended. She looked out the bulb of glass in front of her and blew air past her lips. It was difficult to tell in the dark, but she definitely felt buoyant and was confident they were rising again.

"If you hadn't rushed to be the first one here, if you had done it properly, with a *plan*–"

"This was *planned*?" Trafalgar said in shock. "I hate to see what would happen if you worked by the seat of your pants."

Dorothy said, "My hand was forced. I worked patiently back in London, I set up benefactors to fund an expedition, I arranged for surveys of the lake, all to make certain an excavation was done properly. Then I receive word that you have a team on the ground! I had to be impetuous to ensure you didn't muck everything up."

"Excellent job at that, Lady Boone."

Dorothy sneered at her.

"As it is," Trafalgar continued, "our work has been delayed days. Perhaps weeks. If the submersible is damaged beyond repair we may not get another chance until next summer."

"The damage you cause by going off half-cocked..."

Trafalgar said, "There is no guarantee we'll have a chance next summer. This entire area could be..." She clamped her teeth together and closed her eyes.

"Could be what?" Dorothy said.

"The woman who was with me above. Her name is Adeline. She... sees things. Usually only a few minutes or even seconds in the future. Glimpses and clues to what is about to happen. But in the past year the noises have gotten louder. Bigger and darker. Something is coming, Lady Boone, something that will affect every person in every corner of the world. We must explore sites like this and preserve what we can while we still have time. We can't waste precious weeks gathering funds and writing plans."

Dorothy said, "So we rush in blindly without a care to the locals we may upset or the dangers we risk by removing artifacts from the places where they have been held for centuries or millennia? We 'waste time,' as you call it, to ensure everything is done properly. Doing anything less results in..." She laughed ruefully and gestured at her waterlogged self. "In this!"

The darkness through the glass lessened somewhat as they breached. "I shall remember that the next time we meet, Lady Boone. Perhaps I will be less inclined to save you on that date."

"The day I require your rescue..."

"...is apparently this day," Trafalgar said.

Dorothy slumped against the wall and crossed her arms over her chest. Trafalgar walked back to the hatch and climbed up to push it open. She hung from the ladder and turned back to look at Dorothy. She stepped down off the ladder and gestured for Dorothy to lead the way. "If you think I'm leaving you behind on this ship, you are sorely mistaken. After you, Lady Boone."

Dorothy gripped a rung of the ladder but paused before she began climbing. "Even if this darkness your companion saw does come to pass, this will definitely not be the last time we meet, Miss Trafalgar. Right now I am in your debt. Don't expect that to affect my feelings on our next encounter."

"And just because I saved your life this time does not mean I intend to make it a habit." She nodded up at the opening. "Out. Now."

Dorothy climbed out of the still-dripping submersible and, after taking a moment to inspect the damage, sighed and followed Dorothy out of the ship.

In the end the submersible was able to make the dive after an intense examination from its owner. Dorothy and her team were banned from the site and forced to return to London in defeat. Her benefactor was highly irate with news of the failure but his tempers calmed slightly when word came from Turkey that Trafalgar's team had also come up empty-handed. Dorothy helped him see the silver lining, in that he had only paid for a brief trip rather than a long-term mission that proved fruitless. The other members of her team were less amenable. Several of them decided her rash actions indicated a capriciousness that they were unwilling to deal with. She was still able to find people to fund and accompany her on expeditions but she had to admit the process was much more difficult than it had once been.

And as Trafalgar predicted, the following years were indeed dark for everyone, not just Dorothy. With the advent of the Great War, formerly generous beneficiaries were reluctant to fund any kind of international excursions. She disliked traveling alone but she rarely had a choice in the matter. Able-bodied men were shipping off to war, and those who remained home weren't able to justify gallivanting off to dig for treasures in some distant land when the homefront was under fire.

Dorothy occasionally received word that Trafalgar was spending more time abroad to keep away from the fighting and the air raids. Her expatriate status meant it was easier for her to travel, but she was cut off from her sources of information and the suppliers who made her missions possible. The women did still cross paths from time to time. They frequently only caught sight of each other from a distance, one leaving as the other arrived, but so far they had refrained from further fisticuffs.

From the library of Ephesus, where Dorothy conspired to have Trafalgar evicted from her hotel in order to buy herself time to get the items she'd unearthed to the train station unmolested, to the Ellora Caves of India, where they agreed to a brief truce in deference to the site's importance in the nonviolent religion of Jainism. The truce hadn't extended to the train station where Trafalgar traded Dorothy's bags with decoys and disappeared with the charcoal rubbings Dorothy had made of the various carvings. Generally they were both aware when the other was in London and found ways to avoid one another. Trafalgar tried to stay on the south side of the Thames while Dorothy remained in her own space on the northern shore.

One evening en route to dinner with her male companion, Professor Desmond Tindall, they spotted Trafalgar and one of her cohorts standing on a street corner waiting to cross. He took note of her sour expression but waited until they passed her before commenting on it.

"Surely there are ways you could avoid her entirely, or eliminate her from the playing field. You could buy her out, you could convince any bank-rollers to cease working with her..."

Dorothy sneered. "That hardly seems fair."

"Fair? The woman drives you insane, Dorothy. She's maddening."

"She keeps me on my toes. She forces me to think critically and often on the fly. And if, on occasion, she manages to outwit me, I use that as incentive to try harder the next time. Avoid her? Quite the contrary, my dear Des. What is a woman without an adversary?"

He laughed and shook his head, and Dorothy looked out the window. Trafalgar was already gone, but Dorothy touched the brim of her hat in a subtle but sincere gesture of acknowledgement to her adversary.

Chapter Four

The same day Adeline met her tragic demise, Beatrice received the daily mail from the front stoop and brought it into the parlor. Dorothy was still recovering from her trip to Mexico, but she was awake and working in the library. She was dressed for the day in a lightweight blouse, open at the collar with the sleeves pinned above her elbows. The window was open and a gentle breeze lifted the hair from her neck as she bent over her latest map.

She adored cartography; drawing the lines of the world as she saw them on her own journeys rather than relying on the eyes of others provided her with a much more accurate representation of where she had been should she ever need to go back. Her feet were crossed at the ankles under her chair as she drew the coastline as it was in her memory. She had entire books full of maps depicting places she had traveled. She drew them both as they were now and as they had been generations ago when their civilizations were thriving.

Her tongue was poking between her lips as her head rocked one way and then the other so she didn't have to move the paper. Beatrice took a moment to appreciate the view, the sunlight glinting through the red strands of Dorothy's hair, before drawing attention to herself.

"The mail is here."

"Ah, splendid." She put the finishing touches on the harbor she'd been drawing and put her hands in the small of her back. She stretched and grimaced as her muscles protested the movement. "Anything worth noting?"

Beatrice set each item down as she examined the return addresses. "Correspondence from the archaeology department in Connecticut. Hm. This is curious. Something from Miss Trafalgar."

That drew Dorothy's attention. She looked at the book-shaped package wrapped in pale brown paper. "How very odd." She pushed away from the slanted top of her desk and crossed the room to take it from her. "This is addressed to Dorothy Boone. Curious."

"What?"

"Not once has she ever referred to me by my given name. To her, I am Lady Boone. Why wouldn't she address the package that way? And why would she send me anything at all to begin with?"

"Perhaps a taunt?" Beatrice said. "She may have an intriguing new lead, or gained a new wealthy benefactor."

Dorothy considered that but it didn't seem plausible. They would taunt and mock one another but only if they happened to cross paths. She would never have gone out of her way to gloat about some piece of good fortune, and it seemed impossible Trafalgar would be petty enough to start. She tapped her thumbs on the edge of the package and pursed her lips.

"An intriguing mystery."

"One that could be resolved by opening the package."

Dorothy raised an eyebrow. "Yes. But without knowing what it is... do you recall the story I told you about the sunken temples off the Comoros?"

"Of course."

"The entryway was entirely clear of obstacle. A perfectly formed tunnel leading down into the main cavern. To one side, a handful of torches to light the way."

Beatrice nodded. "The torches were the trap. Whoever tried to pick one up triggered the release of poison darts."

"An innocent enough offering that obscured its true and deadly purpose." She held the package up and looked across the face of it on a horizontal plane. She closed one eye and tried to see any discrepancy in the shape of it. "I would say a box. Slender, not capable of holding much." She brushed her thumbs over the sides. "A hinge along the upper edge, meaning it opens length-wise rather than along the width. Lightweight enough..."

Beatrice said, "There's a way to know how dangerous it is without opening it."

Dorothy raised an eyebrow. "You don't like utilizing that little trait."

"You've driven me to it with this incessant deducing. The suspense is driving me mad."

"Well then." Dorothy put the package down and flourished toward it with her hand. "Be my guest, Trix."

Beatrice rubbed her left thumb in a wide circle against the pads of her first three fingers. She held her hand out, palm-flat, and closed her eyes. Dorothy crossed her arms and watched as the package began to tremble on the tabletop, then began to slowly spin counterclockwise. Something within the package clicked, and the shape of the paper changed as the lid tried to flip open. Beatrice spread her fingers wider, a wrinkle appearing between her eyebrows as she focused. A concentrated burst of magical energy could disrupt simple mechanisms, the sort of mechanisms which would have to be used if such a small package was indeed intended as a trap.

The room filled with a slow, clanking melody. "A music box," Dorothy said. "Oh, that is a shame." She furrowed her brow as she recognized the song. "A funeral dirge? That's hardly–" With sudden realization she threw an arm across Beatrice's torso and pulled her back. They fell to the floor as the box detonated, sending shards and splinters through the spot where they had just been standing.

Dorothy pushed herself up and touched Beatrice's face. "Are you all right, darling?"

"My head hurts."

Dorothy tenderly touched her hair. "From the fall?"

"From using magic. It was my idea, don't fret." She kissed the heel of Dorothy's hand. "You?"

"I rapped my elbow on the floor when I fell. Hardly the worst injury I've ever suffered." She sat up and offered Beatrice her hand, hauling her back to her feet. The room reeked of cordite and charred wood, the paper from the packaging smoldered on the table where it had dropped after Beatrice broke her concentration. Dorothy cupped the back of Beatrice's head and gently massaged her scalp as she considered the wreckage of the bomb. It had been small enough, as bombs go, with highly localized damage, but if it had exploded in her hands...

"What are you thinking?" Beatrice asked.

"I still find it difficult to believe Trafalgar sent the package. It's not her style. Still, I believe this mystery may require an audience with her. Prepare the car. We're going to Bankside."

Dorothy changed into a proper visiting outfit and tucked her hair up under a bowler hat. Beatrice tended to be more casual around the house, so she put on her uniform jacket, cap, and gloves, and brought the car around. She settled in the backseat with the ruins of the music box, rubbing the paper between her fingers as it crumbled to ash. She brushed the soot from her slacks and pursed her lips as she considered the possible suspects. There was no shortage of men who found it untenable that a woman would vie for a position in their field. But resorting to attempted murder was beyond the pale. And attempting to frame Trafalgar was curious to say the least.

They drove south to the bridge and sighted the Thames just as an oncoming vehicle veered into their lane of traffic. Beatrice cursed as she swerved to avoid the other vehicle, which passed close enough that Dorothy could look into the backseat to see Trafalgar staring back at her. Beatrice saw her as well.

"She just tried running us off the road," she said. "Still think she's innocent?"

"Perhaps less so, in light of the new evidence," Dorothy admitted.

"Her car is coming around."

Dorothy took off her hat and tossed it into the seat beside her. "Stop the car. If she intends to hash this out in the street, I'll be more than happy to oblige her." She removed a pearl-handled revolver from beneath the seat and tucked it under her belt. She also unsheathed her dirk, though she had no intention of stabbing anyone with it at the moment. Plans could change in an instant, however, and she very much preferred to have it available and never use it than the alternative.

Beatrice grinned and rolled the car to a stop at the kerb. Dorothy climbed out as Trafalgar and her enforcer, Leola, stormed toward her from a few yards down the street. Trafalgar was carrying what appeared to be a bladed weapon in one hand with a short club in the other. Leola seemed intent on using only her fists for whatever confrontation was to come.

"Miss Trafalgar," Dorothy said. "I was just on my way to see you."

"To admire your handiwork?" Trafalgar said, her lips curling into a sneer. "Your victim's name was Adeline Okoro!"

The challenge faded from Dorothy's expression, replaced by confusion. "My victim? Adeline? What in blazes are you--"

Her question was cut off by a wide swing of Trafalgar's club. She obviously planned to lash out the moment she was in range but miscalculated the distance. Dorothy rocked back on her heels and felt wind on her face from the club's passage. Trafalgar took another step and followed through with her swing. Dorothy ducked to avoid it this time and threw herself at Trafalgar's midsection.

Leola pulled back her fist, but Beatrice stepped in and hooked her arm around the woman's elbow. They spun like dance partners and Beatrice stuck her foot out to trip Leola. Both went down, but Beatrice recovered more quickly. She struck from a kneeling position and punched Leola just under her ribs in the soft skin of her gut. Leola was dazed long enough for Beatrice to get to her feet for another attack. Leola's shoulders rose and fell as she centered herself before launching forward with a second attack. Beatrice leapt out of the way but Leola was prepared. Her hands hit the pavement and she turned her pounce into a somersault. The heel of her shoe clipped Beatrice's chin and sent her reeling.

Pedestrians had cleared the area, and all other traffic was stalled to give the four women space for their brawl. Trafalgar's bladed weapon caught the buttons of Dorothy's vest and popped them off. Dorothy grimaced and captured Trafalgar's wrist to keep the blades from getting a better angle on her.

"I haven't the slightest clue what you're accusing me of, Miss Trafalgar. But

I assure you–" Trafalgar thrust her free hand into Dorothy's gut and knocked the wind from her. Dorothy doubled over and released her grip. They pushed away from each other as if drawn back magnetically, and Dorothy put a hand against her stomach to make sure the clothes and skin had come out unscathed.

"You sent an assassin after me," Trafalgar said. "He failed, but claimed the life of my dear friend. Adeline Okoro. You will say her name before I make you pay for her death."

Dorothy's eyes widened. "Bloody hell." She straightened as much as her bruised abdomen would allow. She took her gun from her belt and tossed it aside, then did the same with her dagger. "Miss Trafalgar, I deeply regret the loss of your companion and I assert wholeheartedly that I had no hand in it whatsoever. Miss Sek and I were also the target of an assassination attempt this afternoon. I have the evidence in the car if you would like to see it. The method was an explosive hidden inside a package allegedly sent to us by you."

Trafalgar's posture relaxed slightly. She flexed her fingers on the grip of her club, and Dorothy saw the bladed weapon was attached to a ring around Trafalgar's middle finger. She was impressed by the ingenuity but forced her mind to stay on track.

"Why do you think I would have sent someone to kill you?"

"The sniper named you upon his capture."

Dorothy nodded. "We must interrogate this man at once, the both of us together. He could be invaluable to finding out what precisely is going on."

Trafalgar had the grace to look sheepish. "I killed him."

Dorothy's shoulders slumped. "You didn't."

"He murdered my friend in cold blood," Trafalgar said through clenched teeth. "Tell me you wouldn't have done the same thing in my place."

Dorothy looked at Beatrice and conceded. "Right. We'll simply have to make do."

"We?"

"Yes. It stands to reason that two attempted murders occurring nearly simultaneously with both victims named as the perpetrator in the other attempt." She sighed. "Someone wanted to eliminate us. They made certain there was a contingency in the event one or both were unsuccessful. Either we both die and our invisible adversary gets what he wants, or one of us dies and the other is held accountable. "

Leola said, "Or neither of you dies, you end up brawling in the street. It's only a matter of time before the police arrive and start asking questions." She looked at Beatrice, who was still rubbing her jaw. After a moment Beatrice nodded, a small gesture of apology, and Leola returned it.

"Right." Dorothy straightened her ruined vest and smoothed a hand across her hair as she examined the crowd around them. "I would like to see the crime scene, Miss Trafalgar, if you would be agree to that. I'd also like to see the man who claims I hired him. It would be interesting to see if I even recognize the bloke."

"Very well." Trafalgar snapped the blade in half and concealed it up her sleeve. Dorothy made a note to definitely get a closer look at the weapon, and soon. "Since it seems we've been targeted by the same person it only makes sense that we enact a temporary truce."

Dorothy nodded. "It's so agreed. Lead the way."

Trafalgar inclined her head slightly, then motioned for Leola to follow her. Despite the apology Leola and Beatrice still eyed each other warily until they were outside of striking distance. Beatrice smoothed down her clothes and checked her hair as she led Dorothy back to their vehicle.

"Someone going after both of you. That's intriguing."

"Isn't it? For the time being it's almost worth joining forces with Trafalgar to determine the true culprit. Needs must and all that."

Beatrice didn't seem convinced, but she slipped behind the wheel and watched Trafalgar's car. "If you say so, mum."

Dorothy sighed as she settled back in her seat. "Ah, I love it when you call me 'mum.'"

Beatrice smirked and started the engine. Trafalgar passed them, and she pulled out into the street to follow her across the bridge.

The spray of blood was still visible on the front steps of Trafalgar's townhouse, and Dorothy was taken aback by how large the pool had been. It had dried by that point, a deep maroon spill, and it chilled her to stand in front of it. Trafalgar stood at her right shoulder, with Beatrice and Leola standing on either side of the front steps to redirect any foot traffic that might pass by. Dorothy took a moment of silence in honor of the woman who had died before she spoke.

"Show me where she was standing, if you would." Trafalgar demonstrated, and Dorothy took position on the third step. "And you were directly in front of her?"

"I was here."

Leola pointed. "The shooter was in that window, between the third and fourth corbel."

"Third and fourth... what?"

Leola said, "The bracket holding up the cornice." She held out her arm and leaned to one side so Dorothy could follow her finger. "See?"

"Ah, yes. Thank you." She chewed her bottom lip and then narrowed her eyes. "Was that his only option? What about these other windows? Do they lead to offices, locked rooms, what?"

Trafalgar shook her head. "It's a loft space. He could have used any of them. He didn't want to be seen when we approached, so he chose a position as far away as possible."

"And sacrificed a sure shot for a riskier attempt. He knew he would be shooting at this position and yet he moved that far away. He was confident in his ability to hit you from that distance."

"He shouldn't have been," Trafalgar said flatly, pushing down her anger and grief.

Dorothy rocked her head from side to side. "Perhaps, perhaps not. But if he missed he knew he wouldn't have a second chance. If any of these windows were as good as the one he picked, why not get a little closer? An assassin would place himself as close as he needed to be, and in this case that was still quite far away. That speaks to his ability."

"What ability?" Leola said. "He missed."

"A man with an assassin's rifle, with an assassin's skill, would not miss so perfectly. He would not prepare a shot for Trafalgar that was off by less than a meter. If he missed, he would have hit the... the..." She gestured at the door.

"The lintel?" Leola suggested.

"Yes," Dorothy said. "If he was aiming for Trafalgar and misjudged the wind, the bullet would have been carried farther. It would have gone into the street or the building." She extended her hand to lay two fingers flat against Trafalgar's temple; her arm was nowhere near at full reach, and her elbow was in fact slightly bent. "The man who chose that vantage point would not miss by this much. And he certainly wouldn't have been fortunate enough to score an unintentional perfect kill. The man was not aiming at you, Miss Trafalgar. He hit his target."

Trafalgar's eyes flashed with anger. "Why would he want to kill Adeline?"

Dorothy dropped her hand. "She was incentive. Beatrice and I assumed the plot was for us both to die, but now I don't believe that's true. The plot was to kill me and set you up to take the fall." She closed her eyes to picture how the plan would have gone down. "A package arrives in the mail, a package with your name and return address. I open it, and the explosion kills me. Meanwhile, here in Bankside, a sniper kills Adeline Okoro. Enraged, you make haste to my doorstep..."

Trafalgar said, "At which point I would have broken down the door when you didn't respond. I would have found your charred corpse on the parlor floor..."

"And I'd wager anything the Met would be right behind. I've little doubt whoever arranged this was poised to make a call to them at just the right moment. I had to spoil the whole thing by surviving the attempt."

"But why go through this production?" Beatrice said. "If someone wants you dead and Trafalgar out of the country, surely there are easier ways to go about making both those things happen."

"True," Dorothy said. "But this method leaves our enemy's hands clean. The police have a suspect for my murder and Trafalgar is arrested and jailed. The only loose end is Adeline's death, and I'm sorry to say the police likely wouldn't expend much energy in solving that."

Beatrice said, "Why not?"

Trafalgar said, "Her skin is the wrong color, and she was too close to a brothel for her death to be a mystery in their minds. The case would have been completely closed before a single police officer set foot on the crime scene. But why us? Let us presume someone is clearing the path for... something... and didn't want us to interfere. Why in Heaven's name would he target us both?"

"It's common knowledge we're enemies. If some constable did get it into his head to investigate, our antagonism would have made the murder charge easier to swallow."

"Yes, I understand that. But why would anyone fear the both of us getting in his way? He was perfectly willing to murder you. He could have murdered me without bothering to line up a scapegoat."

Dorothy chewed her bottom lip as she thought. Finally her eyes widened. "Oh, crumbs. He wouldn't target us specifically. If he wants to eliminate his competition, we wouldn't be his only targets. He would want to clear the entire playing field. Archaeologists, practitioners, and explorers all over London are in grave danger." She hurried down the steps and motioned for Trafalgar to follow her. "Come! We can only pray it's not too late to stop him from massacring all of our peers in one fell swoop!"

Chapter Five

Little more than a dozen King's College students filled the Department of History's main lecture hall, shuffling their feet or staring at the dust motes dancing in the sun that filtered through the arched windows. The young men were well-distributed among the sea of wooden seats, their distance from one another enforcing just how low the turnout for the class was. Those who bothered to show up were mainly there for the spectacle, but one or two were fresh meat who had yet to hear the rumors.

Professor Desmond Tindall finished writing "Mitanni" on the chalkboard with a flourish on the tittle above the last letter. He was young with hair the color of wet sand and bright blue eyes. When he tanned people often said he looked like the beach at low tide. Currently the hairs of his beard were dusted with residue from the chalk, and ghostly fingerprints marked the front of his shirt and the collar of his tweed jacket. He turned away from the board to face his class once more.

"The Hittite, Mycenaean, and the Mitanni kingdoms all fell to the might of the mysterious Sea Peoples. These invaders spread like a plague across the Mediterranean, and they had their sights set on the biggest prize of all: Egypt, and the Nile delta. Their victories had already set in motion the events that would cause the collapse of the Bronze Age. If they had managed to take down Egypt then history would be forever changed. The only thing standing in their way was Ramses III and the full might of the Egyptian navy. Warships and galleys blockaded the mouth of the river and stood to protect the kingdom. In 1175 BCE, Ramses built a fleet specifically to repel the invasion. When the Sea Peoples arrived--"

A hand went up at the back of the room. Desmond nodded to the student, who stood up. "You keep calling them the Sea Peoples. Surely there's a more accurate name for them."

Desmond smiled. "Of course there is. Atlanteans."

The class chuckled, but their humor died when Desmond didn't admit to making a joke. The student said, "As in…?"

"As in people from Atlantis. Now, if you will refer to your textbooks–"

This time the interruption came from the doors at the back of the lecture hall. Dorothy Boone didn't pause as she barreled into the aisle and down the steps. The students who had been startled out of their near-dozing gawped at the woman dressed in trousers and a bowler hat but she ignored their stares. "Des! You must come at once. Lives are at risk."

"Ah. Yes, class, you may have heard of this lovely lady. This is my betrothed, Lady Boone."

She stopped at the bottom of the steps and looked at the students she had just become aware of. "Oh. Right, you're in the middle of a…" She looked past him at the chalkboard. "Oh, Des. Atlantis again? Really? Even Plato admitted that was just an allegory."

He took a measured breath. "The evidence suggests–"

"The evidence suggests you are a lovely man who is susceptible to fairytales and legends."

Beatrice Sek had entered with Dorothy but remained at the door. "Perhaps this is a debate better suited to another time."

"Quite right," Dorothy said. "The timing is unfortunate, of course, but you must come with us. Lives hang in the balance."

Desmond sighed and put his chalk down. "Class, I apologize for the interruption, but I've learned that Lady Boone rarely exaggerates when it comes to matters of life and death." He took his coat and hat from their hooks and stepped around his desk. "We shall pick this up again on Monday. Class dismissed."

"And forget that rubbish about Atlantis," Dorothy said. "It's a myth, pure and simple. The Sea Peoples were actually from Pavlopetri, off the coast of Greece. Don't allow him to fill your head with lies and confusing half-truths. Ta."

Desmond wrapped his arm around her elbow and hauled her outside. "A matter of life and death and yet you still have time to toy with the children."

"All in good fun, Des," she said.

He sighed and looked ahead to where Beatrice was leading them out of the building. "Always good to see you again, Miss Sek."

"Likewise, Professor."

"What exactly is the problem this time?"

Dorothy said, "This morning, someone attempted to kill me and pin the blame on Trafalgar. When Trix and I went to confer with Miss Trafalgar on this occurrence, we discovered that someone attempted to kill her and named me as the mastermind."

"Unthinkable," he said. "But she is unharmed as well?"

"Her associate Adeline was killed," Dorothy said. "Partially as a way to further set me up, but I also believe she was eliminated because of her precognitive abilities. She could have been invaluable to figuring out just what the blazes is going on here."

Desmond put his hat on as they exited the building. He fished for a pair of tinted sunglasses from the inner pocket of his jacket and put them on as well. "Who else is in danger?"

"Trafalgar and I believe we weren't our assassin's only targets. Whoever is responsible might be someone who is also in our unique line of work. Today's attacks may be his attempt to clear the field of competition."

"That's inconceivable. No one I consider a colleague would stoop to those tactics. This is a gentleman's profession." Dorothy shot him a look and he grunted. "You know what I mean. We wouldn't resort to murders and mischief."

"Be that as it may, can you think of any other reason Trafalgar and I would both be targeted for death on the same day? We were each named as the other's alleged assassin. There's no possibility in my mind that this was a coincidence. We must assume the worst." She opened the car door and let Desmond get in first. "Trafalgar is at the offices of Dubourne and Associates, while we have called ahead to Mr. and Mrs. Keeping so they'll be expecting our imminent arrival. I have a list of all those who share our unique occupation, and we shall be paying them all a visit as soon as possible. If we are correct we shall either find more potential victims or the villain himself waiting for word on how his plans have fared. Either way, a bit more exciting than your preposterous Atlantis lecture."

Desmond shook his head. "It infuriates me when you presume you're correct without any evidence whatsoever to support your claims."

"No, that part makes you feel alive. What infuriates you is when I'm proven right."

He grumbled and pushed his hat down over his eyes, pouting as Dorothy chuckled beside him.

Leola wasn't as practiced behind the wheel as Adeline, so Trafalgar found herself jostled about the backseat as they raced through town to warn Dubourne about the potential threat he faced. She braced her hand against the ceiling and said nothing. She knew Leola was doing her best at an unfamiliar task while grieving her friend. Leola and Adeline had been acquaintances by necessity rather than choice, but they got on well enough. They occasionally spent their nights off together, visiting the theater or keeping one another company while shopping.

"We will find the men responsible for her death," Trafalgar said as they followed the curve of the road deeper into Covent Gardens.

"The man responsible for her death was in the butcher's shop," Leola said without emotion. "You found him, and you killed him without a second thought."

Trafalgar started to nod before she understood what Leola was saying. "And in doing so, I prevented you from taking your own vengeance. I'm sorry."

"Make it up to me by finding the man who put the shooter in that window and we'll call it even."

"Deal."

The neighborhood was a red-light district normally only active after dark. In the daylight its denizens retreated to their rat holes and their home was exposed for the tawdry and rundown place it truly was. The parking lot Leola found outside of Dubourne and Associates was partially filled with rubble and debris from various air raids. She parked and settled in to wait; if something went awry upstairs she would be needed for a rescue. Trafalgar examined the street as she climbed from the car. There were attempts underway to revitalize the area, to bring it out of the ashes like a phoenix, but at the moment Trafalgar found those rumors to be spurious at best.

Dubourne's office was above a burlesque house. Despite the early hour music seeped from the blacked-out windows and through the paper-thin walls of the staircase as she went up to the second floor. She paused on the top step when she saw the office door was ajar. The smell of smoke was strong in the air, wrinkling her nose as she dropped the emei piercers back into her hand. She advanced carefully until she was positioned in front of the door, then she stepped forward and kicked the door open wide. Something had burned in the middle of the office, and the source of the flames still smoldered on the carpet. A twisting white column of smoke rose from the device and accumulated in a thin sheet across the ceiling.

Trafalgar stepped over the threshold and glanced to her right. She saw the body of a man, judging by his clothes, lying on the ground as if he had been thrown. His head resembled nothing more than a prune, red and blackened with tufts of hair stuck to the fringes where it hadn't burnt away. The smell was abominable. She ignored it as best she could and scanned the rest of the room. The wallpaper was pockmarked with small dimples that were surrounded by char marks. There had been an explosion in the room, and its shrapnel had been incendiary as well. A nasty combination.

Behind the desk she found Dubourne's secretary. The woman hadn't been as mutilated as her employer, but the damage was done. Trafalgar knelt and touched the woman's throat just to be certain she was beyond help. The flesh was cold, and there was no pulse. Trafalgar closed the woman's eyes and stood up with a weary sigh. Dubourne was a mercenary for hire, the sort of man who could push through borders and get behind unfriendly lines no matter how dangerous the situation was. During the war he had been an invaluable ally to her efforts. She remembered hiring him to escort her into France to explore the basement of a church. He was expensive but he earned every dime.

It appeared as if Lady Boone's theory was correct. Someone was targeting people in their field and, if this was any indication, the plots were already in play. She and Boone would have to move quickly. Some would have Boone's ingenuity and avoid the traps, but those survivors might then become weapons of their persecutor. A red herring or a scapegoat would be named, and the erstwhile victim would set out for justice against their persecutor.

Trafalgar moved to the fuming device and gingerly turned it over to see the exterior of the package. It had purportedly come from the offices of Abraham Strode, a name Trafalgar recognized but a man she didn't know personally. She tore off the identifying piece of the envelope and placed it into her pocket. She hated the idea of destroying evidence but they didn't need the Metropolitan Police stumbling over it and getting the wrong idea. The situation was hazardous enough without a well-meaning officer threatening potential victims.

She checked the inner office to make sure no one else was involved before she went back downstairs. The dance hall music was still boisterous as ever, almost sickeningly sweet after the scene she left behind her. She gathered her coat in one hand as she slid into the car.

"Dubourne and his secretary are dead. It appears as if it was another trap set by our saboteur."

"Lady Boone is correct."

Trafalgar nodded. "So it would seem. Abraham Strode..." She removed the strip of paper and read off the return address. "We should get there at once to warn him, if it is not already too late."

Leola started the car again. "Hold tight, ma'am. I won't go as carefully this time."

"Until now you've been careful? God help us all." Trafalgar braced herself but was still flung hard against the door as Leola backed out of the parking lot and returned to the street. Strode's offices were two miles away, and Trafalgar had the feeling she would be pinned to the seat for the duration of the trip.

Leonard and Agnes Keeping lived on Montpelier Place, not far from the majesty of Harrods. Dorothy allowed herself to be distracted by the store as they passed. It had been a good long while since she had a shopping spree, and several of her outfits had been ruined beyond repair by travel and misadventure. Perhaps once they had settled their current troubles she could celebrate by spending a few hours getting lost amid the racks.

Beatrice parked in front of a terraced house with a red door, the windows of the upper floor shaded with bright blue curtains. Dorothy led the charge up the steps, followed closely by Desmond and Beatrice. She didn't know the Keepings very well but they'd shared polite conversation at a handful of events. Desmond was more acquainted with them and she hoped their relationship was strong enough that they would take him at his word. She paused when she reached the door, the jamb of which revealed a poor attempt to disguise a recent and violent splintering.

"This door has been kicked in." Dorothy drew her gun and noted that Desmond did the same. Beatrice remained unarmed but Dorothy knew she could do just as much damage with her bare hands as anyone else could with a club. Once they were prepared Dorothy tested the latch and pushed the door open. An end table lay on its side, the vase it had once held shattered on the tile.

Desmond cursed quietly under his breath as he followed her inside. The parlor doors were slightly ajar but she could hear nothing from within. Beatrice moved past them and walked deeper into the house. Dorothy pressed her back against the wall, waited for Desmond to take position on the opposite side, and she reached out to push the door open wide enough for them to pass through. She stepped into the parlor and stopped short as the keen edge of a sword appeared against her throat.

"Crumbs..."

"Lady Boone. I must say I'm disheartened to see you are involved in this."

Something crashed behind her, and then Desmond was tossed into the parlor. He hit the floor on his hands and knees, lifting one arm to protect himself from the brute that had obviously been the thrower.

The pressure of the blade lessened. "Desmond? Good lord, have you gone mad? I know you're engaged to this woman, but that doesn't mean you have to follow her into a life of crime."

Dorothy looked at the swordsman from the corner of her eye. "Mr. Keeping? How wonderful to see you are alive and well."

Something heavy fell to the floor upstairs, followed by a feminine grunt and the sound of punches landing on soft flesh.

"I'm sure you're surprised to see my wife and I survived your associates, Lady Boone."

"Leonard, please," Desmond said, "this is all a misunderstanding."

"There was no misunderstanding, Professor! This morning we were called upon by someone claiming he had an artifact for us to authenticate. We arranged the meeting and everything seemed routine until our guest asked for a glass of water. Agnes went to retrieve it and, once we were separated, the brute overpowered me. I was rendered helpless by some gadget he placed on the back of my neck. The same was done to Agnes. We would have been slaughtered if Mr. Elmer hadn't chosen that moment to come by." He nodded to the behemoth who had tossed Desmond into the room like a rag doll.

Dorothy said, "And these men claimed I sent them?"

"They placed the blame on Nigel Mummery. But now here you are with the rest of your lackeys. Here to raid our home for its treasures, ay? If Nigel is too craven to do his own dirty work, we shall have to take the fight to him." Something shattered upstairs. Leonard rolled his eyes and shouted, "Damn it, Agnes, just deal with the blasted girl already!"

"Easier said than done, I'm afraid," Dorothy said. "Beatrice is skilled in several disciplines of self-defense. And I assure you this *is* defense rather than an attack. There is no reason to fight us. We came here to warn you. I was also the target of an attack this morning, as was Trafalgar of Abyssinia. We saw evidence of forced entry on your door, and the damage in the hallway led us to assume the worst."

Desmond said, "She's telling the truth, Leonard. Honestly, do you believe we would arrange for your murder and then ransack your home before the bodies would even have gotten cold? We came here to save your life, man."

After a moment of consideration the blade was removed from Dorothy's throat. She took a calming breath and glared at the man. He was taller than her, gray at the temples and bald on top, with a drooping gray mustache that concealed his lips. His right eye was red and swollen, and there was a bruise on his left cheek that would grow more colorful with the passage of time. Despite that, she had little doubt the man could and would have cut off her head if she had revealed herself to be a threat. There was another crash from above them.

"If you could please call off the battle royale taking place upstairs?"

"Agnes!" he shouted. "We have agreed to a temporary halt to the hostilities."

A shrill voice shouted back from the second floor landing. "Tell that to this insane woman!"

Dorothy couldn't resist a smile. "Lay down your arms, Trix. We've decided to be civil."

The sounds of conflict ceased, and a moment later Beatrice came downstairs with an older, stern woman whose hair had come loose in a wild tangle around her face. Beatrice had loosened her necktie and the top button of her blouse but looked otherwise shipshape. Dorothy winked at her and Beatrice twisted the corner of her mouth upward in a small smile as she joined everyone else in the parlor. Leonard put away his sword as Agnes joined him.

"It would appear we were not the only targets today," he said. "Lady Boone says she, as well as Miss Trafalgar, were also nearly victims."

Dorothy said, "We believe everyone who shares our profession has reason to fear. Trafalgar was sent to speak with Dubourne."

Agnes said, "We know Wallace. We could call him to see if everything is all right."

"Trafalgar would have reached him by now. He is either warned or it is too late. If I were you, I would worry about contacting Nigel Mummery. Trafalgar was blamed for the assault on my life, and I was named as the architect of her assassination attempt." Agnes went to the telephone to make the call. "Whoever is truly behind this has covered his tracks well and ensured that we as a group will be at each other's throats. The question is why."

"He obviously wants us out of the way," Leonard said. "He's trying to rid London of our particular breed so he can take over."

Desmond nodded. "Even if he is only partially successful, our numbers may be greatly reduced. Then he will be free to usurp our funding and our beneficiaries."

Leonard raised his eyebrows. "Any theories on who it might be?"

"I would say present company excluded," Dorothy said. "As well as Mr. Dubourne and those who work with him. And if Mummery was named in your attack we can eliminate him with a certain degree of certainty. We've all been active long enough that we don't have to take such drastic measures to ensure our employment."

Leonard said, "Being caught up in this insanity is hardly a reason to discount anyone as a suspect. It's the easiest thing in the world to foil an assassination attempt you set up for yourself. All you would have to do is pretend you foiled the attempt."

"Like you, Mr. Keeping?" She raised an eyebrow in a show of good-natured joshing.

"Or you, Lady Boone?" He narrowed his gaze at her.

She smirked at him as Agnes returned. She had adjusted her hair and clothes, but her face was now pale and drawn. "There was no response at Mummery's home or offices. Who else do you believe has been targeted?"

Dorothy said, "Anyone who has led or taken part in an expedition, anyone with any connection to seeking out or recovering ancient artifacts."

"That could be dozens of people in London alone."

"And we've covered only a fraction of them," Dorothy said. "Agnes, I believe you and your husband should check on Mummery. I'm not entirely hopeful for his chances, but he may simply be distracted. Be very careful. If he has fallen victim, check the house for clues. It may lead you to the next victim. In the meantime, Des and I shall continue down our list."

Leonard said, "Who is on it already?"

She took a piece of paper from the cuff of her blouse and handed it over.

"If there is a name on there you are familiar with, I'd be happy to let you take it. This news is more likely to be believed if it comes from someone trustworthy." She touched her throat. "For obvious purposes."

"Sorry about that."

"You were on edge," she said, unaware of the pun until she'd spoken it. "No apologies are necessary. For now we must make haste. It seems these traps have been set for a certain timeframe. If so we could already be too late to warn anybody. But perhaps we can be there in time to save a few of them." She held out her hand for the list and Abraham handed it over. "Next on our list is Abraham Strode. Good luck, Mr. and Mrs. Keeping."

"And to you, Lady Boone."

The Keepings escorted their guests out, then hurried to their car. Desmond knew that another person on the list, Arthur Whitmore, kept an office nearby. He could make it faster on foot than if Beatrice drove out of her way, so he wished them luck and headed off. Once they were on the road Dorothy examined Beatrice as best she could from the backseat.

"I hope you weren't brutalized too horribly by that awful woman."

Beatrice grinned. "Nah, it was good. Got my blood pumping, which is always nice. You?"

"Bastard put a sword at my throat." She touched the skin once more to make sure there was no damage. "Haven't had that in a while. At least a year."

"It must be nice to know you haven't lost your touch."

Dorothy chuckled and nodded, but the smile faded as they continued on to their next stop. She had little hope of finding Abe Strode alive and well when they got to his home. Whoever sent the killers and the devices planned their implementation very carefully, down to the last detail. All over London her colleagues were receiving packages or answering the door to find hired killers. Those who weren't killed in the first assault would be given orders of their own. It was diabolical; the madman was taking his failures and turning them into tools of his success.

"Beatrice," she said.

"Yes, ma'am?"

"When we find this blackguard, I do trust you will save a few blows for me."

Beatrice chuckled. "I'll do my best to control myself."

Dorothy nodded. "Fantastic."

She braced herself for what they would find in Strode's home. Their profession was small to begin with, and the thought of even a fraction of these booby-traps being successful would severely diminish their numbers. She had a sinking sensation that even with all their countermeasures and all the running around she was doing with Trafalgar, Des, and the Keepings, that it was all for naught. There was a chance that whoever was behind the frame jobs and the assassins had already won.

Chapter Six

Dorothy recognized Trafalgar's car parked outside of Abraham Strode's office and directed Beatrice to park behind her. The office door was standing open when they arrived, causing her to believe the worst. She entered the house and examined the foyer, but nothing seemed amiss. There were a few smudges of mud smeared on the tile, but it had rained the day before. She assumed someone had simply left their muddy shoes next to the door so they could dry out.

She advanced carefully and found Strode and Trafalgar in the lounge, both completely unharmed. Strode was a tall, slender man with an ash-blonde Vandyck and his hair swept back in a pompadour. He stood behind his desk where a silver tray held a large porcelain bowl, a tall glass, and a pair of seasoning shakers. The room was spotless, a portrait of having a place for everything and everything in its place.

Strode was in the middle of some diatribe when Dorothy entered the room, and her sudden appearance caused him to stop midsentence. "Lady Boone. I suppose it's too much to expect you to knock."

"Your door was open."

He rolled his eyes and removed his tinted glasses to pinch the bridge of his nose. "Of course it was. I hope you left it open to ease your retreat."

"I came here to warn you."

He offered a patronizing smile. "Yes, I am aware. As I was telling your associate–"

Trafalgar and Boone both said, "We're not associates," and Dorothy awkwardly continued, "More like reluctant allies."

"Whatever you may be, I assure you I am in no more danger today than I was yesterday. When one is the best at what he does, there is no small number of people who might wish him harm. You say that someone is attempting to kill people in our profession while framing our contemporaries? Well, you can imagine my skepticism when two of my contemporaries arrive on my doorstep with weapons drawn."

Trafalgar said, "Dubourne and his secretary are both dead. My friend was murdered on the doorstep of our home."

Dorothy said, "Leonard and Agnes Gray were also attacked in their home. We have no idea how high the body count actually may be, but we are doing everything in our power to keep everyone safe."

Strode sighed. "Be that as it may, I am perfectly unharmed. I've received no correspondence, and I have received no visitors until your friend here so rudely interrupted my work."

"Sir..."

Dorothy held up a hand to stop her. "Trafalgar, it's no use. We came here to warn the man that he was in danger, and we have succeeded on that front. There are many more on our list who are more deserving of our time. Mr. Strode, you have been duly warned to keep your eyes open and alert."

He waved dismissively and looked down at his desktop, his mind obviously already returning to what he'd been doing before he was interrupted. Dorothy looked at Trafalgar and motioned toward the door with her head. When she turned to leave she stopped short and held up a hand so Trafalgar wouldn't continue past her. She looked into the entry hall for a moment and then turned to scan Strode's lounge once more. He looked up and sighed when he saw they were still there.

"What is it now?"

"You say we are your only callers today?"

"Yes, and the experience has completely put me off the idea. If I never have another visitor, it shall be too soon."

Dorothy stepped into the lounge. "Miss Trafalgar, please come into the lounge and close the door behind you."

Trafalgar did as requested. The pocket door rattled loudly as it was pulled out and latched into place. Strode frowned at them as Dorothy's eyes panned slowly from one corner of the room to the next.

"What in blazes–"

"Sh."

"You will not shush me in my own home, Lady Boone! The–"

She took out her revolver, and he clamped his teeth shut on the next word. Dorothy crossed to the desk, lifted the pepper shaker off his lunch tray, and unscrewed the top with a deft twist of her fingers.

"What in the world are you doing?" Strode asked.

"Your front door was open. Not unlocked, it was actually standing open. Did you leave it that way when you let Miss Trafalgar inside?"

"Of course not."

"No, I wouldn't think so. A man with a lounge this tidy wouldn't leave his door open like that. Miss Trafalgar, where is Leola?"

"She wanted to check the kitchen to ensure my food hadn't been tampered with," Strode replied.

Dorothy turned in a slow circle as she brought the shaker up to her lips. She tilted it slightly so the granules within were almost to the spilling point. She moved quickly toward the heavy curtains of the window and exhaled sharply through pursed lips. A cloud of pepper spread out across the chaise longue and the end table.

"Are you mad?" Strode demanded. "What in the blazes are you doing?"

Dorothy turned toward the fireplace and exhaled again. Strode rounded the corner of his desk blustering about the mess she was making. She blew again, this time aiming the cloud toward an empty corner to her left.

Someone sneezed.

Trafalgar straightened and looked around the room, while Strode froze where he stood. Dorothy splashed the contents of the shaker toward the sneeze and coated the head and torso of an otherwise invisible woman. The woman recoiled and sneezed again, more violently this time, unseen hands swatting at her face as she tried to clear away the grains.

Dorothy stepped forward and grabbed the woman's wrists. "Why if it isn't Ivy Sever. I haven't seen you in ages!"

"Ugh, such an old joke." The voice came from directly in front of Dorothy, a soft Liverpudlian accent tinting her words. "Never gets old."

The apparent apparition leaned back to brace her shoulders against the wall and Dorothy rocked back from what appeared to be a kick to the stomach. Now that she knew where Ivy was, and with the help of the pepper still darkening her face, it was easier to fill in the blanks for the rest of the woman's body. She released Ivy's hands and stepped back. Ivy tried to make a run for it, but Dorothy blocked her with one outstretched arm and pulled the invisible woman into an embrace. She threw herself onto Ivy's back and wrestled her down onto the carpet.

"What in the blazes?!" Strode said.

Dorothy realized to him and Trafalgar it appeared as if she had just taken a very brief, very rough flight to the ground. She sought and pinned Ivy's arms before she lifted her head to look at them.

"Abraham Strode, Miss Trafalgar, I would like to introduce you to Miss Ivy Sever. In addition to being a private investigator, she is also the unfortunate victim of a failed experiment which left her trapped in an invisible state. I presume she was looking for a way to gain entrance to your home without alerting you and took the opportunity when you let Trafalgar in. After that she was simply waiting until we left to strike. Very sloppy leaving the door open like that, Ivy. I suppose you didn't want any potential passersby to see the door open on its own."

Strode had gone pale. "How did you even know to look for her?"

"She spent some time outdoors looking for an open window or an unlocked door. She traipsed through your back garden. When she came inside she left smudges on the tile. A man like yourself, Mr. Strode, would never abide such a thing."

"I feel faint."

"Fortitude, Mr. Strode. We may have just found the key to unraveling this entire bloody mess. If you would be so kind as to fetch a coat or something similar for our captive to wear, I would be most appreciative. It will be harder for her to slip away once she's clothed."

"Clothed? You mean... oh, goodness." A bit of color returned to his cheeks before he turned away and retreated. All of his bluster and braggadocio faded at the realization of how close he had come to dying. He brushed a hand over his face and went to follow Dorothy's instructions.

Trafalgar stepped aside to let him out of the room. She looked at Dorothy, who appeared to be crouched in an arachnidian manner. For a moment it seemed as if she wouldn't say anything, but finally she inclined her head and offered a weak smile.

"Well done, Lady Boone. Lovely detective work."

"It helps to know in advance that an invisible assassin is a possibility, of course," Dorothy admitted. "Ivy and I have had our run-ins, haven't we dear?"

"To be honest, I much prefer the times I've ended up on top."

Dorothy patted the spot where she imagined Ivy's cheek to be. "Now, now. Just because we're enemies on this occasion doesn't mean things won't be friendlier next time."

Strode returned with a long overcoat, a pair of slacks, and strips of cloth he indicated could be used to swaddle Ivy's head. Leola had come back from inspecting the kitchen and gladly restrained the invisible woman to a chair once she was dressed. While it was still unsettling to see nothing through the gap in the cloth, and while the top of her head was left exposed, it was now obvious to everyone in the room that she was indeed a person rather than a poltergeist. Even with the confirmation, Strode looked lightheaded. He walked to the longue and stretched out with the slender fingers of one hand across his eyes.

Dorothy waited until Leola was finished with the restraints before she stood up and began her questioning. "First of all, I assume that you were left with instructions to frame someone else for this attack. Who was it?"

"Arthur Whitmore."

"And what is the name of the person who actually hired you?"

Ivy scoffed and shook her head. "You'll have to work a little harder than that, Dot."

Dorothy smiled and leaned down, lining her eyes up with the wider strip where Ivy's eyes should have been. She lowered her voice to a seductive coo. "Oh, come on. No special favors for an old friend?"

"Neither of us got where we are in this business by handing out special favors."

"An exchange of services, then. If you tell us what we want to know, we'll make sure you don't get done up for attempted murder."

Strode slapped his hand down on the table. "She entered my home uninvited and planned to murder me! I hope you don't expect me to turn a blind eye to these crimes."

"Ivy was working at her client's behest. If we take the client out of contention, her employment will be terminated and she'll no longer have a quarrel with you." She raised an eyebrow at Ivy. "It's the only way for you to come out of this unscathed. No client, no outstanding assignment, no connection to the string of murders and attempted murders all across London."

"What you said is true?" Ivy asked. "Someone tried to kill you?"

"And succeeded in killing several others. I fear their work is not done yet. We've spent the morning traversing London in an attempt to stop his plans, but it would be much easier if you could simply tell us who hired you."

Ivy considered that for a moment. "He didn't give me his name."

Dorothy smiled. "When has that ever stopped Ivy Sever? Come on. You must have done some digging before you attempted to murder a stranger for him. Tell us what you found."

The shoulders of her borrowed coat rose and fell as Ivy took a deep breath. "Fine. Looks like talking is the quickest way out of this. Felix Quintel."

"I've never heard of him," Dorothy said.

"I have," Trafalgar said. "He wants power, prestige. He does the same work we do, to a point, but his endgame is what he favor he can curry with the items he brings back. That and money, of course. He wouldn't think twice about raiding a tomb or pillaging a holy site for a few baubles if the price was right on the black market."

Dorothy chewed her thumbnail. She had heard of treasure hunters like Quintel, but she'd never had the misfortune to run into any of them. They rarely lasted long, either shunned by the establishment or punished by the local tribes whose relics were being defaced. Quintel was eliminating anyone who could potentially stand in his way. If that was the case he wouldn't think twice about slaughtering anyone at his destination who might protest an expedition.

"Where can we find Quintel?"

"Easier said than done. I used all the resources at my considerable disposal and all I got was a name. Believe me, I looked. The man has firewalls and contingencies like you wouldn't believe. I'm lucky I got as far as I did. I have no idea what the man looks like or where he has his offices. You can waste your time looking but I assure you, you will not find him."

Dorothy stood up and brushed her hands together. "Then perhaps it requires the resources of more than one person." She turned and looked at Trafalgar. "You and I have been at odds since before the war began. But one indisputable fact is that you were a worthy adversary for me, and vice versa. We are both very good at what we do, Miss Trafalgar. Quintel expects to eradicate us while he hides in the shadows like a coward. We are an extremely fractured group. We compete against one another. We lack trust in each other. He's counting on that to make his plan succeed."

Trafalgar nodded. "It's the only way his plan of framing us would even work."

"He managed to hide from Ivy, which is no small feat. We've managed to combine forces today for the greater good. We may have saved a few lives in the process. I propose that we continue this partnership in the interest of stopping Quintel before he can cause any further harm. He wouldn't have gone to such great measures on a single day unless he was planning something big. I would like to stop him, but I doubt I could do it alone." She held out her hand. "What say you?"

Trafalgar stared at Dorothy's outstretched hand for a moment. Finally she reached out and took it. "To obtain justice for Adeline, and the other deaths Quintel is responsible for."

Dorothy squeezed Trafalgar's hand. "I believe that's a cause I can support."

"Are we really going to let her go?" Trafalgar asked, nodding to where Ivy was still strapped to the chair.

"But of course. How else can we follow her to meet up with her client?"

Ivy cleared her throat. "Pardon?"

Dorothy smiled. "Consider it the terms of your surrender and release. You're going to lead us back to the man who hired you and, with luck, he will lead us directly to Felix Quintel."

After checking to make sure Strode would recover from his shock, Dorothy suggested that Trafalgar ride with her, Beatrice, and Ivy. Leola was hesitant but Trafalgar argued that they would have to start trusting each other eventually. She also understood it would be easier to keep track of Ivy with more people in one vehicle. She and Boone sat on either side of the invisible woman in the backseat of Boone's car for the ride back to Ivy's base of operations. Beatrice drove, and Leola waited until they were on the road before she pulled away from the kerb to follow.

Ivy's offices were located in the Barbican Estate, near a bastion of the ancient London Wall. The area had been horribly damaged by air raids during the Great War, and every building they passed bore some measure of damage. Dorothy recalled the terror of the first raids, hearing London's aeroplanes flying overhead with rail guns blazing while something in the distance exploded with ground-shuddering force. Production of their own airships was quadrupled so they could meet the enemy on equal ground, and the air above London quickly became a battlefield. Dorothy recalled the newspapers that urged people to relocate to hovels popping up in the Underground, which reminded her far too much of H.G. Wells' time-traveling novel for comfort. Eventually the German airships were sent back where they had come from. London's Bumblebee Squadrons took up sentry along the coast to deflect any further attacks, and the city began to slowly rebuild itself.

Ivy directed them to one of the many buildings that was still waiting to be repaired. Its neighbor had been completely demolished, either by the initial bomb or by residents who were afraid it would collapse if left on its own. A handful of windows on that side of Ivy's building were covered by wood or plastic that bellowed and caved in with the passage of the breeze as if the building was slowly breathing. Dorothy found it hard to believe they were only a mile or so away from her home on Threadneedle. If the Germans had dropped their bombs just a minute earlier...

She pushed the thought out of her mind. They were escorting an invisible troublemaker onto her own turf. A moment of distraction could be all it took for Ivy to give them the slip. She unlocked her office and dutifully waited in the hall while Beatrice and Leola, unenthusiastic allies due to the agreement between their employers, examined the office for booby traps or secondary exits. Once they had the all-clear, Ivy was allowed inside.

"I have pancake makeup and some clothes through there." She gestured at a door behind the desk. "It might make it a little easier for you to trust me if you can see me."

Beatrice checked the room and made sure there were no windows, but Dorothy insisted on leaving the door open enough that they could watch her while she changed.

Ivy chuckled. "You just want to peek."

"It's nothing I haven't seen before."

"Flirt." Ivy shed the coat she'd taken from Strode as she entered the room, the rags unwinding themselves from around her head and rising to drape across a coat hook. There was a surprisingly dainty vanity mirror hanging from one wall, decorated with brass accents and small lights that cast a solid glow on the empty space in front of it. A small canister rose from a shelf next to the mirror and the cap unscrewed itself. As Dorothy watched, Ivy applied some of the cream to her fingers and began spreading it across her cheeks and the bridge of her nose.

Dorothy met Ivy while they were both investigating a self-described inventor named Colin Pettigrew. He was a grave robber who raided buried cities and sought out lost civilizations solely to find evidence of what he believed to be a long-forgotten advanced society that existed before the rise of humanity. In 1912, Pettigrew discovered a hidden cache deep in the Peruvian Amazon that he believed belonged to such a society.

One of the items he brought back was a sealed jar carved with a formula for a chemical compound of unknown properties. He managed to produce a sample of the compound before Dorothy tracked him down. She tried to stop him from imbibing it and their confrontation quickly turned into a brawl. Ivy stumbled upon the laboratory during their fight and tried to use the opportunity to steal away with the compound for herself. Pettigrew tried to stop her by opening fire on her, but he only hit the sample she had stolen. The highly unstable and untested compound exploded in her hands. Pettigrew fled, but Dorothy couldn't leave the screaming and terrified Ivy behind.

By the time they reached the hospital, Ivy's skin had turned a peculiar shade of pink. When the first doctor arrived on the scene to examine her, every vein and muscle was visible through the thin resin her skin had become. Though they had never met, Ivy clutched Dorothy's hand like a lifeline. Dorothy had initially stayed simply out of curiosity; she watched with detached amazement as the fingers squeezing hers turned to pink muscle and then bone. By the time the bone vanished, Dorothy could no longer feign separatism and admitted she was terrified for the poor girl.

The doctors were completely stumped by her vanishing act. She was bathed thoroughly every hour, her unseen flesh scrubbed until it bled. The blood curiously only became visible a few seconds after it had left her body. Droplets appeared on the floor around the bed, and only after the rags seemed to blossom after being tossed aside did they realize what was happening. Dorothy stayed with Ivy until the doctors kicked her out. They kicked Ivy out of the hospital a few days after that. She was taking up a valuable bed and far too often a nurse tried to place a patient on top of her without realizing.

Ivy eventually came to terms with her new state, embracing it, in fact. Her work as a private investigator had never been easier. She got used to wandering the streets of London in the nude. What did it matter if no one could see her anyway? Eventually she tracked down Dorothy, the stranger who refused to abandon her in her darkest hour, and they struck up a tenuous friendship. Ivy often took jobs Dorothy didn't agree with, and Dorothy's strict guidelines about what was and was not fair game conflicted with Ivy's, but they couldn't make the leap to consider themselves enemies.

In the intervening years Ivy had made quite a few adjustments to make up for her new reality. She wore makeup to meet with clients, and she hid the fact her eyes were invisible by wearing tinted eyeglasses with leather shields on either side to prevent even a sidelong glimpse of her empty sockets. She shaved her head, since letting her hair grow out would be all nuisance with no benefits, and doing so allowed her to wear a variety of wigs when she was "presenting herself," as she liked to call it.

In the small room next to Ivy's office, her visage was slowly coming back into view. She had a Greek nose, flat between the brows and straight along the bridge. Her eyes were spaced widely apart and, if Dorothy remembered correctly, had originally been green. At the moment they were simply dark craters where she hadn't bothered to detail the lids or wrinkles. She instead focused on her cheeks and her wide mouth, applying crimson powder to her bottom lip before rubbing it against the top. She ran her fingers down her throat to the curve of her shoulders.

Her round spectacles and a long brown wig covered the parts she hadn't covered with makeup, and she returned to the room like a bust come to life. She put on a blouse, buttoned it to the collar, and then covered it with a black vest. A pair of gloves twitched in midair and then inflated to give shape her hands. She put on a pair of trousers and shoes and, with those final touches, appeared to have manifested an actual human being out of several disparate parts.

Trafalgar and Beatrice seemed to be the most impressed by the transformation. Dorothy smiled at the sight of her old acquaintance and gestured at the wig.

"New hair?"

"Thought I'd try it. What do you think?"

"It suits you."

Ivy smiled. Trafalgar recoiled and Ivy grunted. "Oh. Sorry." She opened a tray on her desk and pulled out a set of veneers. She snapped them over her real teeth, smoothed her tongue over them, and smiled again. "I sometimes forget to put in the caps. Sorry."

"No apologies necessary. It's quite a remarkable gift."

"I've decided to take it as such, yes." She scooted her chair forward and flipped her journal open. Dorothy took one of the client seats in front of Ivy's desk, while Trafalgar took the other. "I spent three weeks tracking down Felix Quintel. After the first week I began to suspect he was merely a figurehead. Just a name used by a conglomerate of people to strike fear into their competition. But then I found this." She turned the journal around so they could see her sketch of a circle with a cursive F cutting through the center of it. The lower part of the F was stylized to give a tail to the circle.

"F and Q," Trafalgar said. "Felix Quintel left a calling card? Where?"

"Carved on the stone entrance of a tomb in Jordan. His people were the ones who carved it. As far as I can tell he didn't make that particular trip himself."

"From what I hear he never leaves the country," Dorothy said. "So the name acts as their brand. Just because they mark the man's name doesn't mean he actually exists."

"I thought the same thing. But I looked into some of the goons who were present on the majority of Quintel's expeditions. I found their names on passenger manifests of nine different airships heading to the continent, as well as to South America, India, and the Middle East. I figured they were his most loyal employees, so I dug as deep as I could on them. They all receive payments signed by F. Quintel. As far as Barclays is concerned, he exists. And he has a lot of money to throw around."

Dorothy said, "You tracked him to a bank account, but you couldn't follow that thread to a flesh and blood person?"

Ivy held out her hands. "And what does *that* tell you? I know where he lives, but even I couldn't get into the place to confirm he was there. The place is a fortress. He has a guard posted at the door and security watching the perimeter. Even if I got in, I have to believe there would be countermeasures even an invisible woman like myself would have a hard time getting past."

"You've had it too easy," Beatrice said. Dorothy turned to look at her, and Beatrice shrugged. "It's true. She's gotten so used to slipping through places unseen that she doesn't know how to avoid a normal security perimeter. She's lazy."

Dorothy said, "Do you think you could do it?"

"I'd have to see the place first," Beatrice said, "but I got into your place, didn't I?"

Dorothy grinned. "Indeed you did."

Beatrice said, "I'd have a good shot by myself, but with Ivy's intelligence and if Miss Trafalgar is willing to loan me Leola, I think we'd stand a better than fair chance of robbing the National Gallery."

"We'll save that as a possible victory celebration." She stood up and faced Ivy. "Miss Sever, kindly point us toward Mr. Quintel's home. We shall see how much of a fortress it truly is."

Chapter Eight

There was much about the plan Trafalgar disliked, not the least of which was the idea of working alongside Dorothy Boone. But Ivy Sever proved herself to be a valuable source of information and Trafalgar would never have been able to find her without Lady Boone's presence. Now there was the small matter of finding a man who seemed to not exist. And now that they had an inkling of what had caused the day's mayhem she knew she had more to motivate her than mere vengeance, but on the ride back to Lady Boone's townhouse she found her thoughts drifting back to Adeline.

The girl had never known peace, but she'd accepted her ability as a gift instead of a curse. From the moment she fell into step with Trafalgar outside the orphanage, she greeted the world with a smile despite the turmoil in her head. She was very young when she came to the conclusion that seeing more than everyone else was a treasure, but accepting something was far different from actually being at peace with it. There were nights Adeline couldn't sleep for all the turmoil in her head. There were days she locked herself in her room and piled pillows on top of her head in a futile attempt to silence them. The worst part, she'd once admitted, was sometimes she didn't know if her feelings were her own or just castoff from someone nearby.

"I thought I was in love," she once revealed. She and Trafalgar were in an airship over the English Channel, and looking out over the water had helped lower some walls between them. "All the signs were there. I was short of breath, anxious, I was always nervous and babbling whenever a certain person was nearby. I convinced myself the feelings were mine, and they were for him. Then I discovered I was simply siphoning his feelings. Feelings he had for my friend.

They fell in love with each other and got married." She gazed out the window wistfully. "I didn't get to feel that part. The being loved in return part. That was just for them."

"I cannot imagine going through life with such a commotion."

"I can't imagine life without it." She had looked out over the water then and smiled. "In the air, it's easier to pretend. There are fewer people up here, fewer signals to cross with my own."

"Would you like me to leave?"

Adeline had put her hand on top of Trafalgar's. "No. You're quiet. I like being near you."

Trafalgar closed her eyes at the memory, hoping the other passengers of the car wouldn't see the tears on her lashes. Earlier she had been angry but now... now she was livid. Adeline's death was meaningless. She was merely a pawn in some bored rich man's private game. She died as a means to his end, a prop with which he hoped to eliminate Trafalgar from his path. The girl deserved so much better. If there was one bright spot, one small consolation, it had been the look on Adeline's face just before the bullet hit. For a few seconds the girl only had the present with no future overlapping. For a shining moment the world was silent and clear to her.

"The future has finally gone quiet."

Lady Boone... or Dorothy, she supposed she should get used to calling her, looked at her. "Did you say something?"

"I didn't realize I had spoken aloud."

Dorothy seemed to accept that as a reluctance to follow through. "I wouldn't have interrupted, but Ivy says we're almost to the fortress Felix Quintel calls home. I thought you might like to take note, and you seemed distracted."

"Thank you."

They had been traveling close to half an hour, and now she could see they were near Kew Gardens. Here the trains ran aboveground, and the homes were considerably less rich than the neighborhood they had just left. There were hints of wealth, however, and it was on one of these posher streets that Ivy directed them. Dorothy instructed her driver to stay well enough away that they wouldn't attract attention from the homeowner. She leaned forward between the two front seats, and Trafalgar removed a pair of eyepieces from her inner pocket. The glasses had a pair of open frames with various lenses extending out to the side like small flat moons orbiting near her head. She flicked a metallic tongue with her fingernail and a pair of magnifying lenses dropped into place.

"Fancy toy," Dorothy said.

"Threnody the Crafter."

Dorothy said, "Aha. She does excellent work."

With the aid of her lenses, Trafalgar was able to get a very detailed view of the home. It was less ornate and less cluttered than most homes, which she found refreshing. She didn't like all the fancy patterns and ornaments that denoted the Victorian style. The house was two-story, brick, and was a perfect mirror of itself. Two large windows on the ground floor, and two more above on either side of a patio with a high balustrade. The front garden was protected by a gated wall, and to the right she could see a plaque which bore the FQ logo Ivy had shown them.

Ivy spoke up. "He's got guards all around the place, and no one gets through that gate without an escort."

Dorothy pondered that. "He never leaves?"

"Not that I ever saw. He has a maid and she brings in groceries."

"Then how does he hire killers? How did he arrange this whole bloody day down to the damned minute if he's sitting safely in his den? There has to be some way for him to get out and arrange his schemes. The lot behind him... what does it lead to?"

"There's a ten foot stone wall, and then a two-story shop. Believe me, I kept my eye on it. No sign of Quintel going in or out that way. The grass is overgrown, there's weeds and critter nests. He's not going that way with any kind of regularity."

Dorothy twisted her lips at the quick dismissal. "There must be some explanation. No man can pull off something of this magnitude solely using outside contractors. If we uncover how he's getting in and out with no one seeing him, we'll be one step closer to stopping him."

Trafalgar said, "There's something else we must consider. He's not only leaving home without being seen, he's doing it when he's unaware of being observed."

"Ain't that what we just said?" Ivy asked.

Trafalgar said, "What I mean... if he was aware of surveillance, it would make sense that he'd be furtive in his movements. Yet there is no way he could have known Ivy was watching. The street would have appeared empty and his movements unobserved. Why would he go to the trouble of concealing his departure when no one was present to see him? The law of averages states that she should have at least seen something, depending on how long she watched."

"Three days. And she's right. If he knew I was out here, yeah, he could arrange his schedule so I'd never see him. But given my unique abilities..."

"He'd never know when it was safe and when it wasn't." Dorothy stroked her thumb over her bottom lip. "There must be something we're missing. But we're not going to make much headway sitting here announcing our presence. Trix, take us back to the Tube station. We'll ponder the situation from there." She settled back in her seat and checked her pocket watch. "We should also see if we can find a telephone. Desmond will most likely be wondering where we've gotten to by now."

"Hold that thought," Trafalgar said.

Beatrice looked over her shoulder at Dorothy. It was obvious she would be willing to ignore Trafalgar if that was what her employer wanted.

"Do you have an alternative plan?" Dorothy asked.

Trafalgar opened the car door and stepped out onto the street. She heard Dorothy mutter, "Crumbs" and clamber out behind her. Trafalgar's longer stride meant Dorothy had to hurry to catch up with her, and then she was nearly trotting just to keep up.

"You certainly don't intend to walk directly up to his front gate and knock, do you?"

"This man perpetrated several attempted murders today. Who knows how many were successful? We can waste our time by withdrawing to conjure up some scheme or we can act."

The front gate opened as they approached, and two men exited. They wore heavy leather coats buttoned to the collar that were close enough in appearance to give the impression of being a uniform. They each held long-barreled flintlock pistols by their sides. The one closest to them held up a hand, but Trafalgar continued walking until she was close enough for a civil conversation.

"Turn around and go back to where you came from," the man said.

"We would like to speak to Felix Quintel."

The man narrowed his eyes. "Maybe you didn't hear me, madam. I said–"

"I am Trafalgar of Abyssinia. This is Lady Dorothy Boone. Your employer arranged to have us killed this morning. We would like the opportunity to convince him that further attempts would be most unwise. While we could use you as messengers, I believe it would have more weight coming from us directly. So if you would please step aside."

"We're prepared to use force."

Trafalgar smiled. "You shall have to." She flicked her wrist and the emei piercers dropped into her palm.

Dorothy rolled her eyes and withdrew her own gun. As she aimed it at the second guard she leaned toward Trafalgar and spoke sotto voce. "There was no need to create a physical confrontation."

"I shall not cower in the shadows while my friend's body lies cold in my parlor. Felix Quintel is responsible for her death and shall be held accountable."

The men brought up their guns. Trafalgar heard the car doors open and close behind her, then the running footsteps as Leola and presumably Beatrice ran to prevent the other perimeter guards from providing backup. Trafalgar saw one of the men moving to thumb back the firing mechanism.

She took a quick step forward. "Look to the sky!"

The combination of her sudden movement and shouted phrase confused him enough that his eyes flicked upward. His gaze was only off her for a split second, perhaps shorter than a blink, but she closed her hand around his gun with her right hand while slicing his forearm with her piercers. The man howled and clutched at his arm. Trafalgar turned to deal with the second guard, but Dorothy was already engaged. She smacked his gun hand with her club, stepped into his reach, and smacked her hand flat against the center of his chest. He fell back, winded, and Dorothy relieved him of his weapon as he tripped over his own feet. Trafalgar turned her attention back to the man she'd cut. He was trying to stop the bleeding, so he had only one hand free to fight back. He seemed unwilling to try it, however.

"I imagine you rarely get to this point. The majority of people who show up at this gate are likely intimidated by the mere threat of violence, so you've never had a chance to hone your skills against a true attacker. In a way, we've done Mr. Quintel a favor today."

Dorothy said, "I believe we shall accept our gratitude in person."

Trafalgar looked toward the corner of the wall. "Should we perhaps check in with Leola and your girl? They may require assistance."

"Does your Leola generally require backup?"

"No."

"Then she will be fine with Trix." She stowed the guard's gun in her coat pocket and pushed the gate open. "Shall we?"

Trafalgar looked at the guards. "By my estimation, you have only two options. You can pursue us and tell your boss that you allowed us entrance, at which point you will likely be out of a job anyway. Or you can leave now, tend to your wounds, and never return here. Either way you will be seeking new employment tomorrow. If you leave now you can meet your new managers without appearing bloodied and bruised."

The men backed away, but Trafalgar kept an eye on them until they were out of sight around a bend in the road.

"Impressive," Dorothy said.

"Anyone can defeat an enemy in a brawl. To convince one to give up without fighting requires a bit more finesse."

"This from the woman who storms the gates of her enemy's home without a plan."

"Plans make you predictable," Trafalgar said as they entered Quintel's property. "I would expect the woman who stole my submersible would understand that."

"I only stole..." She took a deep breath. "Another time."

Tall grass and overgrown flowerbeds filled the null space between the wall and the bricks of the home, foliage crowding in on either side of the main walkway. Once through the gate they were buffered from street sounds so much that it seemed as if they had crossed over into a completely different world. Dorothy approached the steps but paused to let Trafalgar take the lead to the front door.

"Shall we ring?"

Dorothy shrugged. "We've already come this far. Why not a bit further?"

Trafalgar tested the knob and found it unlocked.

"Assault and battery, breaking and entering..."

"Both crimes trumped handily by assassination and multiple counts of attempted murder."

Dorothy raised an eyebrow. "You raise a fair point."

They stepped into Quintel's atrium and took a moment to get their bearings. A staircase directly in front of them led up to the second floor landing, which wrapped around the walls with a series of closed doors. Dorothy and Trafalgar stepped apart to look beyond the staircase into the back of the house. Trafalgar said, "Kitchen."

"A larder," Dorothy said. They both spoke at a low whisper, and they slid their feet across the tile to prevent their steps from echoing. She moved into the dark doorway next to her, and Trafalgar did the same. She found herself in an unfurnished sitting room, the heavy window dressings preventing the afternoon light from casting more than a sickly beige pallor over the walls. Dorothy reappeared in the entryway.

"Library, but completely barren. Not a book on the shelves."

Trafalgar said, "Your transparent friend lied to us."

"Then who were those apes on the front step? They wouldn't defend an empty building. And the maid who brings in the groceries..."

Dorothy gestured at the cobwebs between rails on the stairway banister. "You truly believe a maid has seen this place?"

"This place... the grounds are protected by armed guards, who patrol around a locked gate. Two lines of defense. Who is to say there's not a third? If someone outwits the guards and gets through the gate, once they see an abandoned house they'll turn around and leave. It's just another layer to discourage people from digging deeper."

Dorothy considered the theory for a long moment. Finally she sighed and started upstairs, motioning for Trafalgar to follow her.

"This could all very well be what it seems. Ivy said the back was just as overgrown as we just saw the front to be. Perhaps the reason she never saw anyone enter or exit is because the house has been vacant this entire time. The guards gave up easily. Perhaps too easily. Whoever put them there may have been gambling on the fact no one would challenge two goons with loaded weapons. This entire fortress could be a red herring to distract people from finding his true stronghold. We're wasting our time."

"Perhaps."

Dorothy reached the top of the stairs and went right, so Trafalgar took the left wing. She took the time to search each room thoroughly, opening closet doors and kicking aside what little furniture there was to be found, but there wasn't a shred of evidence the rooms had ever been lived in. In one bedroom she pushed back the thick curtain and looked down into the backyard. Beatrice and Leola had moved three unconscious men onto the small concrete deck. Neither woman seemed worse for wear, so Trafalgar was confident they had made it through their confrontations without incurring any major damage.

From the other side of the house she heard Dorothy call to her and she hurried to see what had been found. Her boots sounded hollow as she jogged around the perimeter of the landing, their thuds echoing throughout the house and making it sound emptier than ever.

She found Dorothy in the bedroom attached to the balcony they had seen from the street. Unlike the rest of the house, this room had been furnished. A plush armchair stood next to the balcony entrance and angled to look outside rather than to catch the light. There was a bedroll in the corner, a dirty blanket and pillow piled on top of it. Dorothy was crouching next to the bed with a book in her hands. She looked up when Trafalgar came into the room.

"I believe I've actually found a clue. A mark on the inside cover declares it property of one F. Quintel. Our mystery man may at last have shown himself." She stood up and thumbed through the pages. "He wrote it in some sort of code, so we're not overly fortunate. But at least now we may have an idea of who we're looking for. The frontispiece."

Trafalgar took the book and flipped to the title page. The portrait showed a tall, broad-shouldered bald man with a pair of tinted glasses covering his eyes. His smile was wide but uncomforting; she remembered reading somewhere that some creatures considered showing their teeth an act of aggression. This man was revealing his teeth as weapons, something with which he could bite, rend, chew, tear. He wore a light-colored suit, and over it was a very familiar brown leather jacket.

"This is not Felix Quintel," Trafalgar said quietly.

"How can you be so certain?"

She swallowed the fear that had risen at the sight of the man she'd met so long ago. "This is the book of a man named Solomon. I met him twenty years ago aboard the vessel that took me from my home. He attempted to use me for a... a ritual. He put a stone in my mouth and summoned a creature from the depths of the sea. Or perhaps somewhere deeper. I foiled him by spitting the stone out before he was finished. It rolled off the deck and he jumped into the sea in pursuit of it."

Dorothy took the journal back and frowned at the picture. "So whoever

Quintel is, he is studying the work of a man who died trying to summon a creature from the netherworld. Perhaps he wishes to pick up where Solomon left off."

"Solomon was no leader," Trafalgar said. "I've spent the past two decades investigating the operation that sent him to Africa. He was but one small part of a larger organization. Perhaps he was a merlyn."

"Merlin? Like King Arthur's Merlin?"

"Of his ilk," Trafalgar said. "They are powerful mages who are adept at conducting magic and summoning the darkness of the world that came before ours." She held up the journal. "I've seen a book like this before, not long after he brought me to Cairo. I stole his coat after he fell overboard, and I used its contents to fund my journey to London. One of the items I sold was a journal that looked very much like this one."

"You sold this book to Quintel? Then you've seen him!"

Trafalgar shook her head. "Those men had no reason to lie about their names. I was nothing more than a child speaking broken English. I cannot be certain this is even the same journal."

"But the facts indicate it could very well be."

"Yes. If Quintel is continuing the work Solomon began, then it is I who provided him the means. This day would not have happened, and Adeline would be alive still, if I had simply burned that journal when I had the opportunity."

Chapter Eight

THEY SEARCHED the house thoroughly until they both had to concede there was nothing else to find. Even distracted as she was by the journal's discovery, Trafalgar had to admit there was no secret passages or hidden rooms in which Quintel could be concealed. They stood at the top of the stairs after Dorothy confirmed the attic was a cramped, hot space with nothing larger than a coal chute, which she reported was completely empty.

"Ivy believed Felix Quintel was a real person because she found this place," Dorothy said. "All signs point toward his being a decoy. We're not looking for a single man."

"Then who sat in that room watching the street? Who brought this journal here, and who hung that portrait like some sort of idol?"

Dorothy shook her head. "A watchman, someone designated to act as Quintel if the necessity arose. Even if it comes to pass that Quintel is an amalgamation of many rather than a single man changes nothing. The organization who put all of this together will still have a man in charge. Now, we should leave this place and return to our own territory to sort out what we know. Perhaps something will come to light once we hear how Desmond has fared this afternoon."

At the door Trafalgar paused and looked back over the house. "Such an elaborate artifice. Why go to such extremes with something no one should ever see?"

"I haven't a clue." Dorothy now sounded exasperated. "We've searched the entire house, Trafalgar. Everything points to the fact that no one has been here for weeks, perhaps months."

"No one except the maid and the guards. Set pieces that are visible from the street. In fact, from the street, everything points to this being a functioning... home..." She closed her eyes. "Oh, we've been so thick."

Dorothy frowned. "In what way?"

"Ivy never saw anyone go into the house or come out of it the entire time she was watching. But no one knew she was watching."

"Correct. They couldn't have slipped by without her seeing because they'd have no idea what her vantage point was."

Trafalgar gestured at the house. "This is a stage, set dressing for an elaborate ruse. It was built to serve as the public residence of Felix Quintel, whether he exists or not. It is a place for Felix Quintel to perform for the benefit of others. Pray tell, what kind of actor performs when there is no one in the audience to appreciate his craft? This is not a ruse meant to fool people. It's a tar-baby."

"The Br'er Rabbit story?" Dorothy said. Her confusion faded as she realized what Trafalgar was saying. "It's intended to draw attention. Those guards were willing to leave because their job isn't to watch the house. They are employed to inform their master when someone shows an interest in the house."

Trafalgar nodded. "He no doubt intends to trap us here. But to do that he would be required to actually make an appearance. If not Quintel himself, we can assume he will send someone."

"And whoever it is, that will be one more piece of this puzzle."

Outside they reconvened with Beatrice, Leola, and Ivy. They explained what they had discovered and detailed Trafalgar's theory. Leola and Ivy volunteered to stay and keep watch.

Leola said, "Whoever uses this house, one man or a dozen, is the one responsible for Adeline's death. I'd like to be the one who takes him down if I can."

Ivy said, "And I'm just annoyed. The one time being invisible kept me from seeing something."

Beatrice said, "I'd stay as well, but someone has to stick with you for protection." She nodded at Trafalgar and Boone. "You both have targets on your backs. I'd rather not take the risk of being across town in the event of a second attack."

"Thank you, Trix. Now that we all know where we shall be, let us part ways." Dorothy looked at Ivy. "Can we trust you? Quintel may have hired you, but things have changed since this morning. And now you know that I'm involved."

Ivy raised an eyebrow. "You think I care enough about you to take that into consideration?"

"One would hope," Dorothy said in a seductive coo, smiling slightly as she dipped her chin.

Ivy chuckled. "What the hell. Whatever's going on here is a lot more interesting than a simple assassination. But if this Quintel fellow comes after me for not finishing the job, I'm counting on you and yours to have my back."

Dorothy nodded. "Of course."

"Then I'm on your side."

"Excellent. Ivy, play nice with Leola. Whoever is behind this decided Trafalgar and I are his enemies, and the old adage stands true. For the time being the five of us, and Desmond Tindall, are a united front against Quintel. Whoever or whatever he turns out to be."

"Agreed."

They arranged for Ivy and Leola to both check in as needed during the night using street urchins to deliver whatever updates they might have. They climbed into the backseat of Dorothy's car, and Beatrice set off toward home. They sat in awkward silence on either side of the bench, both watching the city through their own windows. Dorothy was recalling a number of encounters she'd had with Trafalgar and had no doubt the same litany of remembrances was occurring just to her left. She looked at the woman sharing her car and decided to try easing the tension between them.

"Tell me about Adeline Okoro."

Trafalgar looked away from the window. "Why?"

"I know we encountered each other time and again, but she was always simply your steward in my eyes. She died because of this nonsense and I would like to know more about her as a person. I know she had a great talent..."

"Some might say a curse."

"Some might. But she used it for the benefit of her friends. An ability like Adeline's is neutral by nature. It's what a person does with their ability that makes it a gift or a curse. From what I can tell Adeline turned it into a blessing for those around her."

Trafalgar considered the argument and nodded slowly. She looked out the window again, her hands folded in her lap. They were nearly to the King Edward VII Bridge before Trafalgar spoke again.

"She was very fond of rabbits. She was fortunate to have a mother who could read and also had access to books. She thought the rabbit was particularly interesting and for one reason or another believed it was a fictional beast. The first time she saw one in real life she was overjoyed. She thought it was magic." She smiled weakly. "In a world where magic was real, she saw proof in a simple long-eared swift-footed pest."

Dorothy chuckled. "Rabbits."

"She would draw pictures of them if her hands were idle for too long. She was quite talented."

"Thank you. We'll stop Quintel in her honor."

"I appreciate that."

The silence that fell between them for the rest of their trip was easier, a touch more amicable. Dorothy knew they still had quite a distance to go before they could consider each other friends, but she felt as if inroads had been made. At the very least she was starting to feel more comfortable working alongside Trafalgar to bring down the mysterious Felix Quintel.

Desmond was waiting at Dorothy's townhouse when they arrived. He reported that Arthur Whitmore and Nigel Mummery were both confirmed dead. Witnesses revealed Whitmore had been killed by what looked to be a large mechanical bird which swooped out of a tree and pierced his skull with its talons. The construct couldn't pull itself free from his shattered bones, so a constable was able to smash it with a truncheon. Attached to the bird's wing was a note which read "Leonard & Agnes Keeping Send Their Regards." Mummery was done in by a compressed-air rifle concealed within a viewfinder. The package was labeled as a gift from Dorothy Boone.

"It would seem to an outside observer that everyone in our profession has simply gone off our nuts."

"I've contacted the Met," Desmond said, "and the members of my social club have been calling anyone and everyone who may be targeted. The loved ones of those who were lost must know that they still have friends willing to help them."

"Very good, Des. Thank you. For now, after the day we've had, I believe we could all use a nice cup of tea."

"I'll put it on," Beatrice offered.

"Thank you, Trix."

Trafalgar hesitated at the threshold, but eventually joined them and sat awkwardly in the wingback chair next to the fireplace. Dorothy noticed her awkwardness and gestured at her.

"Professor Desmond Tindall," Dorothy said, "allow me to introduce Miss Trafalgar of Abyssinia. Trafalgar, Desmond is my gentleman friend."

"I see."

Dorothy could see Trafalgar was revisiting their time with Ivy, the obvious flirtation they'd had with one another. She saw no reason to reveal the true nature of her relationship with Desmond, so she ignored the confusion on her temporary ally's face and took a seat on the couch. They recounted their findings, or lack thereof, at the Quintel house. Desmond made a note of the man's name and the address and promised to see if either was familiar to his brothers in the club who had joined him that afternoon in seeking out more traps and sabotage. In the end they confirmed at least nine people had been killed that day under mysterious circumstances.

When Dorothy noticed how late it was, she suggested they take a recess until the morning. "Miss Trafalgar, we have plenty of food here if you would like to dine with us. There is a room upstairs you can take if you would like to sleep here."

"I appreciate the offer, Lady Boone, but I must decline. I must see to Adeline's arrangements. Would you happen to know where one could find a bus or train?"

Dorothy said, "Ah, yes, I forgot your driver is indisposed. Beatrice, would you mind driving Miss Trafalgar home?"

"I would be glad to."

"That's not necessary," Trafalgar said at the same time.

Dorothy said, "I insist. Either you spend the night in my spare room or Beatrice will see you safely to your door. Those are your options."

Trafalgar sighed and inclined her head to Beatrice. "In that case, Miss Sek, I would be greatly obliged to you."

"It's a pleasure," Beatrice said.

Trafalgar walked from the parlor where the unofficial briefing had been held. Beatrice passed by Dorothy's chair on her way out, checked to ensure Trafalgar wasn't lingering in the hall, and leaned down slightly so she could whisper to Dorothy.

"All on the level? You just want me to take her home?"

"Yes, Trix."

Beatrice nodded. "Sorry, mum, but I had to be sure. But this is a woman who, if she had arrived on our doorstep naked and hungry at this time yesterday, you likely would have been reluctant to even give her directions to a soup kitchen."

"What a difference a day makes," Dorothy said with a sigh. "We've both cheated death today, we fought each other and at each other's sides. It was a hell of a day, Trix, and that deserves a modicum of sisterhood."

"Of course, ma'am." She straightened and looked at Desmond. "Good evening to you, Professor Tindall."

He inclined his head. "And to you, Miss Sek."

They left Desmond and Dorothy alone in her parlor. She leaned forward and removed her shoes, setting them to one side and stretching out her toes. Her stockings were ivory-colored with reinforced panels of black at the heel and toe. She hadn't noticed before but now that the day was over her feet were exhausted. She crossed one leg over the other and leaned forward to rub the arches with strong strokes of her fingers. Desmond, seated in an armchair nearby, noticed what she was doing but made no offer to take over the massage for her.

She didn't expect such chivalry from him. Other than a quick kiss or linking arms at public affairs, she and Desmond very rarely made physical contact. She first met Desmond in a professional capacity when she had several artifacts from the Valley of the Kings she wished to have verified. A few questions to the right people led her directly to Desmond's office at the University. They surprised each other with their easy rapport and, based on their mutual interests, agreed that having dinner together would not be out of the question.

After their first dinner together, Desmond offered to walk her home. She tempted scandal by inviting him inside to see her library. He, unable to resist the urge to take a peek, instantly agreed. Once they were inside she led him upstairs. When the lights came on he gazed awestruck at the collection as she explained that she was only supplementing the collection left to her by her grandmother.

"In many ways, I am stepping into her shoes to carry on the work she left unfinished."

"Remarkable," he said.

Dorothy smiled. "That's not the only remarkable thing here, Professor Tindall. I spend a delightful evening with a man, a man with whom I share a great many interests, and I invite him upstairs without a chaperone. Most men in that situation wouldn't be interested in these covers."

Desmond appeared flustered. "Ah. Yes, well, one... does not wish to be thought presumptuous."

Dorothy smiled. "Professor, I've never been an ordinary woman. I've never exactly been what someone might call traditional. I'm an outsider. We can recognize our own kind when we've spotted them in the wild."

He stared at her nervously.

"My mother told me I was fortunate to live in the age of women's rights. My grandmother was only allowed to own this house because it was bought in the name of my long-dead grandfather, while I am allowed to own it because I inherited it from her. And yet there are still institutions in this town, in this bastion of forward thinking, where I am denied access simply because I don't have a man on my arm. I'm sure you have the same issues with the University. A single man of a certain age may raise a few eyebrows or invite comment."

Desmond sneered. "There have been whispers."

"Confirmed bachelor," Dorothy said, and he nodded. "It seems we have a solution staring us in the face. We enjoy one another's company, we share a variety of interests, and we can help each other professionally. I never have to worry about you wanting more out of the relationship, and you never have to worry about me, either."

"You? Oh. You..."

She smiled. "In my journals and letters home I referred to my first love as Charles. But the name I whispered in bed was Charlotte."

"I see. Perhaps we can come to an arrangement after all."

To the public, they became an item. She attended his work functions and he occasionally spent a night in her spare bedroom. There was a bit of scandal, of course, an unmarried couple spending the evening under the same roof, but it was the sort of controversy that came with a wink and an elbow in the ribs rather than cruel investigations and ruined reputations. They did share a deep affection for one another. Dorothy appreciated his ability to argue and concede when he'd been beaten, and he was greatly enamored with the depth of her intelligence and loved to hear reports of her various adventures.

As far as romance went, on the other hand, they were completely oblivious to one another. So Dorothy rubbed her own tired feet while Desmond stared into the fire and twisted an unlit cigar between his fingers. The house seemed quiet after the bustle of the afternoon, the violence and the threats from all corners. She reached up and touched her neck where Mr. Keeping's sword had rested, well aware that if he hadn't planned to interrogate her the situation could have turned bloody with just a little bit of pressure.

"Dot?"

She looked at him. "Yes, Des?"

"I asked if you were all right. You looked haunted."

"It's been a very busy day, which ended with me offering tea to a woman I've considered my nemesis for half a decade. I'm simply overtired." She stretched where she sat, lifting both arms over her head and rocking her head one way and then the other. "I believe I shall take a bath and retire. You're more than welcome to stay if you wish."

"I believe I will."

She hesitated after she stood. "Are you merely staying here to act as my protector?"

"And if I am?"

"I will be offended at your machismo and touched by your concern. I'm sure the two will balance enough to cancel each other out." She walked to his armchair and bent down to kiss the top of his head. "Pleasant dreams, Professor."

"And to you, Lady Boone."

She smiled and left him to brood. On her way upstairs she passed through the sitting room. The exploded package which would have killed her remained on the table, and the stink of cordite hung in the air. She wished she had thought to ask Beatrice to try cleaning it up but it was too late in the evening for a chore of that magnitude. Instead she opened two windows just enough to create a cross breeze in the hopes the fresh air would dilute or push out the tainted air of the house. Even with the attempted murder she wasn't overly concerned by the idea anyone would take advantage of the opening. If someone wanted to kill her they wouldn't climb her gate and traipse through the bushes in the hopes of finding the windows open. There would be easier and more direct ways to get into the house for a determined murderer, and she would have ample warning if someone did try to break in.

Dorothy returned to the box and picked it up to examine the mechanics of the bomb. It was incredibly intricate work, skillfully done. She brushed her thumb over the woodwork, to the brass latch, and something clicked in her mind. She realized where she had seen work of this caliber before and she cursed quietly at how long it had taken her to put the pieces together.

"Threnody."

If Quintel required elaborate gadgets to use as weapons, there was one place in London he would go for quality work. Threnody had no qualms about working on opposite sides of a conflict. She provided weapons to whoever had the clout to find her in the first place as long as they had the coin to pay her once the job was done. She wasn't cheap but Quintel had proven he wasn't skint. Anyone who could afford to buy and maintain a house and surround it with guards could definitely afford to hire Threnody.

"I shall have to have a discussion with our masked tinkerer," she muttered to herself as she put the device back down on the table.

Upstairs she drew herself a bath and disrobed. She lifted her arms over her head and examined her body in the mirror. No new scars, no scrapes or bruises that would color themselves in come morning. She let her hair down and stepped into the bathtub, sinking down to relax against the smooth curve of the porcelain. Her bag was resting against the corner of the tub, and once she was settled in she opened it to retrieve the journal they had taken from Quintel's home.

She flipped through the crowded pages in the hopes she would find some rhyme or reason. She wasn't expecting to find anything resembling a key or a legend so she focused on the sketches. Artifacts rendered in intricate detail, some of which she knew from her own research and a few that were in her attic and storeroom. She paused to examine full-page landscapes of pyramids and interiors of tombs. "Peru," she said softly, identifying one page before moving to the next. "Ecuador. Egypt. Hm. Don't know that one."

Near the end of the book she was startled to see Trafalgar looking out at her. After the initial surprise faded she realized it was a drawing of Trafalgar as a child. Her hair was cut short over her ears, and her lips were slightly parted as her wide eyes stared forward. There was a challenge in the expression, despite the slender neck and without doubt equally small arms, this was a girl who was prepared to fight. Dorothy wasn't surprised Solomon had been inspired to sketch her so quickly after meeting her, nor that this child had grown to be such a vexing woman.

When the drawings no longer held her interest, she closed the book and put it aside on the ledge with her soaps and creams so she wouldn't drop it into her bath. She stretched her arms along the edge of her tub fell into a light sleep, aware of movement in the house - Desmond retiring to the library so he could read before bed, Beatrice arriving home and cleaning in the parlor even though she hadn't been asked.

Dorothy made a note to thank her for taking the initiative, sinking lower into the seductive embrace of the water as her mind drifted off into oblivion.

Chapter Nine

At some point during the night, Beatrice woke Dorothy by trailing cold water from the bath down the side of her neck. Dorothy shivered and opened her eyes, her protest cut off by a quick peck on the lips. She allowed Beatrice to help her out of the bath and towel her off, and showed her gratitude by taking Beatrice into her own bedroom. As she undid the buttons of Beatrice's blouse she whispered in her ear that they would have to be quiet since Desmond was in the house. Beatrice whispered that she would try, then put her lips on Dorothy's neck and put their silence to the test.

In the morning Dorothy woke when she felt the mattress shift under Beatrice's movements. She rolled over and looked at the other woman's bare back, once again amazed by the intricate tattoo which covered the olive skin. Her spine provided the trunk of a tree, its roots spreading along a thin horizontal line at her waist but the branches were the truly impressive thing. Starting just below the middle of her back they spread out to cover both scapulae in a spiders-web of various thickness. Large branches split off into smaller ones which forked into hair-thin tendrils, and thicker branches twisted and curled around her sides without ever crossing the hemisphere of her body.

The first time Dorothy had seen it she traced the branches and asked who had done it.

"I don't know."

"A tattoo like this and you just don't remember?"

"I've told you before, I don't remember the first few years of my life. I have no memory before waking up on the boat with the old man."

Dorothy frowned. "But you were a child. If you received this tattoo as a child, it wouldn't have… there would be indications. Tattoos do not grow with you."

Beatrice said, "No. I would say you're right."

"How many branches are there?"

"Four hundred and twenty-six."

"And the significance of that?"

Beatrice shook her head. "I haven't the slightest clue."

Dorothy had wanted to pursue the mystery further, but Beatrice's tone brooked no further questioning. In the years since the curiosity would now and again reassert itself, but Dorothy fought the urge to ask. She had made her interest known, and Beatrice would tell her more if and when she was ready. For the time being she was willing to simply accept it for a beautiful piece of art on an exceptionally gorgeous canvas.

Beatrice looked over her shoulder and saw Dorothy watching her. She smiled, stretched, and then pulled on her blouse to block her view of the ink.

"Shall I make breakfast?"

Dorothy sat up and shoved her fingers through the wild tangle of her hair. "Yes, please. Would you ask Desmond if he'll be joining us?"

"I heard him leaving fifteen minutes ago."

"Ah. And any messages from Ivy or Leola?"

Beatrice said, "A runner brought a note last night. No sign of movement from the house, but they were going to stay until mid-morning."

Dorothy nodded. She stood up and wrapped herself in a dressing gown. "It's been hours since Ivy applied her makeup. She'll need to go home and shower before she reapplies it. I'll send a message back to let her know it's okay to put the surveillance on hold for the time being. We may have another angle we can take to find Quintel."

"Oh?"

"Think about the bomb he used on me. Think of the other devices he created for this damned plan. Then think about where he might have gotten them."

Beatrice understood almost immediately. "Bloody hell. Threnody."

"I think we'll be paying the Crafter a visit this morning. After breakfast."

"Of course."

Beatrice left and went to her own room to dress for the day. Dorothy went to her own wardrobe to choose her own outfit. She didn't know if she should anticipate as much brawling as the day before, but she was willing to be safer than sorry. She dressed in trousers and a long-sleeved shirt, both of which had a myriad of hidden pockets sewn in to hold her weaponry. She added suspenders and a necktie and tied her hair into a single plait that ran down to the middle of her back. She chose her shoes for comfort more than style, tying the laces as the doorbell rang downstairs. She put on a jacket over her ensemble and went down to see who their guest was. She was surprised to see the woman standing with Beatrice in the foyer, wearing in the same coat she'd worn the day before.

"Miss Trafalgar! What a surprise to see you here."

Trafalgar seemed anxious at the false joviality, but she nodded a greeting. "I was thinking about the means by which Quintel attacked our peers yesterday and I have a theory. The Crafter, Threnody..."

Dorothy nodded. "Great minds think alike. I made the same connection yesterday when I was examining the bomb he sent to us. I was planning to pay her a visit later this morning. First we were going to have breakfast. Would..." She hesitated. "Would you care to join us?"

"I couldn't impose."

"You're here now, and you're going to accompany us to Threnody's shop, correct? It would be incredibly rude to make you wait outside while Trix and I eat. Please, it's no trouble."

Trafalgar seemed to be searching for a way to refuse, but finally she nodded. "Very well. It would be my pleasure to join you for your meal."

Dorothy nodded. "Trix, if you wouldn't mind?"

Beatrice kept her eyes on Trafalgar. "Of course not. Lady Boone, may I have a word in private?"

"Of course." They moved into the dining room, Dorothy's cheerful demeanor fading once they were out of sight. "I know what you're going to say."

"That woman is the enemy," Beatrice said. "We've gone against her time and again. Sometimes she won, sometimes we did, but I am finding it very difficult to understand why you're trusting her."

"Quintel targeted both of us. He killed Dubourne, Mummery, Whitmore... whether we like it or not, he has allied us together against him. He has resources beyond most men, and he was able to sow this confusion mainly because we work in a very fractured profession. He won yesterday because we don't trust one another. If sitting down to a meal with Trafalgar and working with her to unravel this mess helps take away some of his power, then I am definitely willing to take that step."

Beatrice took a deep breath and looked back toward the foyer. "You make a compelling argument. All right. If you say she's on our side then I'll go along with it for now." She smoothed her hands down the sleeves of her jacket and looked at Dorothy again. "What shall I prepare?"

"Nothing fancy. We shouldn't take long to eat. I'd like to speak with Threnody before she has a chance to prepare for our arrival. Word may have reached Quintel by now that some of his traps failed. She may be expecting us to come after her."

"I'll get started on a fry-up."

Dorothy nodded and went to retrieve Trafalgar. She had drifted into the parlor to inspect the remnants of the bomb. She looked up when Dorothy joined her, but there was no guilt in her eyes despite being caught snooping. She held up the bomb.

"This could have caused quite a bit of damage. You're fortunate you realized what it was before it detonated."

"Caution is what's kept me alive this long. I see no reason to start being foolish now." She clasped her hands behind her back and chose her next words carefully. "Beatrice wanted to know if I thought it was wise to join forces with you on this endeavor. I told her that our very lives may depend on trust. If we were a bit less wary of one another, Quintel's plan would have had a much smaller chance of succeeding. I told her that I can put aside everything that's happened between us in view of the larger picture. I hope you're able to do the same. I know I've caused you a fair amount of headaches over the years, and it might not be easy for you to overlook that."

Trafalgar tilted her head to the side. "Headaches?"

"The submarine in Turkey, for instance. Canceling your train reservations in France, stranding you at the station."

"Oh... yes, I remember now."

Dorothy narrowed her eyes. "I have been a major inconvenience to your plans for the past four years. You can't tell me it didn't even register."

Trafalgar smiled and put down the bomb. "Well. Perhaps a nuisance..."

"A nuisance? I..." Dorothy stopped. "You're trying to wind me up."

"Perhaps a bit." Trafalgar's smile widened slightly. "You have been a pest to me, Lady Boone."

"I told you yesterday. For the time being, we are partners. Perhaps you can see yourself to call me Dorothy."

She thought about it and said, "I shall try."

"For now, help me clean off the table so we can eat. I'd prefer not to pick pieces of burnt paper out of my beans."

After they'd eaten, Dorothy went upstairs to retrieve "a few items" from her armory before they left. She offered to loan something to Trafalgar, who demurred and said she had her own weapons if the situation came to that. When they departed Dorothy placed a bowler had over her hair and covered her eyes with blue-lensed pince-nez.

It was early enough that the rising sun was still flooding London with a mixture of yellow, orange, and pink that reflected from the windows of Threadneedle Street. Dorothy blended with the bankers and stockbrokers on their way to work at the various financial institutions with whom she shared her street, but Trafalgar was an anomaly. She wore the same much-mended coat she stole from Solomon so long ago, and underneath her beige cotton wool shirt had also seen the needle far too often to blend with the finery all around them. The two of them cut quite a dashing pair as they stepped out of the house, and they drew more than a few sidelong stares as they made their way down to the car.

To her credit, Dorothy didn't seem to notice the sidelong glances they received. During the evening she had made arrangements for Adeline's remains, and she sat with the body until a pair of morticians arrived to take her to the crematorium. Adeline had once mentioned that was how she wanted to leave the world; she wished to become one with the wind and the sea, rather than buried and forgotten somewhere. Trafalgar would receive the ashes and take them back to Africa where they could be spread over the Red Sea.

Beatrice parked across the street from Threnody's building. She stayed with the car while Trafalgar and Boone crossed the street.

Trafalgar said, "I assume you already know the procedure to get inside."

Dorothy nodded. "Of course. But we're not going to follow her instructions. Not today. We don't want her comfortable for this conversation." She stopped on the sidewalk and looked both ways before she removed an elegant pair of what looked like brass knuckles from her coat pocket. There was a small suction cup in the center of the device, and a small phial with a thick white liquid inside. She stood close to the front door and pressed the suction cup against the keyhole and thumbed the side of the device. The liquid was forced out through the cup into the keyhole. She twisted her wrist and the construct snapped, existing just long enough to turn the mechanism to release the bolt.

"A convenient device to have," Trafalgar said.

"It's come in handy once or twice." Dorothy winked and pushed the door open.

Threnody's entry hall was dark, with newspapers covering the windows to let in only the barest hint of light. Scattered envelopes littered the curling tile under their feet like fallen leaves in September, and the paper shuffled as Dorothy stepped forward and pushed open the inner door. Trafalgar had never seen the front rooms of Threnody's home. She could tell from the way Dorothy scanned the foyer that it was new to her as well.

The door opened into a wide, empty space filled with furniture hidden under white sheets. They could see into the kitchen where the windows were similarly blocked to keep the sun from intruding. Dorothy removed her brass knuckles and returned them to her pocket. When she brought her hand back out she was holding a sheathed blade.

Trafalgar moved toward the stairs and peered up to the pitch black second floor. There were no ambient sounds coming from elsewhere in the house; no voices or footsteps, not even the eerie creak of the foundation settling. Dorothy continued toward the kitchen and Trafalgar heard a door open with a moan of warped wood. Trafalgar was aware it was the second unusually empty house they had searched together in as many days, but Threnody's home had a different feel from Quintel's. His home had felt completely abandoned, whereas the room they currently stood in was more of a tomb.

Despite the neglect, there was a certain disturbance to the air that made the hairs on the back of Dorothy's neck stand up. Someone had passed through this space maybe minutes before their arrival.

Dorothy returned from the kitchen. "Downstairs is dark," she said in a whisper. She looked upstairs and gestured with her chin for Trafalgar to lead the way.

They climbed as quietly as they could, hugging the wall so they wouldn't step in the creaky middle section of each riser. Dorothy had taken out her revolver at some point, while Trafalgar had her club held tightly in her right hand. There were only three doors on the second floor, and all but one stood open wide to reveal the rooms within. The first room they passed had a drafting table set amid an army of dented filing cabinets and mountains of precipitously stacked papers. The second room was a narrow water closet. At the end of the hallway they flanked the closed door and eyed each other in the darkness. Dorothy was on the side with the knob, and she gripped it lightly so the tongue wouldn't rattle against the latch. She listened for a moment, then threw the door open and stepped inside.

"Threnody! We'd like..."

Her voice died in her throat, and the silence was filled with a desperate shriek from the woman sitting on the edge of the bed. She threw her hands up in front of her face and dove for the plague doctor mask currently sitting on a mannequin's head. Dorothy retreated a step, her eyes wide as she watched the Crafter shuffle across the room with her shoulders hunched, turning her back so she could slip the leather over her head.

"I'm sorry," Dorothy gasped.

Threnody growled in a voice rougher than Trafalgar had ever heard. "How dare you invade my personal private space? What gives you the right?"

To Trafalgar's surprise, the woman seemed to be crying. Dorothy's face had gone so pale that her freckles stood out like match heads across the bridge of her nose. Dorothy gulped heavily and looked at the floor, suddenly abashed. Threnody settled her mask into position and turned to look at them again. Instead of her normal attire she wore a threadbare nightgown that looked as if it had been mended several times in several places. Her hands were shaking by her sides.

Trafalgar knew exactly what Dorothy had seen; she'd seen the same thing once, and the image remained burned in her mind. Threnody had been born as Ida Kearney, the daughter of an inventor whose accomplishments she had long ago surpassed. When she was a teenager she was assaulted by a young man. She fought back, and he responded by hitting her in the face with a piece of masonry until she stopped fighting. She survived the attack and crawled back into her father's lab. She created a new jaw for herself and reconstituted her right cheekbone with bolts and braces. Metal was bolted onto bone, and leather straps served as tendons between her new parts.

Over the years she had upgraded and refreshed her tech. The result left her functional but the result was far from attractive. The right side of her face above the damage was scarred and lined like a road map. She kept her hair cut short in order to fit the mask more comfortably over her head. Without the mask she looked like a shattered doll which had the scissors taken to it. Adeline once theorized that Threnody wore the mask not to hide her mechanical parts, but to hide the attractive side of her face that was relatively normal. She didn't want people looking at her and seeing what could have been, so she covered everything with her mask.

Trafalgar didn't know how many people had seen under the mask, but that number had just grown by a factor of one.

"You are banned for life," Threnody finally said. "Both of you. I will not have my private residence violated in this manner."

Dorothy seemed to regain a portion of her control. "We will gladly walk away and never again darken your door, but first we require answers. In the past twenty-four hours, several items you created have been used in a series of murders. Nine people are dead."

Threnody was trembling, her body half-turned away and her shoulders hunched as if protecting herself from them. "I do not create floral arrangements, Lady Boone. I create weapons. I assume a great many of them end up bloody."

"One of them was used on me," Dorothy said. "Someone tried to kill me and framed Trafalgar for it. The same thing has been happening all over London. I'm willing to wager a fair amount of the victims also bought weaponry from you in the past. Mummery? Strode? The Keepings?"

Threnody stared at them. "Someone is targeting my clientele?"

Trafalgar said, "It is curious that anyone would be knowledgeable about so many people in our profession. How were we found?"

"An excellent question." Dorothy had regained her bearings after the shock of seeing Threnody unmasked. "Of course, it would be child's play to someone with your records."

"I only create the weapons. I don't use them myself. And I would certainly never hand over my records to someone who planned to decimate my paying customers."

Dorothy said, "Then help us find who is responsible. We believe his name is Felix Quintel."

Threnody hissed and turned away. She took a pair of folded gloves from a drawer and shook her head as she pulled them on. "That blasted man... I knew I shouldn't accept his commission, but the money was too good. I lost a fair amount of money during the War just paying for my supplies. I thought it would be a good way to build the coffers back up. He told me that he was just building up a surplus. Just in case he needed it in the future."

Trafalgar said, "Quintel himself commissioned the devices?"

"Yes. He sent me a letter describing what he needed and when he needed them to be completed."

Dorothy sighed. "And the shadow remains elusive. Did you keep the letter?"

"I made a copy. I had to refer to it several times to complete the devices." She gestured for Dorothy and Trafalgar to lead the way out of the room. "I have it downstairs. I'll show you." They turned to leave, but Threnody said, "Dorothy. Trafalgar. I am furious with you both for bursting into my home like this. For invading my privacy, which is the one thing I have always..." She caught herself before emotion overtook her. "But if I am responsible for the attempts on your life, then I suppose I can't hold you in much contempt. I would have done the same in your situation. You are not banned for life, you are not banned at all. It is the least I can do to atone for my part in your near-death experience."

"Thank you," Dorothy said. "And for what it is worth, what I saw... no one will ever know."

"I appreciate your discretion. Now..." She gestured again. "Down the stairs... I assume you already found the entrance to my laboratory when you were snooping earlier. Please lead the way, Lady Boone."

Dorothy glanced at Trafalgar before they left the bedroom. The haunted look lingered in Dorothy's face; she knew that the shock of seeing such devastation without warning would take some time to fade. She nodded to Dorothy to indicate she understood and, once he was past, nodded to Threnody to show that she understood as well. Threnody took a deep breath which she exhaled through the filters of her mask before she returned the nod. She stopped at the threshold and watched Dorothy descend the stair, then looked at Trafalgar.

"Of all the duos who could have burst into my room this morning, never would I have dreamed it would be you and Lady Boone working in concert."

"It's a temporary arrangement, I assure you."

Threnody shrugged. Dorothy had stopped at the foot of the stairs to look back at them, but she apparently sensed their conversation was not for her ears and continued to the basement door.

"Allegiances forged in fire, even among bitter enemies, have a strange way of becoming permanent. It takes great will to open a heart to trust anyone, let alone a person you don't particularly like. Once those doors have been opened they are exceedingly difficult to close."

Trafalgar snorted. "We're talking about Lady Boone."

"We are. You followed Dorothy Boone into this house with your weapons drawn. You provided cover while she advanced. I never thought I would see the day." She chuckled behind her mask. "It may already be too late for you to close the gates on this one, Miss Trafalgar. You may have to create space in your life for Lady Boone whether you like it or not."

She walked past and down the stairs. Trafalgar considered her words for a long moment before she closed the bedroom door and went down after her.

Chapter Ten

When Ivy originally staked out the house, she didn't have to worry about concealing herself from sight. Now that she was visible and partnered with Trafalgar's lady, they were forced to find a vantage point that wasn't overly obvious. They broke into another house that looked equally abandoned and set up a little camp on the second floor.

She wasn't entirely onboard with the theory that knowing the mysterious house was under surveillance would make Quintel show up, but stranger things had happened. Some men liked an audience. She smirked at the thought and glanced over at Leola. The African woman was extremely still and quiet, almost as if she was a wax figure placed in the chair and left to gather dust. Once in a while she drew a deep breath, not quite a sigh, but enough for Ivy to know she was alive and bored. There was no light to play cards, no pen or paper for a game of noughts and crosses, and the effort of staying awake was difficult enough without worrying what the woman sitting across from her might do if she drifted off. She trusted Dorothy, to a degree, but Dorothy hadn't trusted Trafalgar until that morning. As far as she was concerned she was on a stakeout with the enemy.

When the darkness became infused with color that slowly brightened with the oncoming dawn, Ivy could see Leola's features more clearly. The woman didn't seem to have any trouble staying awake. She looked as alert as she had when they first broke into the house and started watching. Ivy needed some sort of stimulation to get through the next hour or so, and finally she cracked and broke the silence.

"So how long have you known Trafalgar?"

"Since I was a child."

"Oh. So you're childhood friends."

Leola said, "No."

Ivy waited for her to elaborate. After a moment she sighed and looked out the window again. It was difficult to see in the darkness; the street had no exterior lighting so she was forced to rely on the ambient glow from Quintel's neighbors. In the time she'd spent watching the house she had become familiar with the shape of the neighborhood; the bow of that tree's branches and the low brick wall that enclosed that home's lawn. She would be able to see better if she removed her goggles, but she hadn't bothered to detail the makeup around her eyes. People tended to panic when they saw ragged open craters where her eyes should be.

"I've known Dorothy for years myself. We don't always agree with each other, but sometimes it's the fighting that makes life worth living."

"Hm."

"You don't say much, do you?"

Leola looked at her. "I lost my friend."

"Right. Sorry about that."

Leola looked outside again. "The existence of this house proves to you that Felix Quintel is a real person, not an organization using his name as a title."

Ivy nodded. "That's right. Dorothy and Trafalgar may think he's just a figurehead, but I'm not so sure. He has followers, people who do his bidding and present a public face to the world. He has his maid picking up groceries for him."

"His compost heap was rather full."

"Mm-hmm. I suppose she could just dump everything out."

Leola drew a finger along her bottom lip. "His maid is definitely a woman? Not a man in disguise?"

Ivy smiled. "I thought the same thing, but nope. She moves like a woman, but not in a contrived way. It seems too natural to be a put-on. Plus I managed to get up close without her knowing. She's definitely as female and as old as she pretends. She's just a woman who, according to Lady Boone, should be fired if her job is to clean up the house."

"It's Felix Quintel's house, and yet he is never seen entering or leaving. It's his home and yet no one seems to live there." She lifted her chin slightly and raised an eyebrow. "It's Felix Quintel's house, but he doesn't live there."

"You've got the high points, yep."

"The man who took Trafalgar from her home twenty years ago is represented in a picture in the one furnished room in the house, the house is empty, and Felix Quintel is the purported owner." She worked her jaw back and forth as she stared out into the darkness. She seemed to be talking in circles, but it was obviously helping her put the puzzle together in her mind. "This is Felix

Quintel's home, but he has not arrived to claim it yet. The guards protect it for his eventual arrival. The maid brings food for the same reason. When a week goes by and he has not come, the food is put in the compost heap and fresh groceries are brought in."

Ivy leaned forward and put her elbows on her knees. "So where is he?"

"The man in the portrait, Solomon. He attempted to use Trafalgar's body to summon an entity from the netherworld. She was to be its host, but she thwarted his attempt. The stone with which he was using to draw the being to her body was lost in the Gulf of Aden. He gave his life trying to retrieve it. The house belongs to a man rich enough to build these devices and pay assassins, and yet his garden is overgrown and his home is falling to disrepair."

Ivy started to say something but didn't want to risk interrupting the other woman's train of thought. She seemed to be close to making the final connection, and if doing so got them out of the blasted room, then more the better.

"The group to which Solomon belongs is intent on bringing a creature of great power into this world. Trafalgar foiled their plans all those years ago without even realizing it. To her it was simply self-preservation. Perhaps that was simply a trial run, as I cannot imagine them putting their messiah into the body of a young female child from Abyssinia. She took away their magic stone and with it their ability to summon a creature to a particular body." She closed her eyes and held her hand out in front of her as if rearranging pieces of a puzzle. "The War is over. Travel between countries is easier than it was a year ago. Quintel's men now have the ability to go wherever it is they must be to perform this ritual. But they may not have the means. The War was expensive for everybody, plus there is the cost of maintaining this house and its servants all this time. They may not have the funds to travel. They will require funding, a patron who will hire them for the expedition."

Ivy said, "And the best way to ensure they are the team chosen is to eliminate anyone else who might take the job. Lady Boone, Trafalgar, the Keepings..."

Leola opened her eyes and looked at Ivy. "Quintel wanted a monopoly on expeditions. He wanted to be the only option when it came time to fund the trip."

"Why now?"

"Because the time has finally come for another attempt to finish what was started with Trafalgar. They cannot afford to do it themselves. But they can afford to wipe out the competition here in London so anyone with the means for an international expedition has no choice but to come to them. Whoever this Solomon fellow was intended great things for Trafalgar. He told her she would have Power, and that she would lead everyone on the boat. It was the only thing that saved her life. He was summoning his leader. Felix Quintel does not exist because he has not yet ascended from the depths. This home is set up so he will have someplace to go immediately upon waking."

"That was remarkable," Ivy said.

"It's my gift. Adeline could see things as they would be, and I could connect disparate facts to see how things are. It takes me a while sometimes, but eventually I can see the entire picture as if it's drawn on the wall in front of me." She stood up. "We must find Miss Trafalgar and Lady Boone at once to tell them what we have learned."

"We?" Ivy questioned.

Leola nodded. "I'm not certain how my gift works, but I know it works best when there is someone with me. Thank you for giving me a focal point for my mental wanderings."

Ivy chuckled and stood up as well. "I've been called a lot of things in my life, but 'focal point' is a new one. Considering *my* gift. Lead the way."

Ivy wasn't entirely certain about leaving their post outside of Quintel's house, but if Leola was correct then it wouldn't matter if they saw anyone or not.

Threnody let them into her lab, and Dorothy was intrigued by seeing the familiar space in a new light. Ordinarily she would have entered from the other side of the room, and now knowing what the rest of the house looked like, she had a new perspective on the cluttered lab. Threnody obviously spent the majority of her time here among her designs and devices. Considering what Dorothy now knew was concealed under the mask she felt sad about how Threnody had cut herself off from the rest of society. She swore that if she was still welcome in Threnody's home after the current events were finished, she would endeavor to be more friend than client.

Threnody made her way through the maze of tables to a roll-top desk tucked into one corner. It stood at an angle that prevented it from being seen on the other side of the room, reaffirming Dorothy's feeling of pulling back the curtain to see the workings of the performance. Threnody pushed up the desktop and shuffled around the papers within until she found what she was looking for. She turned back and held up a sheet of paper which had been folded into quarters.

"This is the letter I received from Felix Quintel. It lists the items he required but, as you can see, he gave no indication on whom they would be used. The same goes for all of my clientele. I make what you want and I don't ask questions."

Trafalgar took the paper and held it up for Dorothy to see the FQ brand on the front square. "It certainly seems as if it's our man."

Dorothy said, "How many devices did you make for him?"

"Seventeen."

"There could still be some out there."

Trafalgar nodded. "We'll speak to Professor Tindall to see which devices have already been found. And he didn't use one for me. A simple rifle. Nothing fancy... just a bullet in a head. As if we were an afterthought." She grimaced.

"That's not true and you know it. He sent Ivy after Abraham Strode. The man utilizes the resources he happens to have at hand. When people will do, he uses them. When a device is the most expedient way to attain his goals..." She ran her eyes down the list. "That doesn't change the fact that there are a great many items out there either waiting to detonate... or we have several more bodies waiting to be found." She brushed her thumb over the paper, then held it up to the meager light. "There's some sort of watermark on the paper. I can't quite make it out."

Threnody went to her workbench and turned on one of the lights. Dorothy thanked her quietly and held the sheet of paper over the bulb.

"The Quintel crest, no doubt."

"Not this time. It appears to be a creature of some sort. The head of a man, the body of a beast..."

Trafalgar said, "A lion?" She moved closer and Dorothy angled the paper so she could see. "The head of a man, the body of a beast, and a pair of great folded wings along its back."

Dorothy squinted at the smeared and faded insignia. "How on earth can you make out such detail? The paper is old and faded."

"Yes, but this is not." She opened her coat to reveal an inside pocket with the same crest sewn into the material. The details were much easier to make out even with the embroidery, but it was undeniably the same as the watermark. "The creature is called a manticore. I read about it when I... inherited the coat. It's an eater of men. A beast with the mind of a man, the body of a lion, and the teeth of a shark. I always knew it was the symbol of Solomon's organization, but after the discovery of his portrait yesterday I can no longer deny that his organization is the same one which Quintel heads."

Threnody said, "Solomon? Enoch Solomon?"

"I never knew his Christian name," Trafalgar said. "A bald man with a British accent and vaguely saurian features. He... went missing twenty years ago."

"Then I believe I know the man you're speaking of. When he disappeared he was the highest ranking member of a sect dedicated to gaining power over the United Kingdom by any means necessary. I thought they vanished when he did, simply fading away without their leader to guide them." She took the letter back and gazed at the watermark through her goggles. "But if this is their insignia then perhaps they were only hiding in the shadows, waiting to strike."

"Does this sect have a name?"

"They call themselves the Watershed Society. They believe that can create a situation which will be the tipping point for the future of our world."

Trafalgar said, "I saw the power they want to tap. It was something large enough to make the seas churn. If these men acquire that power for themselves, there will be no limit to what they can accomplish."

Threnody said, "I wish I could tell you more about them. All I know is what I've gleaned over the years. My father refused to work for them. He saw them as elitist warmongers who only wanted to destroy and build a world of their design from the ashes. I've never knowingly worked for them before. I thought they were defunct."

"They may have silenced themselves in order to prevent anyone from realizing what a threat they posed," Dorothy said. "Do you have the envelope this came in?"

"I'm afraid I don't. But there was no further information on it. The envelope lacked a return address or any identifying marks."

Perhaps to your eyes, Dorothy thought, but she left it unspoken. She scanned the list of items, along with the price the client was willing to pay for each one. At the bottom of the letter, she was instructed to send a note to a post office box. Threnody saw where she was looking and answered Dorothy's question before she could pose it.

"I sent the letter, obviously. They told me a man would arrive to pick up the finished items on an arranged date. The man was of no consequence, an urchin paid to do some heavy lifting. I made no note of his features so I couldn't hope to track him down again."

"A shame," Dorothy said. "Perhaps something can be gleaned from the letter itself, or the post office box. I may have Beatrice stake it out to see if it's still in use by the Society." She held up the letter again. "May I keep this? I'll return it when this business is complete."

"I don't see any need to have it back."

Dorothy nodded her thanks and placed the letter into her pocket. "I suppose there's little else we can gain here. We should check in on Ivy and Leola, see if they've found anything. Threnody... thank you for your help. And I cannot apologize enough for..."

Threnody cut her off with a wave of her hand. "Please, I would prefer to forget it ever happened. And if I provided the Watershed Society with the means to kill my other clients, then I'm glad you burst in the way you did. Take them down and I will consider us square."

Dorothy nodded and touched the brim of her hat. They left through the alley entrance so they wouldn't violate Threnody's refuge any more than they already had. When they reached the street Beatrice saw them and started the car to come pick them up. Dorothy put her glasses back on and looked at Trafalgar. When she became aware of the scrutiny she met Dorothy's gaze.

"Will you be all right with this?" Dorothy asked. "These people have tried to kill you twice, by the looks of it."

"I will be fine. They've tried to kill me twice, and they have failed. Now it is my turn."

Dorothy grinned. "Jolly good point of view." Beatrice stopped the car and Dorothy opened the door for her. When they were seated she told Beatrice to take them back to Threadneedle Street. She waited until they were underway before she spoke again. "We now know who we're up against. I want to see if Des is waiting for me at home before we venture out to Kew Gardens. There's a chance he's heard of this Watershed Society. He may even know some members."

"We also must be wary of further attempts on our lives. Seventeen devices does not necessarily mean there were seventeen victims."

"A salient point," Dorothy said. "He may have contingency plans for those who didn't fall victim to yesterday's attacks. We should warn the Keepings and Mr. Strode to be on their toes until this sordid business is finished."

When they arrived they found Desmond's car parked in front of the house, with Leola waiting on the front stoop. Beatrice let them out so they wouldn't have to walk, then continued on to park the car where it wouldn't be in the way. Ivy's absence was disturbing to Dorothy, so she asked after the private consultant before Leola had even gotten to her feet.

"Her makeup was fading, so she asked Professor Tindall if she could wait inside. She didn't want to upset any of the pedestrians."

"Ah, I see. You would have been more than welcome to wait inside as well. You didn't have to wait for an invitation."

"Yes, I did," Leola said. "Would've been rude not to."

"Then by all means, let us all go inside. We have a great many revelations to share."

"I may have a revelation of my own to provide," Leola said. "Watching an empty house all night was just what I needed to put together a few pieces of this puzzle."

Dorothy gestured at the front door. "Then by all means, lead the way."

They entered and found Ivy waiting in the lounge. She had borrowed some makeup to freshen her disguise and was speaking with Desmond about her condition. When Dorothy, Trafalgar, and Leola joined them the conversation shifted to the newly-identified Watershed Society. Desmond affirmed he had heard the name whispered around campus from time to time, and he recognized the crest when Trafalgar showed the embroidery inside her coat. Leola put forth her theory that the house was being held in anticipation of Felix Quintel's ascendance, which Trafalgar agreed with.

"They are looking for a leader. They want someone to serve. I foiled their attempts by stealing the stone away from them. I spit it into the Gulf of Aden and their de facto leader went into the water with it."

Dorothy said, "So even if you are responsible for the Watershed Society getting this journal back, you are also responsible for crippling their efforts when you were just a child. I would say that more than makes up for the journal."

Trafalgar met Dorothy's eye and nodded quickly, thanking her for absolving her guilt. "But that is moot. They are obviously moving quickly now. I can only imagine that means they found the stone."

"Or they know where they can find another," Desmond offered.

"Yes," Dorothy said. "They are eliminating anyone else who could take a commission. They want the field clear so they are the only option when they seek funding."

Trafalgar said, "If there is another stone, they cannot be allowed to find it."

"Definitely not," Dorothy said. "But how can we prevent them? They have all the cards at the moment and we're not even sitting at the table. We don't know where the stone is, we don't know who is involved in this society, and we have no way of getting any information without the society learning we've figured out as much as we have."

Ivy said, "You could force their hand."

Desmond said, "How so?"

Ivy shrugged. "You don't know where the stone is, but you are confident it's out there somewhere. I would be willing to bet all these murders on a single day means the society is ready to move. They will most likely try to clean up their loose ends..." She nodded at Trafalgar and Boone, "...and then they will head out to retrieve their prize. They've waited twenty years, so I imagine they will be very eager to get underway. They may already be gone."

Trafalgar shook her head. "They would need to gather the backers before they left, and they couldn't have done that in one day. If only we could force their hand, trick them into revealing themselves."

Dorothy said, "We could go after the stone ourselves."

"We haven't the slightest idea where to even begin looking," Desmond said.

"No," Dorothy said, "but the Society won't know that. By now they only know the bare facts. Trafalgar and I survived their attempt on our lives, and we spent the rest of the afternoon saving their other attempted victims. They'll know Trafalgar and I were inside Quintel's home. If we were to make a mad dash to the Rookery, board an airship, and set out for the Continent, they'll assume we have connected all the dots rather than just a handful."

Beatrice said, "Minty. We could use her airship."

"Mm-hmm," Dorothy said. "We have her take us out and we wait at the mouth of the Thames. Des, you could stay behind and see if anyone leaves in pursuit of us."

Ivy said, "It would increase the odds if you had a stowaway aboard their ship. One they'll never see coming."

Trafalgar said, "How will you know which ship is theirs?"

Dorothy said, "They would be the ones rushing to depart at once. They'll be in a hurry to stay one step ahead of us. It would be dangerous."

"Call it penance for nearly killing Mr. Strode."

Desmond said, "If Miss Sever can tell me which ship is theirs, I can wire you when they've taken off in pursuit."

Dorothy and Trafalgar looked at each other, and Dorothy shrugged. "It's worth a shot. And it would be a far sight better than just sitting here waiting for them to take another shot at us."

Trafalgar sighed. "I suppose that is true. And if they don't take the bait we can simply turn the ship around and return home." She stood up. "Leola and I shall return home to pack. We should be ready by... shall we say one? Will that give you enough time to arrange for transportation?"

Dorothy grinned. "Oh, plenty of time. I already have a ship to take us wherever we want to go."

Chapter Eleven

The Rookery was a clutch of airship hangars joined together as a single entity along the banks of the Thames. It had replaced the rickety Battersea Bridge, one of the last remaining wooden bridges in London, and its bloated flotilla served to ferry people back and forth from one side of the river to the other. Amid the small airships used for commuting, a handful of larger craft were available to hire for longer trips.

The most majestic ship in the fleet, the *Skylarker*, was often docked outside of the Rookery where it could be seen for miles. When the sun was out the light would glint across the gridwork of its rigid structure to make the entire thing seem as if it was aglow from within. It was nine hundred feet from nose to rudder, with a top speed of ninety miles per hour. The gondola, an elongated hexagon, held up to seventy passengers but its captain rarely took more than twenty at a time.

The captain was Araminta Crook, a British Indian who stood just a hair above five feet, and perhaps an inch or two more with her boots on. She had been an engineer before she was a captain, serving about the *Skylarker* during the War. They were part of the infamous Bumblebee Squadron, England's first line of defense against the enemy. In the first year of service, they took heavy fire during one assault, and the entire flight crew was either incapacitated or killed. Minty gathered her engineers and took over command. She kept the line intact, helped force the Germans into retreat, and received a promotion as soon as the ship limped back home for repairs. The ship was officially hers, and she spent the next three years of fighting as its captain.

After the war she to have the ship outfitted for commercial use. She much preferred the quiet life, and she appreciated the opportunity to see England's coast and northern France without worrying over enemy attacks. It was a peaceful way to see the world, flying above it in an airship, and she was grateful for the opportunity.

She was in her cabin, folded into her bunk with an open book propped against her thighs, listening to the creak and groan as her ship pulled against its mooring. The ship wanted to be out, wanted to skim through the clouds, and she couldn't blame it. With the recent peace they were free to take any commission they wanted. The alternate side of that freedom was that very few people felt the wanderlust which kept her in business. Even those who might want to travel were still pinching pennies.

There was a knock on her door and she closed the book on her finger. "Enter."

Bodhi, her first mate, opened the door and leaned in. As if her thoughts had been heard by the goddesses, he said, "Captain Crook, a potential passenger would like to have a word with you."

Araminta marked her page and stood up. She stretched her arms out to the side and then over her head, standing on her toes before bending forward with her fingers pointed. Her joints popped and creaked from being pent up so long, and she smiled when she straightened up.

"I assume the passengers have already spoken to Meera about the fees?"

"About that," Bodhi said. "The passenger claimed special circumstances. Said you would know what it meant."

"Special..." Araminta's expression became serious. "Lady Boone. Is it Lady Boone?"

Bodhi nodded. "Yes. She has--"

Araminta cut him off with a wave of her hand. "She doesn't pay. Not a dime. Tell Ravi to set up the master suite. How many in her party?"

"Three, besides her."

"The master suite and two first-class suites. Whatever else she needs, give it to her without question. As far as the crew is concerned, her orders supersede mine. Is that understood?"

Bodhi seemed dazed but he nodded his assent.

"I'll be down in a moment to greet them. Have Ajay prepare us for departure immediately. Lady Boone will tell you the course he should set."

"Yes, Captain."

Once he was gone Araminta went to the head and wet her fingers under the tap. She ran them through her thick dark hair. She was wearing her standard on-duty uniform, so there was no way to smarten that up unless she went all the way and changed into her dress uniform. She knew that Lady Boone would be annoyed at any pretense, so she left her jacket and slacks untouched. She knew that if anyone saw her preening this way they would accuse her of fawning over a rich passenger, but her reaction had nothing to do with Lady Boone's wealth or notoriety.

Years earlier, Araminta had been married in all but name to a beautiful woman named Miranda. Araminta saw Miranda on the docks, helping to load, her sleeves pushed up to reveal powerful biceps and pale white skin that glowed in the sun that bounced off the Thames. She learned the dockworker's name and took to the library to read Shakespeare, memorizing lines until she found the perfect way to greet the beautiful goddess. She chose her moment carefully, conspiring to cross paths with the blonde when they were alone on the docks.

She almost backed out at the last moment, nearly offered a casual hello before moving on and never speaking to her again. But just as they passed one another, as Araminta's sleeve casually brushed the bare skin of Miranda's arm, Araminta said, "O, brave new world, that has such people in it."

Miranda stopped and looked at her. "Pardon?"

"From the play. *The Tempest*. By... Mr. Shakespeare."

"I've never seen it. Sorry."

Miranda started to walk away, but Araminta couldn't let all of her planning come to naught. "I could take you to see it. Or I could loan you my copy. Well, the library's copy." She cringed. "The... character is named Miranda. The one who says the line I said to you. I thought you might, um, have heard it or knew it or something."

"Why would I have heard it?"

"I'm sure people tell you you're beautiful all the time."

That made Miranda smile. "No. You're actually the first in quite a while."

Araminta smiled. "Well, then. It was all worth it. Have a good day, Miranda." She turned and tried to flee, but Araminta whistled to get her attention.

"I still don't know your name."

"Crook. Araminta Crook. You can call me Minty."

Miranda smiled again and nodded. "I may have to do that."

Three months later they were lovers, a change so life-altering that Araminta almost instantly couldn't remember a life without Miranda in it. They read Shakespeare together, and attended performances in the park where they held hands in the grass and spent more time looking at each other than the actors onstage. They were blissfully happy for almost five years before Miranda fell ill. The doctors they contacted couldn't give any relief. The medicine only provided brief respite from the pain. The War was over, and Araminta had been given the *Skylarker* only weeks earlier, but she was prepared to sell it in order to pay for experts to see if they could help. She was literally writing a letter to a potential buyer when Lady Dorothy Boone appeared at their door.

She explained that a cursed artifact from a tomb in Cambodia was improperly packed following an expedition. The people who uncovered the artifact had already succumbed, and Dorothy had been called in to see if there were any other victims along its path from the subcontinent to England. Araminta rushed Dorothy to Miranda's side, confident that there was now a cure or some sort of salve that might bring Miranda back to her. Dorothy sat by the sickbed, took Miranda's hand, and very kindly revealed that there was nothing she could do.

By that time Miranda was comatose. Araminta lost every shred of hope, every filament of potential salvation severed and dropping her to her knees. Dorothy gathered the weeping woman in her arms and rocked her until the tears stopped.

"I am terribly sorry," Dorothy whispered, "but there's no remedy. When the illness has advanced this far, it is impossible to bring the victims back. But there may be some solace to be had."

Araminta brushed away her tears only to have them replaced by fresh tracks. "I've lost the only person who matters to me. What solace could there possibly be?"

Dorothy said, "A chance to say goodbye."

It turned out that she had in her possession a tablet which could temporarily draw the ills from one person and give it to another. She explained kings and pharaohs had once used it to give final pronouncements if they fell too sickly to serve. It gave them a chance to name successors or ensure their work was finished before they finally passed on. Dorothy offered to take Miranda's illness on herself so that she and Araminta could say a proper farewell.

Araminta felt guilty accepting the phenomenal gift from a perfect stranger, but there was no possibility she would say no. The ritual was brief and to the point. Almost instantly after the incantation was finished, Dorothy clutched her stomach and had to be helped onto a bed. While they were tucking the blankets around her shivering form, Miranda sat up and asked for Minty. Araminta explained what had happened and that their time together would be brief.

They said their goodbyes. They held one another and whispered everything they wanted to be their last words to each other. They kissed one last time, knowing it would be their last, and Miranda made Araminta promise she wouldn't be lonely or alone. "I know that it will be difficult, I know you'll feel as if you're betraying me, but the betrayal would be abandoning the vibrant, alive person you've become. Don't let all my hard work go to waste."

Araminta promised, and they lay quietly together until the effects of the table wore off. Araminta felt Miranda slip away, and looked over to see Dorothy was awake. Miranda passed on that evening, and Araminta made a point of inviting Dorothy to the funeral. They had very few friends, as Miranda was private and secretive about their relationship. They stood alone at the gravesite and watched as she was lowered into the ground.

"I can never repay you for what you did."

"It wasn't a gift. It was necessary. One human to another. I hope it brought you peace."

Araminta nodded. "It hurt like hell, but my goddess." She smiled and shook her head. Tears were caught in her eyelashes. "My ship is yours."

"Never."

"No, I... I only mean..." She turned to face Dorothy. "I know your work takes you far afield. It requires traveling overseas, to the continent and China. And I know that this blastable War has been making that sort of travel nearly impossible. I may not be capable of taking you to the far reaches of the globe, but if you ever require an airship, it's yours. I will drop whatever I am doing and your journey will take precedence."

Dorothy was shaking her head. "That is far too high a price."

"It's cheap," Araminta snapped. "For what you gave me... for every sleepless night you took away from me, for every unanswered question I might have had for the rest of my life that you let me ask, a few flights here and there is a pittance. From this day forward, I am your personal ferryman."

To her credit, Dorothy only took advantage of her generosity on the rarest of occasions. In the past year, Dorothy had come to her only once, and then for a short trip. They did meet up a few other times, but only for tea and brunch. Dorothy knew that Araminta would still be lonely and grieving her wife, so she provided companionship and conversation. Her discretion convinced Araminta that whatever had brought her to the Rookery today, it was a matter of vital importance. Araminta convinced herself that she was presentable enough and finally left her cabin to greet their esteemed passengers.

Dorothy grimaced and crossed an arm over her abdomen to apply pressure next to her navel. Trafalgar glanced at her but said nothing, and Dorothy didn't offer an explanation. They were waiting at the base of the *Skylarker*'s gangplank with Beatrice and Leola standing behind them. The woman who had told them to wait was lingering near the entrance to the ship, and her posture changed as a man came hurrying toward them. The two crewmembers whispered back and forth for a moment, and then the woman approached Dorothy with a large smile.

"Lady Boone! My apologies for the delay, but we needed the captain's approval."

"I understand entirely. How is Captain Crook?"

"Captain Crook is doing better now that you have graced us with your presence!" The reply came from deeper in the ship. Araminta Crook, resplendent in her blue leather jacket and tan slacks, took long strides across the staging area. She held her arms out and laughed. "Dorothy Boone! It is wonderful to see you again. You look magnificent."

Dorothy laughed and hugged the captain. "Minty! It's been far too long."

"Well, you can stop by for reasons other than taking advantage of free airfare." She squeezed Dorothy's shoulder and looked at her companions. "Trix, I know. I don't believe I've had the pleasure of meeting your other friends."

"Ah. Trafalgar of Abyssinia, this is Captain Araminta Crook. This is her associate Leola... ah..."

"Leola Kidane," Leola offered.

Dorothy nodded. "Yes. My apologies for not knowing your surname. Completely rude of me. Araminta is the owner and captain of this fine vessel."

Trafalgar said, "They allow women to own airships?"

Araminta chuckled. "We're preferable. Back when people were first taking flight, it was a benefit to be as lightweight as possible. Men could fly, of course, but it was easier to adjust for an operator who weighed closer to a hundred pounds than two hundred. So we got our place in the pilot seat before anyone even know an aeroplane existed. Now it's not so much of a consideration, but people still tend to believe smaller is better even on a beast like this. Follow me and I'll show you to your rooms. I'll have someone see to your baggage."

Beatrice and Leola both stooped to pick up the bags, indicating it wasn't necessary to bother the crew, and Araminta linked her arm around Dorothy's elbow to lead them into the body of the ship. Dorothy patted Araminta's hand.

"I do hope we're not keeping you from anything important. We might have quite a long journey ahead of us."

"Might?"

"The length of our trip depends on what our quarry does when he sees we've departed."

Araminta raised an eyebrow. "Intrigue and skullduggery. I don't know why I claim you fly for free when you more than make up for it in excitement. Is there anything else I can do to make your stay more comfortable?"

"The standard perks should suffice. I'm not sure of Trafalgar and Leola's diets, so you'll have to confirm with them. And, ah..." She lowered her voice as a crewman passed. "If you've a hot water bottle aboard, I would be greatly obliged."

Araminta winced sympathetically. "Oh. Unfortunate timing for one to get her monthlies."

"Well, it could be beneficial that it's happening now while we're in transit. By the time we reach wherever we're going, I should be my normal self once again. But until then..."

"I'll get you the hot water bottle, of course. Rags?"

"I have plenty. Thank you."

Araminta nodded and led them to the large, luxurious cabins near the front of the vessel. "This is where you'll be staying. Once you're settled you can join me in the passerelle to help plot our voyage."

Dorothy kissed Araminta on the cheek. "Thank you, Araminta."

"A drop in the bucket compared to what you're owed." She smiled and slid her hand down Dorothy's arm before turning to the others. "Make yourselves comfortable. The crew serves at your command, should you require anything. The galley is open at all hours so please feel free to help yourselves. If something arises that you need, don't hesitate to ask me or a crewman. I hope you have a very pleasant journey about the *Skylarker*."

Once Dorothy was unpacked and had changed into more comfortable sailing attire, she met Araminta in the passerelle as instructed. The bridge was shaped like a seashell, with a forward-slanting wall of glass that currently looked out over the greenish-brown water of the Thames. Araminta's crew of blue jackets manned their stations, going through their final checklist to prepare for a long-term trip. She approached Araminta's station, a plush seat flanked on one side by an intercom and on the other by a ticker tape machine that fed her information from all points of the ship, and Araminta directed her toward a map of England and Europe hanging on the back wall.

Dorothy explained the situation in hushed tones. When the Watershed Society came up, Araminta tensed. She waited until the story was done and then said, "Watershed. They're the ones... they..." She was shaking, so she crossed her arms to pin both hands against her sides. She looked at the floor. "I did some digging and I discovered the man in charge of the expedition that brought back the improperly packed relics was a member of the Watershed Society. I couldn't find much about the group, and what I did find indicated they were defunct. His money came from them. If it wasn't for them, Miranda... she..."

"Oh, crumbs," Dorothy muttered. "Minty, had I known..."

Araminta looked at her with fury in her eyes. "If you'd known, I hope you would have come here sooner. I've been waiting years to bring those blaggards down."

Dorothy nodded. "If you're certain."

"Absolutely. For Miranda." She looked at the map and began to mentally plot their journey. "We must look as if we are setting out, but without actually setting a final destination. We'll head out from here and follow the Thames to its estuary. Anyone paying attention will think we mean to follow the coast rather than flying overland. We'll wait at Southend-on-Sea until your men on the ground get word to you about movement back here in London, then we'll adjust our plans accordingly. We have a range of twelve-hundred miles, so we should be able to reach France, Germany, or Spain. We can stop in Paris for refueling and to resupply if necessary. We should be ready to shove off within the hour and we'll reach the estuary an hour after that."

Dorothy nodded. "Sounds fine to me."

"Depending on where we are tonight, I would love to have dinner with you. It would give me a chance to get to know this Miss Trafalgar of yours."

"Of course. But be careful of her. She's still a mostly unknown quality. We're allies by convenience, not choice."

Araminta smiled. "Ah."

"Do not 'ah' me, Minty."

Araminta drew her finger across her lips as if sealing them. Dorothy smiled and they both addressed the map again. After a moment Araminta said, "If this voyage does eventually lead to you destroying the Watershed Society, then we may come out of this with me indebted to you even further."

"If we come out of this with those bastards in shambles, we'll consider it even."

An hour later the ship slowly lifted from its perch, angled east, and set off following the serpentine trail of the river Thames. The center of the gondola was taken up by a common room that included dining facilities and a relaxation area. Oval floor-to-ceiling windows on either side provided a view of the countryside. Araminta's crew followed the river without keeping strictly to its edge, drifting sometimes to cut a corner or avoid a bend. Trafalgar and Leola were seated in one of the booths near the galley, and Dorothy nodded to them without violating their privacy. She walked to one of the river-side windows and peered out.

The scope of what they were planning to do was starting to hit her. They had next to no information on the Watershed Society, no knowledge of its members or practices, no way of knowing who or what would come after them. Or if their adversary would even take the bait. There was a very real chance that they were just wasting their time as well as that of Araminta and her crew. Dorothy remembered the day Araminta swore allegiance to her; taking Miranda's illness on herself had been an equally spontaneous decision. The moment the ague settled onto her she had wished there was a way to back out of the arrangement. The instant agony was unlike anything she had ever experienced. She was terrified she had mistranslated, that she would discover there was no way back.

She hated taking advantage of Araminta's kindness because she had regretted her decision from the moment she made it. She would have taken it back if she could, reversed the beautiful gift she had given to a stranger. She liked to think she would do the same thing again - the opportunity to say goodbye to a loved one was next to miraculous - but she doubted she would have the courage. Since that day she had tried her damnedest to make sure she never dove headfirst into anything without at least the semblance of a plan. But the damage had been done and, deserved or not, Araminta now considered herself in Dorothy's debt. Dorothy often agonized over it was a greater sin to use Araminta's ship or to refuse her a chance to repay a kindness.

The ship was traveling at a steady pace of sixty-two knots, which would get them to the coast in another fifteen minutes. She had taken out her fob watch to check the time when Araminta entered the common room with an unreadable smile on her face. "Lady Boone, Miss Trafalgar. I thought you would like to know we just received an odd transmission."

"Odd how?" Dorothy asked, rising as Trafalgar and Leola crossed the room to join them.

"It seems the airship *Kestrel* wanted me to know it was setting off twenty minutes behind us. There was quite a fervor at the Rookery after we left. Calls going out, passengers arriving without baggage as if they were in a great hurry... someone saw Lady Boone and Miss Trafalgar boarding my ship, and that someone became very rushed to get in the air."

Trafalgar looked at Dorothy with something like approval. "Our plan seems to have worked."

"For the time being. What was odd about the message, Minty?"

"Other than the fact there is no reason for two unrelated ships to keep each other apprised of their movements? The message contained none of the standard identifying codes, no hails, nothing that would indicate it had been sent from the communications officer. In fact, it's almost as if someone sat down at an unattended station and sent the message without the proper training. There were two letters at the end, and I assume they were someone's initials."

"I.S.?" Dorothy guessed.

Araminta touched the side of her nose and closed one eye. "Got it in one. I'll refrain from asking how you set that up. For now we're keeping course, but the message also relayed our opposition's next stop. Ladies, I hope you packed for warmer temperatures. We're going to Rome."

Chapter Twelve

THE COMMUNICATIONS officer aboard the *Kestrel* opened the door to the head, peered out, and carefully shut the door behind him before starting back toward the front of the gondola. The passengers on this trip were a bunch of demanding bastards and creepy as anything, and he told himself they had made him paranoid and confused. But there was some downright strange things happening on the ship and they'd been happening since they took off. Footsteps in empty hallways, the smell of perfume... faint, but there. He would feel eyes on him but when he turned around he would be alone on the passerelle. His skin crawled even when none of the passengers were nearby.

His captain saw him slinking down the corridor and barked his name. "What in the devil are you doing?"

"Sorry, Captain. Just visiting the head, sir."

"Did you soil yourself? Why are you walking that way?"

"I... n-no, sir. Just, uh, just... jumpy, I s'pose."

The captain rolled his eyes. "Back to your station. We'll be at the North Sea soon."

"Aye, sir."

He went to his station on the bridge, pushed his hair out of his eyes, and looked at the console. To his surprise, it seemed as if a message had gone out while he was in the loo. The message itself hadn't been copied, and there was no way of telling who received it. He checked the tape and saw the messages he remembered sending. If it wasn't for the gap in the records he wouldn't even have noticed the errant delivery. He sucked his bottom lip into his mouth and looked over his shoulder to see the captain standing at the window the watch their progress.

First slinking back from the head looking like a scared cat, now claiming there were ghost messages being sent from his station? He'd be relieved from duty at best or sent to a headshrinker. The best case scenario was that he'd get a reputation for being spooked easily. They'd give him hell, they'd give him nicknames... no. It would be best if the ghost message remained just that, and vanished into the firmament.

He scrolled the tape forward and settled in. As he did, he could have sworn he heard a woman laughing over his shoulder. But as he suspected, when he turned to look, there wasn't a woman in sight.

They could see the *Kestrel* when the ships were angled properly in relation to one another. The *Skylarker* turned to follow a bend in the river and exposed their port side to the west. Dorothy and Trafalgar stood at the windows in the galley. Trafalgar had found the ship's mascot, a small dappled cat named Ditto, and held it in her arms, scratching the docile creature under its chin. Dorothy pointed out the ship that chugged along behind them at a distance of ten or fifteen miles.

"There they are. Who knows how many members of the Watershed Society are aboard that ship, on their way to what they believe to be their treasure."

Trafalgar said, "And what is to prevent them from simply shooting us out of the sky?"

"Other than the fact these ships aren't equipped with weapons anymore? They were caught flat-footed. They wanted to take their time and get patrons to fund this trip but we forced them to start before they were ready. They think we know more than we do, and they believe time is of the essence. They won't waste time with us when they can go directly to their prize and prevent us from advancing."

"These men have proven they aren't shy when it comes to murdering people who stand in their way. They killed at least nine people because it was convenient."

"They blindsided us, taking us unawares. They hid behind sniper rifles, they employed subterfuge. They acted cowardly because they are cowards. We have the advantage of knowing they are coming this time. We can prepare for their attacks. And there is one more thing making me confident." She turned to face Trafalgar. "We are working together."

Trafalgar raised an eyebrow. "And that is a benefit in your eyes."

"We are enemies because we are professional rivals. But I respect you, and I can admit you are an excellent fighter."

"You are recalling the time we grappled over a cabriolet to reach the train station before it departed."

Dorothy said, "I'm sure I don't remember what you're talking about. My jaw, on the other hand..." She rubbed her chin as if it were still sore and Trafalgar couldn't help smiling. "We spent a lot of time in conflict with one another. I believe it's made us both stronger and smarter. With a common enemy I have little doubt that we will come out victorious."

The ship took another slight change in trajectory and the *Kestrel* dropped out of sight. Trafalgar said, "What shall we do while we await further word from Ivy?"

"I brought the journal we found at Quintel's home. I've poked at it a little to see what I could translate from the code but so far I haven't made any headway. I thought perhaps you could offer some insight that I lacked."

"The two of us, working together," Trafalgar said.

Dorothy shrugged and walked toward one of the booths. "We've been thrown together by circumstance. The number of people doing what we do has been greatly diminished in the past thirty hours, largely due to the fact that none of us could trust one another. We could finish this quest and return to business as usual, or we can learn from it. We can test the waters to see if we work well together. I'm willing to give it a chance."

Trafalgar sat across from her. "Of course you are willing."

"What is that supposed to mean?"

"It means that by joining forces, I bring much more to the table than you could."

Dorothy offered a mock laugh. "Yes, I am quite sure I would be lost without your bullheaded approach to situations."

"If you had your way we would still be watching the guards outside the Quintel house."

"And if you were on your own, there is no chance you could have found an airship to take you to Rome at a moment's notice."

Leola spoke up. "Sounds like a mutually beneficial partnership to me."

They both looked at her, the anger of their exchange dissipating from her interjection. She had left the room to see what was available in the galley and had just returned with a small bowl of fruit. She popped a yellow-orange square into her mouth, shrugged as if their confrontation didn't affect her either way, then continued on her way. Trafalgar and Dorothy looked at one another, and then Dorothy retrieved the journal from her bag. She placed it on the table between them.

"You've spent the majority of your life searching for these people. It would be fair to assume you might have a head start on translating it."

"Thank you," Trafalgar said.

"Oh." Dorothy flipped the book open and turned to a page she had marked. "The work of Enoch Solomon, I've no doubt."

Trafalgar looked at the pencil-and-charcoal drawing of her face without betraying any emotion. "He saw me on the docks. I fought back against one of the guards. He stopped them from killing me. Perhaps he thought my willingness to fight would make me a good host for whatever he wished to summon."

"It would seem that error was his undoing."

"Yes." She flipped through a few pages, leaving her portrait behind. It was one of the final entries, naturally, and she began looking at the pages that preceded it. She noticed patterns, blocked off areas of text with a series of numbers along the top edge of every square. "Plus eleven-thirty-two and minus forty-three nine."

"Latitude and longitude," Dorothy said. "I've figured out that much at least."

"Djibouti," Trafalgar said. "We left from there. Apparently he spent quite a bit of time there preparing for our trip. He made sure everything was in place before he sent his men out to gather us up. His little experiments."

Dorothy said, "How many children did he gather?"

Trafalgar shook her head. "I have no idea. On the trip I took there were more than two dozen, perhaps as many as fifty. When they believed their plan had worked, I told them to set the girls free in Cairo. I... I've never even tried to find out what happened to them."

"Wait. You survived the journey to Cairo by pretending the plot worked? And then you sold all of Solomon's items... how long did you continue the pretense of being in control of whatever Solomon tried to summon?"

"Until I was able to book passage to Istanbul. I lost myself in the crowd."

Dorothy ran a hand over her face and looked out the window. "You were the only one of Watershed's victims who was not targeted. Everyone else was a direct target, but you... they killed your partner instead."

Trafalgar said, "You claimed they wished for me to be imprisoned for your death."

"Nah, that doesn't work," Dorothy said absently. "No. They had to have a larger goal for keeping you alive. They think you're still in their thrall."

"It's been twenty years. Certainly they would have realized by now..."

Dorothy shrugged. "Perhaps, perhaps not. The fact remains that you were spared."

"I was spared because if they had shot at me, Adeline would have seen it and interfered."

"The fact remains is that despite what happened to Solomon, these people had reason to believe his plan worked. You were a young girl snatched away from her parents and cast into an alien and unforgiving world. Despite having every disadvantage, you managed to thrive in their field."

"I was only trying to understand what had been done to me."

Dorothy said, "They won't see it that way. Yes, they believe you to be a rival. But because they believe you turned rogue. As far as the Watershed Society is concerned, they believe the ritual granted you some power. They believe they turned you from a weak-willed young girl into a formidable opponent."

Leola said, "If they think she's the thing they summoned, why are they trying to summon it again?"

Dorothy considered the question. "The ritual was interrupted when you spit out the stone. They don't know how far along it got, but to their mind there was a definite change in you. How else would a child from the grasslands of Africa be able to tear into their organization the way you have? They know the entity is still waiting for a host but they might believe a part of it was transferred to you. You're proof the ritual works. Even interrupted it seems to have made you stronger, smarter..."

Trafalgar closed her eyes. "I have spent my entire life fighting that thought. Staring at myself in the mirror and wondering if you are correct, if some... thing was left behind in me. The ritual was underway, the stone was in my mouth. I felt something I cannot describe. And then my entire life changed. I could speak in a new language, although becoming fluent took much time and effort. I walked among people I didn't recognize on streets that were as alien to me as the moon would have been. And I wondered. I wondered if Solomon had indeed turned me into something I was never supposed to be."

Dorothy hesitated, then stood up and moved to Trafalgar's side of the booth. Trafalgar instinctively cringed away from her, but Dorothy took her hand.

"You are yourself. The very fact you've been tortured by the question proves to me that there is nothing hitchhiking in your mind. The creature would not only be certain, it would destroy any part of you still capable of doubt."

Trafalgar smiled slightly and put her hand on top of Dorothy's so that it was sandwiched between hers. "Thank you, Lady Boone."

"Dorothy."

"Sometimes I need to call you Lady Boone just to remember this woman... this woman who is helping me is the same one I've spent the past few years cursing."

Dorothy laughed. "Very well, if that helps. But I hope I can earn your trust enough to be called by my proper name more often than not."

"You are making good progress on that. Dorothy."

Dorothy nodded. "Well, then. Now that we have that sorted, if the opportunity arises, would you feel comfortable exploiting their possible belief in your... status? If they think you have some connection to the creature they wish to awaken, we may be able to use that to our advantage."

"For Adeline's sake," Trafalgar said, "I would be willing to move mountains."

"All right. Let's begin by seeing what sense we can make of this blasted journal."

As they didn't have to wait for Watershed to catch up to them, there was no reason for the *Skylarker* to wait off the coast of Southend-on-Sea. Once they reached the North Sea, Araminta ordered Bodhi to set a course around Botany Bay and heading south toward France. Dorothy was on the bridge when they changed course, and they asked Azitha, the third mate, to keep an eye on their tail. Once they were over open water Azitha reported that the *Kestrel* had turned south as well, but it seemed they would be traveling overland.

"Trying to make up time," Araminta posited. "We'll wait to see what happens in Paris. If it looks like they're going to overnight, we'll keep going. If it looks like they're going to keep going, we'll have no choice but to keep on."

Dorothy said, "Can the 'Lark make it to Rome on a straight shot?"

"Oh, sure. We'll be near-empty but we won't be running on fumes. Azitha," she said, turning to a member of her flight crew, "did you happen to see what model they were in?"

"ZX-XII."

Araminta grinned. "The twelve? They're definitely going to stop in Paris, then. Unless they're planning to crash in Nice. Alert the crew. We're going nonstop."

Bodhi nodded and said, "We'll arrange for a rotating shift."

Dorothy said, "Is there any way to keep track of them? Make sure they do stop in Paris?"

"Only if your stowaway friend manages to send us another message. But I assure you, they have no other option. That particular vessel has a range of eight hundred miles. That's why they're cutting across the land rather than following us over the water. That way Paris is approximately two hundred and fifty miles into their trip. They'll refuel and continue to Rome, and even then they'll only just barely make it to Rome with anything in their gas bags. It'll be a rough trip... they better pray they don't hit any headwinds or they'll be without recourse." She laughed under her breath. "I know you said they departed without a plan but this is reckless even for me. I can't imagine what they're paying to get the crew to risk this."

"Can't they refuel somewhere further along their route?"

Araminta shook her head. "Nowhere big enough until..."

"Geneva," Bodhi supplied.

"Thank you. And England's airships have hardly been welcome to the Swiss ever since the unpleasantness in 1915."

Dorothy remembered it well; a lost airship had inadvertently bombed a town just over the border of Switzerland. They refused to join Germany's forces, but they also turned their backs on England. She put thoughts of the War out of her mind.

"We're fortunate we got the superior ship then, eh?"

Araminta winked at her. "Always bet on the *Skylarker* when it comes to a race. We should arrive in Rome tomorrow morning at half-two. You and your companions should take an early dinner in order to be awake when we land. I'll let you know if your friend on the other vessel sends an update about their final destination."

"I believe we shall. Fair winds, Minty."

Araminta touched her eyebrow with two fingers and tossed off a salute as Dorothy departed the passerelle. Once she was gone Araminta straightened her jacket and went to take her seat at the command console. They would soon reach the other side of the channel, using the town of Calais as their landmark before turning to follow the coastline of France until it was time to turn south toward Paris. She crossed one leg over the other and smiled as she watched the water stretched out before them. They might not get a monetary reward for this trip, but she could always count on Lady Boone making her journeys worthwhile.

After dinner, Trafalgar excused herself to her cabin. Araminta invited her to the passerelle to look at the water before they turned inland, but Trafalgar politely passed. Her first encounter with the ocean had been at night, and seeing the moon reflected in the waves still brought up bad memories for her. Leola excused herself before dinner, and Trafalgar was surprised to find she was still awake. Their cabin was comfortably large, with a bed on either side and a window on the wall directly across from the door. Leola was sitting cross-legged atop her still-made bed, her elbows resting on her knees and hands dangling.

Trafalgar went to the window and closed the blinds before she sat down across from her friend. "You look troubled."

"I miss Adeline."

"Ah. I have been trying to focus on the task at hand. We can mourn once her killers have been brought to justice one way or another."

Leola nodded and twisted her fingers together, watching them like they were a separate creature. "The life you've given me, Tiffy, it's more amazing than I ever could have imagined. I was a bruiser, I was destined to get my brains knocked out one way or another. The men who brought me to Cairo wanted to make me a nursemaid or a governess. I would never have survived. But you gave me a purpose and you showed me things I never even dreamed about. I don't want to sound ungrateful, but now that I'm a different person..."

Trafalgar said, "You want to go."

"Ridiclous, isn't it? You do all this for me, pull me up so far in society that I'm riding to Rome on a damn airship with a proper lady... and then as your reward, I turn 'round and run away just 'cause things got scary." She shook her head. "I'm being a kid."

"You're doing no such thing. I would be alarmed if you weren't having these thoughts, to be honest. We both have Adeline's blood on our hands. I can still feel it on mine. Perhaps that will change once we've gotten vengeance for her, or once we put her to rest, but I don't know if it will ever go away. I can't ask you to stay out of sheer loyalty to me. I won't."

Leola had tears in her eyes. "I don't want to leave you alone."

Trafalgar laughed. "I've been alone most of my life. You and Adeline made things easier, but..." She looked toward the shuttered window. "Adeline was ripped from my life. If you remain with me there's a chance you will meet the same fate. I would much rather be alone knowing you're out in the world than have solitude forced upon me by our enemies. And I would not want you to stay with me out of blind loyalty. If you wish to go, then I wish you well."

Leola stood and knelt in front of Trafalgar. "I'll stay with you until we complete this mission. For Adeline. And then I will seek other employment."

Trafalgar said, "I will help you. Whatever you require." She leaned in and kissed Leola's forehead. "Thank you for being honest with me."

"Of course."

"For now, we should get some sleep. It's another ten hours before landfall in Rome." Leola nodded and stood up to return to her own bed. Trafalgar gripped her hand. "I couldn't have gotten as far as I have without you watching my back. Thank you."

Leola nodded. "If you ever need me again..."

"I'll remember. But I will try to not need you."

Leola smiled and kissed Trafalgar's knuckles before getting into bed.

Trafalgar turned out the light to be polite, but she remained seated in the darkness for a long time after Leola drifted off to sleep.

Chapter Thirteen

It was still early by Dorothy's internal clock, but the ship went into nighttime mode in anticipation of making landfall in the middle of the night. Rome's terminals operated around the clock, so they would be greeted by a full staff. Araminta wanted the crew to be alert and responsive as well. Dorothy retired to her room, took a pill to help alleviate her monthly issues and changed into her nightgown. She'd warned Beatrice she wasn't up for spending the night together, and Beatrice suggested they could share a bed and just sleep. Dorothy accused her of just wanting the bigger room, which Beatrice curiously did not deny.

They passed Paris close to an hour ago and now all she could see below them were dark squares of green, yellow, and brown, the Mondrian pattern of France's countryside. So much of it had been torn apart and scarred by the war, so much beauty needlessly shredded by boots and bombs and burials. She had been behind enemy lines, she had witnessed some of the horrors being wrought in the name of... what? Ideals? Fighting to protect your country whilst simultaneously ripping the country apart, fighting to protect your people while sending those people to die for it... the whole thing made no damned sense.

She had a feeling perhaps her anger was due to discomfort and exhaustion. At the moment Beatrice was sleeping in the bed behind her, nude with the sheets twisted around her waist like a rope ladder. Dorothy was at the cabin's built-in desk with the light turned low and angled so she could see her book. She looked over her shoulder at Beatrice's bare back, the intricate branches of her tattoo blending with the shadows and the loose curls of her hair.

Though she longed to cross the room and crawl under the blankets, there was too much to be done before they reached Rome. She turned back to the journal and focused on the nonsensical words. There had to be some sort of pattern to the code, some system she could crack. Taking notes in the field required speed and shorthand. If Solomon couldn't decipher what he had scrawled down then there was no reason to take notes at all. He had to have a system.

The teletype embedded in the wall next to the desk came to life, beeping and scratching out its message. The noise startled her enough that she put her palm against her chest and turned to make sure the clatter hadn't disturbed Beatrice's sleep before taking the slip of paper from the feeder.

"Sorry for the lateness. New message from IS. Kestrel tucked in for night in Paris. Resuming trip tomorrow 0430. Should have a twelve-hour lead on them. Sweet dreams. AC."

Dorothy smiled and whispered, "Sweet dreams to you as well, Minty." She folded the note and looked at the journal again. She would never be able to explain why everything slipped into place for her then; whether it was looking away for a moment and then re-focusing, or if looking at Araminta's shorthand from the teletype had pushed her brain into the proper position to see it, but suddenly the words in Solomon's journal didn't look quite as random as they had before. She placed her hands on either side of the book and looked down at the swirls and loops of ink, willing the letters to make sense. It was like trying to hold onto the snippet of a dream long enough to remember everything that happened in it.

"Come on," she whispered. "Come on, stay with it, Dot. You can see it. It's right there in front of you." She ran her bottom teeth against her top lip and narrowed her eyes.

Her grandmother had slapped the top of her head just hard enough to make her flinch. "If you expect every answer to be spelled out, you won't last very long in this profession. Look harder."

"I'm looking, Grandma," she whispered. "I can't see it... I... wait."

A single letter seemed to stand out to her. The letter T, by itself, unconnected to the letters around it, and capitalized. Dorothy found a blank sheet of paper and wrote T=I. She flipped back to the coordinates Trafalgar had identified as Djibouti. There were two Ts in it, and she translated the word into the new alphabet. T was a substitute for I, and that meant D was an O. It was the most simplistic cypher he could have used, but the use of random spacing between words would have made it impossible to crack if he hadn't made one mistake. He had been writing too swiftly and his brain told him the personal pronoun needed to be on its own and capitalized.

Dorothy rapidly scribbled the code on her paper, then began translating the final entry. "Believe we have found the perfect receptacle for our host. Willing to defend herself against stronger opponents, willing to fight unarmed, strong, intelligent (learned language in a matter of days to a degree that she was able to converse in English). The girl lacks a name and therefore has no sense of self. The host will easily overwhelm whatever personality the girl may have and subsume her completely. As a child she will be pliable. The host will be like a child and therefore susceptible to whatever the Society wishes. We can mold it into our own champion with minimal effort."

This paragraph encircled the drawing of Trafalgar's head. Dorothy touched the cheekbone, horrified at what Solomon and his ilk had planned for an innocent child. She closed her eyes and pinched the bridge of her nose, settling her brain back into its proper channels. It had taken her nearly an hour to translate one paragraph, and she'd been helped by repeated words. Translating the entire journal would take too long to be very helpful.

If they worked backwards, perhaps they could learn what the Society had been planning for Trafalgar. If they knew that, they might have a clue about what to expect in Rome. She looked at the clock and winced, knowing she should get to bed if she had any hope of getting rest. She sharpened her pencil with the blade of her penknife and wet the nib with her tongue. Behind her Beatrice murmured in her sleep, speaking rapid and desperate Mandarin. She had done it before; Dorothy only waited for the burst of language to fade away before she bent over her page again.

Another hour and she could have the page translated. Then she could lie down and take a quick nap so she was rested when they reached their destination. She put a finger on the journal's page and dragged it along each letter to keep her place as she began translating as quickly as she could.

Beatrice woke to the sway and sweep of the gondola. Her fingers tightened on the bedding and she took a moment before opening her eyes to remind herself that she wasn't in the hold of the ship. Her earliest memory of clinging to the moth-eaten sweater of an old man fading as her brain caught up with her body. She wasn't at sea, she was in flight. She was an adult, she had more memories than blankness, and she knew precisely who she was. Her first years, her mysterious years, didn't matter as much as the years that came afterward.

The fear subsided and she opened her eyes. The room smelled ever so slightly of Dorothy's perfume, but she was alone in the bed. She let the sheet fall away as she sat up and looked at the desk. Sure enough, there was her employer and sometimes lover, head down on the desk and fingers still curled around her pencil. Beatrice climbed out of bed and draped the sheet over her shoulders like a cape, walking on the balls of her feet to wrap her arms around Dorothy's slumbering form. She gently removed the pencil from Dorothy's grip and massaged the divot in the pad of her forefinger until it faded. The gentle massage stirred Dorothy.

"Mm."

"You fell asleep," Beatrice whispered against the shell of Dorothy's ear. She nipped at the lobe as Dorothy tried to sit up and pressed against her.

"Miss Sek, I do believe you are nude."

Beatrice said, "I do believe that is the way you prefer me."

Dorothy reached back and ran her hand over the curve of Beatrice's hip. "What time is it?"

"Quarter to two."

"Damn. We'll be landing in Rome soon." Beatrice took a step back and let Dorothy up. "I should dress and join Minty on the passerelle." She turned and pushed the sheet out of the way to admire Beatrice's curves. "Or... perhaps... a quick shower first. These rooms are equipped with private bathing facilities. I think I definitely require a bit of a wake-up if you're willing."

Beatrice nodded and pecked Dorothy's bottom lip. "Always willing, Lady Boone. I'll get those hard to reach places."

Dorothy lowered her voice to a seductive purr. "And maybe a few of those that are easy to reach, but are just no fun reaching by myself."

They kissed, and Beatrice's sheet drifted to the floor around their feet. A minute or so later when they retreated to the head, they didn't bother to retrieve it.

Dorothy arrived on the passerelle in a snug brown waistcoat, the collar of her shirt open to reveal a crimson ascot. Her hair was still wet from the shower and bundled in a loose braid that fell over her shoulder. The brief slumber at her desk had been enough to screw up her sense of time. It felt like morning to her and yet the world outside the front windows was full dark. Araminta was once again in her station in full uniform, the only difference being that her hair was now styled in a looser and more casual do. Dorothy wondered if she had actually been to bed.

"Good morning, Dot." Araminta cast an appreciative eye over Dorothy's outfit. "You missed the Alps. Always a spectacular sight to behold, even by moonlight."

"Sounds romantic," Dorothy said.

Araminta arched an eyebrow and smiled. "We shall be descending into Rome in approximately twenty minutes. Make sure everyone has their papers ready."

"I shall."

"Did you receive my text regarding the *Kestrel*'s overnight plans?"

"I did, thank you."

Araminta said, "We've received no further missives since then, but they should be on the ground in Paris as we speak. Shall we make life difficult for them? Send a missive to the authorities that they're smuggling contraband?"

Dorothy smiled. "A tempting thought, but no. We need them to arrive eventually so we can follow them to whatever their next destination might be. We'll take advantage of our early arrival to arrange a surprise once they arrive. Is Trafalgar awake yet?"

"She passed through here about half an hour ago. I believe she's in the galley having some breakfast with that bodyguard of hers."

Dorothy nodded and went to the window. They were flying over the hills that surrounded Rome, and even at the early hour she could see lights burning in some of the windows. She loved ancient architecture like this, cities that seemed to grow organically from the countryside like strange flowers. Cities like London razed the fields, flattened the hills, and shored up the waterways to make the world more convenient. It made for comfortable and cozy towns, but she had to believe there would be a point when the world had become too torn apart to sustain them further.

When Dorothy arrived in the galley, she saw Beatrice had already joined Trafalgar and Leola in their breakfast. She helped herself to a banana and peeled it as she sat beside her friend across from their former quarry.

"Minty says we'll arrive in twenty minutes. Still no word from Ivy since last night."

Trafalgar said, "Should we be worried about that?"

Dorothy shook her head. "Hardly. There's no reason to believe she's been captured. I know from experience that she can be slippery even in an enclosed environment. She once managed to elude a constable while riding in the backseat of a car with him. She may not have any further information, or it may be impossible for her to gain access to the teletype to send another note. Whatever the reason, we're stuck waiting here until someone arrives to point us in the right direction."

"Let us hope Miss Sever is still aboard when they arrive," Trafalgar said.

"In the meantime..." Dorothy took a few folded pages from her pocket and spread them out on the table. "I managed to find the key for unlocking Solomon's journal. I translated a swath leading up to his encounter with Trafalgar, and he wrote briefly about the stone he attempted to use in his ritual. It's something he called chalcedony, unless my cryptography was off."

Leola shook her head. "It's a fibrous variety of quartz."

"All right," Dorothy said. "This particular variety of the stone is extraordinarily rare. It was excavated from a site which had been saturated with mystical energy by ancient wizards. The stones have long been rumored to open a channel between two beings. One mind is opened and another is given the opportunity to step inside. Much like opening a window and letting a burglar crawl inside. Even a thousand years ago there were only a handful of the chalcedony stones, but today even finding one was considered to be a monumental discovery. The Watershed Society took it to mean their plans were blessed. Apparently they had been searching for it since the middle of the nineteenth century and finally found it in a tomb near Athens."

Trafalgar said, "Perhaps they found another tomb. Our final destination may be Athens."

Dorothy nodded. "It's likely, but I don't want to jump to any conclusions. If we tell Minty to prepare the ship for Athens and the second stone turns out to be in Majorca..."

"True. Then we shall wait. Are we being allowed to leave the ship once we arrive?"

Dorothy said, "Of course. We can investigate Watershed's presence in the Mediterranean and gear up for a potential assault. If Ivy can't provide any more information before their ship arrives we may be forced to hijack them and ask them what their plans are. We cannot allow them to achieve their goal. I don't know what they have in store for this Felix Quintel, but I've no intention of finding out." She took out her fob watch to check the time. "Now, we'll be coming in for a landing soon. I suggest we get our papers in order and strap ourselves in."

They took the last of their breakfast and retired to their rooms. When they were strapped securely to the chairs in Dorothy's suite, away from the ears of Trafalgar and Leola, Beatrice said, "Do you really believe Ivy is still at liberty aboard the *Kestrel*? It's a long time to avoid someone running into her. Even invisible she might have accidentally revealed herself a dozen times by now."

"I have faith in her. Even when we're at odds, the woman has proven herself to be a formidable opponent. I'm sure the Watershed Society would have a difficult time capturing her even if they became aware of her presence."

Beatrice said, "Or they became aware of her presence, found out her intentions, and offered her a big payday to play us for fools. The woman is only interested in money. She could've been bought."

Dorothy said, "True. But if we begin second-guessing every piece of intelligence we receive from her, we'll render her useless. She's far too valuable to ignore at the moment. Either her information will prove worthy or the truth will be revealed soon enough."

Beatrice pressed her lips into a thin line but said nothing more on the subject.

The landing was as gentle as they could hope for, and Araminta was waiting by the gangplank to see them off. She had donned her uniform cap and revealed she was sending her crew out to see if there were any cargo contracts heading back to England.

"No reason for this trip to be a complete lark."

Dorothy wished her luck and kissed her cheek before leading her unlikely crew out into the hangar. The Burattini Docks were located at the very furthest reaches of Rome, a fact Dorothy found utterly inexplicable considering the winds coming in off the Tyrrhenian Sea. The potential for a dirigible to be knocked against the mooring masts or sent careening off-course would have been enough for her to suggest a location on the other side of the city, but Araminta had handled their arrival with aplomb.

As predicted the docks were as lively as a market in the middle of the day. Four other airships were circling the area as they awaited permission to land. Crewmen in bright orange jumpsuits were running to and fro on the tarmac, checking their lists before sending a signal to one captain or another that they were cleared for takeoff. Ahead of them, Dorothy could see into the terminal. Even at three in the morning there was a crowd of passengers waiting to be ferried to the far reaches of the globe. She wondered how humans satisfied their wanderlust before airships and sea travel were commonplace. She passed two tourists in brown leather jackets who paused to appreciate her suit before continuing on their way. She winked at them before getting to the matter at hand.

"We shouldn't have time to get settled," Dorothy said. "In two hours, the *Kestrel* will once again be on her way. I'd like to have a larger section of the journal translated by that time. We'll find a quiet place in the terminal where we can split up the pages."

"You don't mean to take the book apart," Trafalgar said.

Dorothy said, "Needs must, Miss Trafalgar. We'll do it as carefully as possible, but I agree that we must... preserve the... content." She furrowed her brow as they approached the terminal. When she spoke again her voice was quieter and more distant. "The Watershed Society, and Mr. Solomon in particular, has been at this for decades. We have no idea how much valuable information lies in these pages. But time is... of the essence."

Beatrice had tensed as soon as Dorothy's tone changed. "What is it?"

"Those men by the door. Brown leather jackets. The two tourists who passed us..." She scanned the tarmac and saw another brown jacket. "Oh, crumbs."

Trafalgar said, "You say that often. What does it mean?"

"In this instance, it means something small and insignificant has been overlooked, and now it may lead to a larger problem. The guards outside the Quintel house wore brown leather jackets. Like this, but shorter." She flicked the mantle of Trafalgar's coat. "I thought it might constitute some sort of uniform. Now I believe that has been confirmed. I never considered that they're a large enough organization to have satellite agencies in other countries. They must have called ahead to tell them we were coming. I count six."

Beatrice gestured slightly with her head. "Seven. The fellow with the newspaper."

Trafalgar rolled her wrist and the emei piercers slipped into her palm. She refrained from extending them, however, choosing instead to look at Dorothy for guidance.

"How should we proceed?"

"If we cause a spectacle we risk being subdued by security. We'll continue on as if we haven't noticed them, but the moment we have an opening, we take it."

Beatrice kept her arms down, but she fanned out her fingers. Dorothy saw a dim spark pass in the space between her fingertips and knew she was gathering energy from the static electricity in the air. If she built up a big enough charge she could provide a distraction for them to get away.

"We can still salvage this, despite the Society having us surrounded. They'll be privy to the next step in the plan. If we can-"

"Insurrectionists!"

The bellow echoed across the tarmac just as they reached the door. Dorothy turned and saw one of the leatherjackets running toward them. His fellow Society members were also taking flight with weapons drawn. They were close enough that they were reach Dorothy and Trafalgar before security did. Dorothy looked at Beatrice and nodded, even though there was no chance she'd built up enough of a charge to do much damage. Beatrice turned and brought her right hand up, cupped her wrist with her left hand, and squeezed her hand into a fist. The blue electric charge built up around her hand like ball lightning as she waited for all the Society men to get close enough that they would all be affected.

Three men came at them from the side. Leola grabbed one and disarmed him by a swift cutting blow to his forearm. He dropped his weapon and she slammed him against the wall. Dorothy drew her baton and dropped into a crouch, swinging at the knees of the closest Society member. He went down hard and Dorothy disarmed him easily. The doors of the airdock had opened to reveal more leatherjackets coming at them from behind. Trafalgar swept her piercers at their chests to hold them back.

"Trix!" Dorothy said.

Beads of sweat appeared on Beatrice's forehead as she fought to gather as much energy as possible before unleashing it. When she determined the men were all close enough, she flashed her fingers outward and released the energy in a blinding flash. Trafalgar and Leola were knocked to one side, only staying upright because Dorothy grabbed their coats to keep them from toppling. Beatrice stumbled, lightheaded from the display, and Dorothy took her hand.

"Quickly! While they're stunned!"

They retreated into the building, through the crowd of stunned fliers who had been preparing to depart. Airdock security were similarly confused as to how they should proceed. Behind them one of the leatherjackets called out the 'insurrectionists' cry again, and this time even civilians tried to stop their forward progress. Dorothy and Leola both had to tear away from the grips of well-meaning Samaritans. As far as the eyewitnesses were concerned, Beatrice had just set off an incendiary on the tarmac. If they were captured they would be imprisoned and most likely put on trial as terrorists. They just had to escape the general vicinity and Araminta would pick them up at the nearest airdock in the morning.

Klaxons began to sound, their jangling bells making Dorothy's head ring as she struggled to think. She had been pursued by the polizia before, during a retrieval at the Vatican that had gone pear-shaped. She knew a few bolt-holes they could use until the coast was clear. One thing in their favor was the early hour; the security was operating with a skeleton crew, and there were few civilians to get in their way as they fled.

"I should have seen this coming," Dorothy growled as they ran.

Beside her, Trafalgar said, "You could not have anticipated this."

"I should have. We had a good head start. We could have detoured and landed outside of town, instead of flying directly into their bloody hands."

Something hit her in the shoulder hard enough to throw her forward. Her foot slipped out from beneath her and she went tumbling, hitting the tile of the terminal hard enough to rattle her bones. Whatever the Society member had thrown at her had pierced her jacket and clothing and penetrated the skin of her shoulder. Her heart had been protected by the hard shield of her scapula, but the numbness from the wound was fast spreading through her left side. Trafalgar and the others skidded to a stop, but Dorothy pulled the bag from her shoulder and shoved it across the floor. It bumped Beatrice's boot and she scooped it up.

"They mustn't get the journal. Run!"

Beatrice looked as conflicted as she ever had, but she looped the bag's strap over her head and started running again. Leola followed her, but Trafalgar hurried to Dorothy's side and grabbed her arm.

"They hit me with a Sandman," Dorothy snapped. Her words were quick and slurred. "My arms and legs aren't working and in thirty seconds I will be unconscious. Go while you still can."

"I will not leave you."

A second Sandman hit Trafalgar in the side. She dropped to one knee and grabbed at the small oval device, grimacing as she pulled its spike from her side. Blood poured from the wound, her efforts to toss it aside hindered by the drug already in her system. Dorothy slumped to the floor seconds before Trafalgar went down as well. The boots of the leatherjackets entered her blurry vision like shiny black trees, their feet stomping against the tile as they surrounded their prisoners.

Dorothy managed to lift her hand in one final and futile attempt to reach her weapon. She was already unconscious by the time the leatherjacket secured her still-raised hand in a metal shackle.

Chapter Fourteen

Olive oil, sea breezes, salty air. Comfortably warm, like a favorite sweater. Dorothy felt as if she was waking from a dream, or as if the dream was wrapping itself slowly around her. As the ship around her came into clearer focus everything else faded away. She knew she had been thinking about something important just a few seconds earlier but it was fading into her subconscious with every lazy sway of the deck under her feet. Her grandmother had just died and, as per her wishes, Dorothy was set to take over. That meant traveling the world, seeing those far-flung civilizations that seemed like something out of H.G. Wells' stories.

Before she got to work, her grandmother urged her to take a "fun" journey. No exploring, no mysteries to unearth, just a pleasure trip to spread her wings. She'd chosen the Mediterranean, the cradle of life. Her plan was to bounce from one port to the next and explore culture through food. She was eager to reach Greece, uncertain about what awaited her in Egypt or Istanbul. At the moment she was having a hard time with even the food she was sure about. The ship's dinner menu had settled poorly, and she found herself on the deck bent over the railing to release some of the meal back into the sea.

"Oh, dear. That doesn't sound good at all."

Dorothy saw the handkerchief first, and she took it to dab at her lips as she looked at the new arrival. The woman smiled kindly and introduced herself as Charlotte Blake. She was a widow, a former actress, and currently a globetrotter. Dorothy felt young and childish in Charlotte's presence, the elegant woman with her dark hair streaked with gray at the temples. Charlotte quickly put her to ease, however, asking questions about her family and her life as they strolled along the deck.

When they reached Dorothy's cabin, she thanked Charlotte for making sure she got there safely. "I don't know what I'm doing out here. Grandma Eula spent a lot of time getting me ready for this, but I always thought she would be there to hold my hand. To show me what to do. Now I'm on my own and it doesn't seem right. I don't know if I'm going to be good enough."

Charlotte said, "One reason I'm taking time away from the stage is to figure out who I am outside of my characters. I wanted to stop reciting from scripts and say my own words for a change. I was terrified when I set out, but I knew one thing for sure. I didn't want to miss out on the opportunity just because I was scared."

She had touched Dorothy's hand. Dorothy stared at Charlotte's fingers for a very long moment, doing a mental run-up before she jumped off the cliff. Twenty years old and she had never been kissed. Two decades of her life without a lover simply because the only ones who intrigued her were forbidden. From the moment she was old enough to want companionship she had cursed her inability to find boys who lit her up the way other girls did. Now, on a boat in the darkness with an exotic stranger, the solution seemed so ridiculously easy.

"Can I kiss you?" Dorothy was surprised to hear the words come out of her mouth, even in a hurried whisper.

Charlotte seemed surprised by the question. Before she could answer, Dorothy realized she had just thrown up. She didn't want her first kiss to be sullied by that, so she put her fingers over her lips and took a step back.

"No. I'm sorry," Dorothy said. "Goodness. I have no idea what's come over me. Lightheaded, or maybe still just out of sorts."

"Dorothy," Charlotte said, "let's go into your room to talk some more."

Dorothy stared at her. Finally she nodded, and she almost immediately poured herself a drink and rinsed her mouth out. She dampened a brush and applied tooth powder, scrubbing furiously before spitting the frothy mixture out into a basin. She touched her wrist to her lips as she joined Charlotte in the main room once more, and they sat next to each other as casually as old acquaintances. Charlotte brushed a stray hair behind Dorothy's ear and smiled at her.

"Are you certain you want to do this?"

Dorothy swallowed, her mouth tasting clean and slightly numb. "For the past two weeks, I haven't been certain of anything. I know I'll be kicking myself the whole way home if I don't." She touched Charlotte's chin. "I really would like to kiss you, Miss Blake."

"I've never done this before, you know," Charlotte whispered as she leaned in. "Never with another woman."

"I've never done this at all."

Charlotte smiled. "Then perhaps we will both learn something tonight."

Dorothy wet her lips just before Charlotte kissed them, and she rested her hands on the older woman's hips as she leaned in. Her fears and confusion evaporated until the only thought crowding the edges of her mind was a low, insistent "Yessss." She moved her hands to the small of Charlotte's back and scooted closer on the divan, moaning when she thought Charlotte was trying to push her away. A moment later she realized she was being pushed down onto the cushions. Dorothy opened her eyes and looked at Charlotte, then let her eyelids drift closed to allow whatever was going to happen without overthinking it.

She pressed her thighs together as the weight lifted from her, as her hands drifted to the sturdy arms of a chair. The familiar scents of her first lover - the sea, olive oil, jasmine shampoo - faded to be replaced with the harsh chemical scents of an airship. Dorothy was aroused even after she realized she had been unconscious, fighting the tingle of desire brewing in her lower body as she struggled to organize her thoughts.

She was no longer lying back on a divan, she was strapped to a chair. Her head ached, her stomach twisted with nausea, and her shoulder throbbed from where the Sandman had stabbed her. She knew there were at least three other people in the room; she could hear them moving quietly about the space and breathing. The ship creaked and groaned, and she knew they were in the air. Her mouth was dry. She pushed her tongue between her lips and tried to work up some moisture as she opened her eyes and took in her surroundings. There was a light shining down on her, the rest of the room cloaked in darkness, but she could see silhouettes in the shadows.

"Welcome back to the land of the living."

She kept her head steady and moved her eyes toward the voice. The room seemed to swim and she grunted helplessly as a tall man stepped into the light. He was gorgeous, a face of hard lines carved from stone to create a titanic jaw, dimpled at the chin, and sparkling green eyes that were partially magnified by his eyeglasses. His blonde hair was parted in the middle and long enough to frame his face on either side, luxurious without being feminine. He smiled and clasped his hands behind his back.

"The infamous Lady Boone. It is a pleasure to make your acquaintance. My name is Orville Weeks. My brother Dan and I have been fans of yours for a very long time."

"I assume it was your fan mail that nearly killed me two days ago."

He smiled. "Yes, that was us. However you must understand that what we did was a necessary evil. We did not wish to kill you, but we knew that if you were alive and got wind of our plan, you would do everything in your power to stop it. Your death was..."

"A convenience," Dorothy said.

"Perhaps, to put it bluntly."

"You tried to murder me. I'm fine with blunt."

He sighed. "Very well."

"It was a stupid plan. Your ham-handed attempt to kill me only alerted me to what you were doing. You might as well have sent a gilded invitation."

"Perhaps so. But the fact remains that you are here now, and that is in fact a reason to celebrate. I believe your presence here will benefit us greatly in the days ahead. Our society is on the precipice of a very important discovery. With your help, we could usher this world into a new age."

"The age of Felix Quintel."

Orville smiled. "Ah, yes. The future King of England. It's high time for a revolution, don't you think? Think about it. We have a new world at our fingertips. Magic is at our fingertips. We glide through the air in these remarkable dirigibles. We race through our streets in motorized carriages. Humanity is poised to take a great leap forward and we deserve a leader who is prepared for the troubles such an age can bring. Quintel will take England as his rightful stronghold, and then he shall advance. Europe, Asia, America, Africa. The Quintellian Age will be a great leap forward in the evolution of our species. We will be a world united under a single god."

"Fallen angel, more accurately," Dorothy said.

"Devils and demons." He sighed and shook his head. "Sunday school does its indoctrination well, doesn't it? God is good, Devil is evil. So simplistic and childish. God did not cast Lucifer into the pit as a ruler. Why would he? Why would he give his enemy an entire realm to punish mortals who were only guilty of the same sin the Light-Bringer had committed? God and the Devil are partners running the longest confidence game ever devised. Benevolence versus malevolence. God has his army of angels and the Devil rules his demon soldiers. I'm simply reassigning one of Hell's generals to clean up here in the mortal realm a little."

Dorothy shook her head. "You're delusional."

Orville ignored her. "With the stone you and Miss Trafalgar will help us find, we will call forth one of the most powerful entities that ever walked this planet. Before gods, before Heaven and Hell, before anything like recorded history, there was Him. His story was only shared orally for millennia by people too afraid to write it down. But eventually word got to us, and we built our society around his eventual awakening. His time is now."

"You know nothing about the creature you're trying to summon. If you succeed, it will crush you and your followers like ants."

"Perhaps some will die. But those who have earned our god's respect and gratitude will be rewarded. We have gone to great lengths to awaken him. We have spilled blood in pursuit of this quest. Enoch Solomon gave his life in an attempt to preserve the sacred stone. We thought all hope was lost when that blasted girl spit out the stone, but now... don't you see? That was all part of our master's plan. Her actions changed her, and now all these years later we have her in our grasp again. She will guide him into this world. We will provide for it a host, and that host will become Felix Quintel. That host will rule this world, and the Watershed Society shall stand at his side like the trusted lieutenants we are. You could stand up there with us, Lady Boone. You could be an acolyte of the strongest leader this world has ever known."

"What would possibly persuade me to help you?"

"We expected you would need some convincing. That's why we took your hands."

Dorothy furrowed her brow and looked down. Both of her arms ended at the wrist with bloody stumps, the pain only just registering as Dorothy saw the wounds. Her chest clenched so she couldn't cry out, but her lips twisted in horror and disbelief. Her forearms were bound tightly to the chair with rope, and her muscles tensed as she tried desperately to break free. The wounds were jagged, hideous, and she knew even if her hands had been salvaged they would never be reattached without scarring, and she doubted they would ever work the same way again.

She was babbling, she realized, moaning, "No, no, no," in a rapid-fire murmur as tears streaked down her face. Her strong front had been shattered in one instant as she saw how she had been mutilated.

"I believe that is enough," Orville said softly. "Lady Boone, look at yourself."

She couldn't bear to. Orville stepped forward and rapped her knuckles with his, and the pain shot up into Dorothy's arm. She stared in shock at the back of her hand, complete and intact, attached seamlessly to her arm with nary a sign of cutting. She spread her fingers and chuffed softly as she curled her fingers into fists. She dug her nails into the palm hard enough to hurt, and fresh tears rolled down her face as she realized what her cruel captor had done.

"I would like to introduce you to Milena Petric," Orville said as a woman stepped forward from the shadows. She wore a brown leather coat like the rest of Watershed's members, but her head was completely shaven. Her eyes were obscured behind tinted sunglasses even in the barely-lit room. Orville smiled at her and said, "Milena is the one responsible for the little illusion about your hands. It seemed real, didn't it? The pain, the shock. If I'd allowed the deception to go on a little longer, your body would have started reacting to the trauma. It would have actually thought you were losing blood. Scary, isn't it?"

Dorothy glared at him. She knew her skin was ashen and her face was still wet with tears, but she refused to let the bastard hold the upper hand.

"Milena is also responsible for the little dream you had while we were waiting for our ride. It was a good dream, wasn't it? She can put you back in it."

She felt Charlotte's breath on her ear, heard the nasty things that had been said on that long-ago night. She closed her eyes and brought her knees together, half-expecting to feel Charlotte between them. Dorothy squirmed in the chair and, almost against her will, let out a quiet moan of pleasure. She arched her back and pushed herself down against the wooden seat to prevent her hips from thrusting upward in an obscene caricature. Then, as quickly as it had started, the phantom released her.

"So much easier than actually causing the damage. No mess to clean up. I can cut off all your fingers, move on to your toes, and then I can start all over again. It doesn't matter if you know it's all an illusion. Your body won't."

Dorothy cried out in agony as her right hand withered, desiccated and died.

"And I can give you your pleasant memories..."

Once again she was on the ship, guiding Charlotte's hand between her legs. She looked up and recoiled when she saw that Charlotte's flushed features had been replaced by Orville's.

"...and I can destroy them from within."

"Stop," Dorothy gasped.

He put his hands on her shoulders and leaned down so they were eye-to-eye. "Then help me. When we land, you will help me find the stone. You will not stand against us when we depart, and you will allow the Society to create Felix Quintel without interference."

"Fine."

Another flash of her night with Charlotte, once again with her lover replaced by Orville. She sobbed as he whispered, "Say the words Dorothy..."

"I'll help you. I'll help you find the stone and I won't raise arms against you. Now get out of my fucking head."

The cabin faded and was replaced by her cell. Orville leaned back and tugged at the cuffs of his coat. "I do apologize for the violation. Before we found Milena we were forced to take physical measures. Did you know it's more sensible to cut off a person's index finger than any other? Some think it's the pinkie, but no. Once the forefinger is gone, the secondary finger adapts to take its place. The things you learn by trial and error." He laughed softly and shook his head. "We should be landing in Heraklion within the hour. You should get washed up. And dressed."

Dorothy looked down and saw she was nude. Her face flushed and she squeezed her eyes shut. She could feel the cotton on her skin, knew without a doubt she was fully-clothed and had been the entire time, but her brain was stupid and slow to process the physical information. When she opened her eyes, Orville and the other men in the room were gone. Milena moved to stand guard in front of Dorothy, blank lenses of her glasses locked on Dorothy's face.

"You toyed with something precious," Dorothy said. "You used it as a thumbscrew. I will not forget this."

Milena said nothing and made no outward acknowledgement of what had been said, but Dorothy suddenly felt the seat drop out from underneath her. She was falling, tumbling end over end, plummeting through the bowels of the ship and out into clear air. She bit her tongue and squeezed her eyes shut, her head swimming with the sensation of weightlessness. Her body braced for the inevitable impact. Her heart raced.

"You bitch," she growled. "You bitch whore, I will make you pay for this..."

She began falling faster. Against her will, Dorothy began to scream.

The screams echoed through the airship, rising in volume before being choked off. Trafalgar kept her eyes straight ahead, focusing on the ceiling above her rather than speculating on what was being done to Dorothy elsewhere on the vessel. She had a feeling her dose of the Sandman had been less than what Dorothy received; the coat had provided a thicker barrier to penetrate and she had pulled it out almost immediately. But she had still lost consciousness and, when she woke, her arms and legs were bound to a table in what appeared to be a medical examination room. Her jacket and clothing had been taken from her, leaving her only in a thin undershirt and underwear. She was gagged by some sort of hard plastic that she couldn't get her tongue around to dislodge, though she spent most of her time after regaining consciousness trying to.

The door swung open and admitted a verminous-looking man in an unbuttoned leather coat. It swung open to reveal the manticore design on the inside pocket. His cheeks were sunken and his eyes pronounced, his graying his cut short to give him a large forehead. His ears stuck out on either side like small horns, and when he smiled his lips crept across his face like a crack opening in an arid landscape.

"Good morning. My name is Daniel Weeks. And you... well, we all know who you are. There has been much speculation about you over the years, miss. Enoch Solomon's men spoke of a young girl called Trafalgar who killed their master, urging him to commit suicide in front of them. Then she stole his jacket and took command of the vessel. And then..." He waved his spindly fingers in front of his face. "Just vanished into the world. Some of us thought you were just a myth. But you're not. Are you?"

A beautiful bald woman in glasses stepped into the room behind him and closed the door. He looked at her and then began to circle Trafalgar's bed.

"I apologize that we had to undress you so completely. A bit crude, I know, but once we discovered those nasty blades you had hidden up your sleeve we had to be certain there was nothing else concealed in the folds of your clothes. Never fear, we have several female acolytes who did the deed. You have nothing to worry about in terms of being violated in that manner."

Trafalgar clenched her fists and tightened the muscles of her arms, testing the restraints she'd already confirmed couldn't be broken. Daniel patted her shoulder.

"Save your strength, Miss Trafalgar. I suspect you'll need it once we land." He stepped around the table and extended an arm to the bald woman. "I'd like to introduce you to Mircea Petric. She and her sister have a unique gift. I like to call it archaeology of the mind. A bit like time travel. They can reach into your mind and dig out a moment, a day, or just a feeling, and bring it to the surface. Every sensation is exactly as you remember it. Only better. The human mind filters the world down to its most important elements so we can keep it. Colors dim, details fade. Mircea and Milena can bring the memory back so vividly that it's as if you have physically traveled back to that moment."

Trafalgar could think of a few moments it would be torture to revisit, but she had a feeling she knew what the Watershed Society would be most interested in.

"Solomon put the stone in your mouth and began the ritual. The forces were at work, they just weren't allowed to complete their job." He leaned over her and rested his hand on her forehead. His palm was cold and clammy, and she tried to shrink away from it. "Something was started that night, Trafalgar, and a seed was planted. A small piece of darkness in your mind, like a lighthouse on the shore calling to our friend in the other realm. When we find the second stone, Mircea will expand that piece of darkness to fill your entire mind and call forth the creature that will soon rule this world. You will be a lighthouse upon the shore of this realm, guiding it safely to us."

Sounds as if I will be more like bait, Trafalgar thought.

"For the time being, however, we need to ensure you won't attempt to escape before we arrive at our destination. Like I said, we need you to keep your strength up. So Mircea will stay with you, and she'll make sure that your mind remains occupied while we're in transit. I would say pleasant dreams, but that's really up to Mircea, isn't it?" He grinned and nodded at Mircea on his way out of the room.

Trafalgar looked at the woman who seemed to loom over her bed. Her mind was racing, as if her memories were nothing more than cards that this stranger had picked up and started to shuffle. She imagined the words DON'T DO THIS writ large in her mind, but the words scattered as soon as she constructed them. As Mircea dug deeper into her mind, the screams elsewhere on the ship started again.

It was late afternoon before the *Kestrel* took off from Rome. It turned on a south-southeastern trajectory that would take it across the boot of Italy to

Athens. They would refuel there and continue south to the city of Heraklion, on the island of Crete. The trip would take twelve hours, plus however long they were delayed at the Athens airdock. The skies ahead of them were clear, and the skies behind them were full of the bustling Roman air traffic.

There were so many other airships aloft, so many gondolas reflecting the setting sun, that no one would have paid much attention when one of them altered course as if in pursuit. The second airship gave the first a good head start, hanging back until the *Kestrel* was little more than a pumpkin-seed shaped object on the horizon.

Once its captain was confident they wouldn't be observed, the *Skylarker* gave full thrust to its engines and set off in pursuit.

Chapter Fifteen

Dorothy's torture continued for a hundred years. No. She squeezed her eyes shut and tried to focus. One hundred years was impossible. She took a deep breath and remembered she was dealing with someone who could play with her mind, who could make her see and feel things that didn't exist. She lifted her chin from her chest despite her brain telling her she was too weak, and she gazed at the bald bitch standing in front of her.

"You'll have to do... a lot better than that."

She thought she saw a hint of a smile cross the woman's face before the trembling subsided. Once again she was young, but she was exhausted. She had no idea how long she'd actually been strapped to the chair. Her waistcoat and fob watch were gone. Her ascot was gone. Her socks and shoes had been taken off, and the floor was cold to the touch. She tried forcing her feet down onto the metal to let it absorb her body heat, but it didn't seem to work.

"You know," Dorothy said, "we've spent this whole time learning about me. What about you? Hopes. Dreams. Fears. Let's get inside your head for a little while."

The bones in Dorothy's chest were crushed. She sagged forward and gasped for air as her vital organs were punctured by the shards...

...and then released. She panted to catch her breath and looked up at Milena through her bangs. "Okay. You don't want to talk about yourself. That's fine."

The door to her cell opened and Orville came in.

"Orville," Dorothy said. "Nice of you to join us. We were just about to talk about Milena's childhood. Apparently she wasn't hugged enough as a child."

Orville ignored her and focused on Milena. "We'll be landing soon. It would be best if she was a bit less of a handful."

Milena nodded and approached Dorothy. For the entirety of their session, however long it had been, Milena had never spoken out loud or touched her. Despite herself, Dorothy cringed when the silent woman reached out and tapped her middle finger against Dorothy's forehead. Orville was the one who spoke, moving so Dorothy could see him.

"You will be asleep when we arrive in Athens. You will sleep throughout our time on the ground so as not to cause problems with the airdock crew. You are falling asleep as we speak."

"Sorry to disappoint. But you throw such lively parties that I'll be up for hours."

Orville smiled. "I'm afraid that's not the case. How long has it been since you slept, Lady Boone? Twenty-four hours? Thirty-six? Forty-eight?" She felt her head growing heavy, her eyelids sailing downward of their own volition. She jerked her head back up and forced her eyes open. "Certainly not sixty. Seventy-two? Dorothy, have you been up for eighty hours?"

She wanted to toss out a quip, wanted to take one last dig at him, but sleep was crowding in on her senses. She couldn't gather the strength to open her mouth, and her thoughts were far too jumbled to be clever. She slumped forward in her chair, her entire body slack in a deep and unbroken sleep.

Airship crew gathered in small clusters on the rainy airdock tarmac, stamping their feet to stay warm in the cold drizzle. Some of them held cigarettes cupped protectively in their hands, curled protectively around the burning tips so they wouldn't be extinguished by the surprise downpour. Above them the massive airships glistened and cascaded more water down, as if each one was its own steel-and-canvas raincloud that had been tethered to the ground. The newest arrival, the *Skylarker*, rested a few slips down from a smaller craft designated *Kestrel*. Two ships among dozens, nothing to distinguish them from their neighbors.

Normally the crews were unflappable, having seen a large swath of the great big world during the War. They flew across Europe, to the furthest reaches of Asia and Africa, and to a man they claimed there was nothing that could make them shake in their skins. But today every man on the Athens dock was skittish. Out on the Saronic Gulf, the waves were dappled by sunshine that had escaped from behind the cloud hovering over the city.

It started with rumors about wet footprints on the concrete, impressions of a woman's bare foot that crossed a dry space with no women - shod or not - anywhere near. And then when the drizzle began in earnest, some people said they saw the shape of a woman outlined in the droplets. She, or it, ran when anyone tried to get close to it. The last reported sighting was underneath the *Skylarker*, but no one was willing to risk career suicide by telling its captain that she may have a ghost aboard.

The *Kestrel* left a few minutes past seven-thirty in the morning. Some of the first people to report the ghostly footprints said they seemed to be coming from the *Kestrel*. A few minutes later the *Skylarker* requested permission to disembark. Departure was granted, and it lifted off with its ghost apparently still aboard.

The roughnecks on the dock said nothing nor did they react outwardly. But they all breathed a sigh of relief as the two ships - one that had lost a ghost and another that had gained one - drifted off over the Mediterranean. Whatever fate tied the two ships together, and whatever the true nature of the invisible woman might have been, it was no longer their problem.

Dorothy was jarred from her slumber to discover she had been transferred to a vehicle. She was once again fully-dressed, although she could feel that her gun was missing from her belt. They were on a road cut into the slope of a hill, with lush vegetation rising high overhead to her left with a soft decline on the right. In the distance she could see the rise of a neighboring hill covered with a blanket of greens and yellows. The sky was utterly clear save for a few clouds near the far horizon. She pushed her shoulder against the door to sit up and turned to see Milena seated beside her in the backseat of the car. The bald woman didn't acknowledge Dorothy's waking.

Orville was seated in front beside the driver, and he looked back at her with a smile. "Good morning, Lady Boone. We're almost to our destination. Have you ever been to Crete before?"

"Once." Her voice sounded odd to her own ears, and she worked up a bit of saliva before she spoke again. "What day is it?"

"The day after we captured you in Rome. You haven't been unconscious the entire time. I simply asked Milena to remove some of your memories from the past twenty-four hours."

That information didn't put her at ease, but she had to assume that was his intention. "Where is Trafalgar?"

"She's in the truck ahead of us. Once we arrive at the site, we'll be requiring you to help us search for the stone. I know Milena left the memory of what will happen if you refuse or attempt to delay us in any way."

Milena slowly turned her head to look at Dorothy. The memory of severed limbs and physical violations flashed in Dorothy's mind, and she shuddered.

"I've been hired by people I don't particularly like in the past, but I haven't let that get in the way of doing my job. I do believe you may have the distinction of being the most despicable client I've ever had. So there is that."

Orville laughed. "That's the spirit. Do it for the love of discovery." He faced forward again. "This has all turned out for the best, all things considered. We have archaeologists in our employ, people who I'm sure would have served us well here, but I cannot tell you how happy I am to have someone as revered as you on our side."

"Is that why you tried to kill me?"

"Well." He shrugged. "It was the easiest course of action. We hired that masked miscreant to make weapons that would dispose of anyone who might stand in our way, and then it didn't matter if we were working with second tier professionals. There was no longer anyone who might pull the rug out from under us, as it were. But then you and Trafalgar fell right into our laps..." He laughed and slapped his thigh. "Trafalgar! Who could have imagined the luck? We sent word back to London about having her with us, and our people are positive it's a sign we're destined to succeed."

Dorothy chose not to respond to that, instead looking out the window at their surroundings. She was more clear-headed now and found it easier to focus. It was good to know there was a society left behind in London; it would give them something to do when they got back. When she looked behind them she could see the airship traffic above Heraklion, five or six fat ships riding high enough to be seen from so far away. When she faced forward again she saw Orville was watching her. There was something unsettling about his gaze, something *knowing*.

"Knossos," she said. "I should have known when you said we were traveling to Heraklion. You want to excavate Knossos."

He nodded. "Very good."

"Arthur Evans..."

"Mr. Evans did a lion's share of the work for us, but he and his men were... ultimately misguided. They wanted to protect the ruins from further degradation. What good is preserving a site if no one is going to appreciate it? There are treasures here waiting to be found, treasures that the Watershed Society believes will change the course of history. We managed to convince him to focus his efforts elsewhere and hand the site over to us."

Dorothy said, "If ancient civilizations had the means to change the course of history, don't you think it's telling that they chose not to? They hid these items away so they would never fall into the wrong hands."

"And who is to decide which hands are wrong? Who is the arbiter of worthiness? You do the same thing we do, but you couch your thievery in terms of exploration and knowledge."

"You're trying to take over the world," Dorothy said. "Believe me, while our interests occasionally intersect, we are far from the same person."

He sighed. "The events of today will dictate the rest of your life, Lady Boone. You can choose to be friend of the society or you can decide we are enemies. If you intend to deceive us, I should remind you that Milena had a full day to get acquainted with your mind. She'll know even before you do."

The truck turned onto a heavily-rutted dirt road. Grass and weeds clawed at the sides of their vehicle as it bounced and rocked through the scrub. The trees parted and ahead Dorothy saw the crumbling yellow brick of a wall on either side of the dirt path. Another truck was parked on the grass just beyond the fortification and Orville's driver took them past it to a wide, open area that butted up against a stone courtyard. Trafalgar was standing in the courtyard surrounded by four leatherjackets and a woman who looked identical to Milena. The wind caught Trafalgar's coat, which Dorothy was surprised to find she had been allowed to keep, and she held her arms behind her back so it was impossible to tell if she was restrained or not.

Once they were parked Milena gestured for Dorothy to get out of the car first. She walked onto the stone slab with her captors following.

"Miss Trafalgar. Glad to see you're in one piece. Although you could have avoided any injuries by fleeing when you had the opportunity."

"Lady Boone. If that's your way of thanking me for coming to your rescue..."

"Some rescue!" Dorothy said, gesturing at the leatherjackets around them.

Trafalgar shrugged. "The day is not over yet."

Orville greeted one of Trafalgar's guards with a hug, patting him hard on the back before letting him go. "We are here, Daniel. We've done it. We're a step away from everything we've dreamed."

Dorothy remembered Orville mentioning his brother was named Daniel. The man had the countenance of a weasel or some other vermin. If he was truly Orville's brother then there had definitely been winner in their family's genetic lottery. The weasel-faced brother looked at her and smiled with tombstone-spaced teeth.

"Is this her? The infamous Boone? I expected her to be much older."

"You're thinking of her grandmother." Orville looked at her. "Mr. Solomon and our society had a few dealings with Eula Boone. She was a thorn in our side."

Dorothy narrowed her eyes. "Someone sent a box of dead roses to her memorial. I had forgotten it until now. Was that you?"

Orville smiled and put a hand on his chest, bowing at the waist. "Not me personally, but the society felt it was necessary to mark the occasion."

"Aha. That is... enlightening."

Orville ignored the threat in her tone and stepped out across the courtyard. Even in its state of decay, lost and forgotten for over a thousand years, the site was still impressive. A large hill to the north would have protected them from the sea, and any attackers coming from inland would have been forced to attack from a downhill position. Standing in the courtyard, even though it was open on three sides, Dorothy couldn't help but feel snug and secure. Imagining the grounds in their prime made her realize just how powerful Minos had been.

"Welcome to the Palace of Knossos, the home of the Minoan dynasty," Orville said. "First inhabited eight thousand years ago, threatened by earthquakes and volcanoes and floods but always rising again from the rubble to regain their strength. The first kingdom to have a navy, which helped them rule the Aegean Sea. This was the heart of civilization and King Minos had his hand around that heart like a steel vice." He turned to face them. "King Minos also possessed the chalcedony stone. It's still here somewhere, hidden in this palace. It's your job, Lady Boone and Miss Trafalgar, to find it for me."

Dorothy held up her hands. "I can't do much while I'm bound."

Trafalgar looked at her oddly. "You're not bound."

Dorothy looked at her wrists and saw the ropes had faded. She glared at Milena, who didn't even have the grace to offer a smile. Dorothy envisioned a bullet puncturing the insufferable woman's forehead directly between her eyes, imagining all the gory details that went along with a good headshot, and she thought she saw Milena's cheek twitch in response to the image. Dorothy looked away from her and faced Orville again.

"We'll need space to work. And we've never collaborated, so there may be a bit of a learning curve. Don't expect immediate results."

Daniel said, "It's disturbing that you're starting off with excuses..."

"This is a science and an art, Mr. Weeks," Dorothy said. "It cannot be forced or strong-armed into providing the results you want on a set timetable. You have kidnapped us and dragged us here and now we have no option but to help you. We intend to do that but you must understand that a lack of results won't necessarily be for a lack of trying. I will not be executed or further tortured simply because the site isn't cooperating."

Orville nodded to his brother, who accepted the terms with a dismissive flap of his hands. Orville looked at them and smiled. "You have your space."

Trafalgar said, "And we will not have your twins interfering with our work."

Orville waved them off. Milena and the other one seemed to relax slightly as they moved off to stand together near one of the stone pits. Dorothy watched as they joined hands and turned to face the hills in the distance. Though silent as always, she had no doubt the sisters were engaged in a deep conversation that only they could hear. Orville moved to speak to his brother, and Dorothy found herself alone with Trafalgar.

"Well," Dorothy said as she scanned the courtyard. "I see you had your own inquisitor."

"Mircea Petric," Trafalgar said. "She was... unpleasant."

"Her sister Milena is no walk on the beach, either." She scanned the horizon. "If we make a run for it, I doubt we'd get far. Even without the skittles-ball twins, we have no means to get home. This Watershed Society would only catch up with us and drag us back kicking and screaming. The only bright spot in all of this is that Beatrice and Leola seem to have gotten away."

Trafalgar said, "What do you intend to do?"

"We help them. It's not ideal, but for the moment I don't see that we have any other option. Yes, they may intend to kill us when we've outlived our usefulness, but up until that time–"

"They don't intend to kill me. They intend to use me as bait and then as the host for this demon they are summoning."

Dorothy said, "Still? After all their work establishing the identity of Felix Quintel, it seems odd that a female host would still be viable."

"They claim it is destiny."

"Damn. You have my assurances I won't allow it to get that far."

Trafalgar looked at her. "Why?"

Dorothy frowned. "What do you mean 'why'? This entire debacle has made us allies."

"Yes. But if you have to risk your life to preserve mine..." Trafalgar let the thought trail off. "Perhaps I have been wrong about you, Lady Boone."

"You're not entirely to blame. I've acted like you're my enemy in the past. If you believe me to be the kind of person who would leave you at the mercy of these scoundrels... then I share the fault. Right now neither of us is going to get out of this mess without the other's help. I doubt they left you with any weapons?"

Trafalgar shook her head. "Of course not. You?"

"No. But if we want to stay on their good side, we should get started. Any ideas?"

She gestured at the wide space around them, an open area reminiscent of a forecourt. "This area we're in now is called the caravanserai. Pilgrims coming to visit the king would stop here to bathe before they entered the presence of the king. There were facilities for running water and drainage..." She looked around and then pointed at three large openings in the center of the space. "Along there."

"These pits are drainage pipes?"

"No. They were most likely used for storage. They lead far below the palace grounds. The courtyard would be, for the most part, a staging area. If we're actually going to look for this stone, we'll need to start in the palace."

She started walking and Dorothy fell into step beside her. The Weeks brothers noticed and followed them across the courtyard. The eastern wall was unbroken by any obvious entrance, and the southern expanse was a sharp descent marked by trees. Trafalgar turned north and led them along a wide path that took them past what was once a large theatre. They were forced to walk in a single file, and Dorothy scanned the ground they crossed for any rocks sizable enough to act as a weapon.

There was a point where the wall had been destroyed enough for them to pass into the palace's interior. Dorothy was about to ask for a torch when Orville stepped forward and held one out to her. It was a sleek black tube with brass fittings, the lens angled outward so she could aim it directly ahead without raising her arm. She turned it on and twisted the end cap to widen its beam before she swept it across the room ahead of them.

"Remarkable that it's still intact." Trafalgar looked up at the ceiling. "Imagine the work that must have gone into this. Even though so much of it has fallen to rubble the fact that any of it–"

Orville said, "There will be time for sightseeing later. Please, let us carry on. Treasures await."

Trafalgar glared at him. "It is precisely that attitude which renders you unworthy of whatever we find here. The history of our species, the world from which we grew–"

"Has fallen to dust and rubble," Orville interrupted again. He picked up a stone and hurled it at the far wall. "Nothing but bricks and faded artifacts. These people had their moment and it passed. The Romans had their moment. England's moment is fading. Now is the time for a new society to rise up and take control, to lead the world into the new millennium. The only thing we have to gain from these people is whatever trinkets they left behind that can help us hold onto our power for as long as possible before the next era comes along."

"Oh, my God," Dorothy said. "You're a child who just wants to play with his big brother's toys."

Orville glared at her. "Need I remind you of what Milena is capable of, Lady Boone?"

"Spare me," she said, rolling her eyes as she moved the light along the far wall. "We should explore as much of the palace as we can before it gets dark. I think your depilated goons would be better served setting up light sources so we won't be cast into darkness as soon as the sun sets."

Trafalgar said, "On the other hand, the veil of night could provide us the perfect opportunity to escape."

"An excellent point," Dorothy said. "By all means, Mr. Weeks, leave your bald-pated twerps to linger and threaten us while we do our work. A much better use of their time."

Orville's good humor seemed to have completely faded, but he motioned for Milena and her sister to go fetch the lights from their vehicle. Dorothy motioned for Trafalgar to follow her to the other side of the room.

"Do you believe it's necessary to antagonize them?" Trafalgar asked when they had nearly reached the far wall.

"Antagonizing them makes them angry. Angry people act with their guts rather than their brains. Just remember that if I provoke them too far, I'm the expendable one."

Trafalgar snorted. "I would prefer a bullet in my head to some arcane beast."

"What do you say we try to avoid either?"

"Sounds like the best plan. Lead the way."

Dorothy fanned the light across the wall until she found an opening that led into a wide corridor. She led the way, with Trafalgar behind her and the Weeks brothers bringing up the rear as they ventured deeper into the ancient palace.

Chapter Sixteen

The first time Ivy went out completely naked, she had to overcome the fear and anxiety of the act before she could even leave her front walk. Her mother grew up in an age when flashing the ankle was considered scandalous. Women in trousers were still given a sidelong glance in mixed company. But there she stood on the street outside her house, the wind hardening her nipples and caressing her most private curves, and no one glanced at her even once. In a way it had been an experiment; it seemed likely that her invisibility would fade at the worst possible moment, and what moment was worse than standing in public without any clothes on?

Her theory failed, but she found herself emboldened to start walking. She stood among commuters at a street corner and no one even turned their head. Occasionally people would look up as she approached, but then they would check left and right before furrowing their brow and going back to what they were doing. It was an interesting revelation at how people can sense someone is nearby even without sight. They heard her footsteps, they became aware of her breathing, or her passage disturbed the air. Soon she was more comfortable going out in the nude than she was clothed. Dressing was armor, caking makeup on her face so it would be seen was literally a mask between her and the world, and she felt separated from everything that happened when she was seeable.

At the moment she was striding confidently through the Heraklion airdock with her shoulders back and her chin up, scanning the crowd for signs of the leatherjackets. Her eyesight had changed after she became permanently invisible; shapes were sometimes indistinct if she didn't hold her head still. Sometimes right after she woke up the entire world was a blur of colors and abstract objects. She'd lived with it long enough that she could manage. She barely even remembered what it was like to see like everyone else, and her invisibility let her see far more than anyone else ever could.

She let herself into the airdock security office, slipping through when someone else held the door open a moment too long, and scanned the chalkboard hanging above the departures desk. When the dispatcher left, Ivy stepped behind the desk and scanned her paper.

"Ooh."

"What is it, Myra?"

"Felt like someone just walked over my grave, that's all."

The reports were written in English, to Ivy's relief, and she scanned each page until she found the name she was looking for. She memorized the information and went back to the door. She rapped her knuckles against the wood. The heavyset man who had spoken to Myra came to open the door, but he blocked her exit. He looked out, shrugged, and shut the door again. Before he could get far she knocked again. He sighed, opened the door, and stepped outside.

Ivy ducked out behind him. He scanned the area with his hands on his hips, searching for the prankster as Ivy ran back to the *Skylarker*.

Bodhi, a member of Captain Crook's crew, was smoking by the gangplank. She whispered, "Back onboard," as she passed him. He casually smashed his cigarette and walked up the ramp. He secured the door behind him, nervous and fumbling. Ivy smiled, knowing he was anxious about the fact he was standing in a small room with a naked woman. Even if he couldn't see her he knew she was there and his body was betraying that knowledge. She decided there were more pressing concerns than teasing the poor boy, and she slipped into the uniform she'd borrowed when she came aboard in Athens.

Ivy tugged the collar of her turtleneck up over her nose, covered her eyes with goggles, and pulled a knit cap low on her forehead so she wouldn't be a headless specter when she met with the others. She found them waiting for her in the passerelle standing in front of a map of the world: Araminta, Leola, and Beatrice. The four of them were the only chance Dorothy and Trafalgar had of getting out of their current predicament unscathed.

"News?" Araminta asked.

"They're here. According to their slip request, they expect to be parked here for a week. The question is what they're looking for."

Beatrice said, "The Palace of Knossos. We know the Watershed Society is looking for an ancient stone. Dorothy has done a bit of research on the palace here, but she's never had the time or patrons willing to fund a full excavation. If I was looking for some ancient stone, that's where I would look."

Araminta looked at the map. The scale was such that she couldn't see much detail on the island, so she walked to her command chair and pressed a few buttons. There was a click behind the wall and the map receded, replaced by another closer view of the Mediterranean. She used the nib of her pen to point at Heraklion. "We're here. Where is this palace?"

Beatrice reached out and moved the pen about a centimeter. "It's right outside of the city. Heraklion probably grew from the caravans coming to see the king back in the day. The problem is that they'll see us coming no matter how we approach. Air or land, they'll see us. It used to be a fortress. They built the place to see intruders before they got close enough to cause problems."

Leola said, "Do they have any idea we're coming?"

Ivy said, "They knew you got away in Athens, and they knew about the *Skylarker*, but they were pretty confident the ship was just a standard passenger service. When I left their ship in Athens, they didn't think you were worth much concern."

Beatrice said, "I'll see what I can put together to act as a distraction. It may have been a fortress thousands of years ago, but now it's a ruin. A little magic could go a long way toward a successful raid."

"Can you conceal the ship?" Araminta asked. "If we could just fly over the site without being seen..."

"Possibly," Beatrice said, "but it would take all of my energy. I'd be wiped by the time we engaged the enemy. I'm assuming we'll have to fight their captors."

Leola nodded. "I've seen you fight. I would like to have you on the ground fighting alongside me more than I'd want magic tricks."

Beatrice seemed to weigh the comment for any hidden insult before she nodded carefully. "Thank you, Leola."

Ivy said, "I could go in first to see if the coast is clear..."

"You'd have no way of contacting us," Araminta said. "Besides, it's too dangerous. Wait. You can't conjure us out of sight... could you make them see something that isn't there? The airship will still be visible but if there was, say, the insignia of the Archaeological Advisory Committee? We can make them think we're there to investigate reports of an unauthorized excavation. We fly in from the north to scare them while you and Leola come in from the south."

Beatrice chewed her bottom lip as she considered the plan. "I believe that would be possible. The difficult thing will be projecting the image onto the gondola while you're in the air and I'm on the ground. But I think it can be done."

Ivy said, "I want to be on the ground, too. No telling when an invisible agent will come in handy."

"Okay. Just make sure we know where you are if the bullets start flying."

"My blood turns red as soon as it leaves my body."

"Really." Beatrice shrugged. "Okay. So if I see blood coming from thin air, I'll shoot somewhere else. We'll head out now. Give us thirty-five minutes to get into position before you come swooping in. I'll do what I can to manifest the proper AAC credentials on the body of the airship, but if they start shooting..."

Araminta said, "We'll maintain an altitude that makes it moot. Sounds like we have a plan, ladies. Do you want to take a few members of my crew with you?"

"No. The smaller our ground force is, the better."

"Okay. Then let's get this rescue underway."

Portions of the corridor's roof had crumbled away or been knocked down, letting in enough light that they didn't need to use their torches. Dorothy paused at a plinth which held an ornate vase carved in the form of a lioness, its lips curled into something that looked almost like a smile. Dorothy touched the detail, brushing her fingertip along the smooth limestone. Orville came up beside her and frowned at it.

"Does this provide a clue to what we're searching for?"

"Not as such. But it's–"

Orville picked it up and hurled it against the wall. Dorothy closed her eyes so she wouldn't see the priceless artifact shatter, then turned her glare on Orville.

"You're a bastard."

"And you are wasting time." He shoved her shoulder to force her to continue. "We're here for one item and everything else is decoration. We're not interested in ridiculous baubles."

Dorothy said, "It would serve you right if some other idiot who collects clay goddess figurines arrived here six months ago and destroyed your precious stone as a ridiculous bauble." She pressed her lips together and grimaced, leaning forward to spit out whatever had suddenly appeared on her tongue. The first bat wriggled free, and then an entire swarm flooded forward. She threw herself against the stone wall, unable to scream as the colony of bats - dozens, hundreds of winged black vermin - flew forth and vanished into the shadows. Even as it was happening she knew Milena was to blame, but that did nothing to help her terror.

Finally the swarm ended. She clutched her chest and tried to catch her breath, panting and trembling at the sensation that was sure to bring her nightmares if she survived this ordeal. Orville leaned down and pinched her chin, forcing her to look into his eyes.

"Never forget you are my prisoner. If necessary I can hollow out your mind and let Milena drive you like a motorcar. Do you want that?"

She could tell he wanted her to actually answer, so she said, "No."

"No what?"

"No... please."

He grinned. "The word you're looking for is 'master.'"

Orville was suddenly pulled from her and slammed against the opposite wall in a single smooth motion. His eyes were wide with outrage, but Trafalgar ignored it as she pressed her forearm against his throat. Daniel pulled his gun, but Orville croaked at him to stop. Milena and Mircea both looked eager to jump in but neither of them had permission.

"You will not humiliate us for your amusement. You will not belittle those whose assistance you require. We are helping you because it is in our best interest, but there is a line you would be wise not to cross. You need the darkness in my mind. You need me to be your host. Very well. If you ever lay a hand on Lady Boone again, I will force your demented twins to put a bullet in my brain."

Orville sneered, but Dorothy could see the threat hit home. "Fine."

"Apologize to Lady Boone."

He took a deep breath, but then he looked past Trafalgar's shoulder. "I apologize, Lady Boone."

She nodded, and Trafalgar let him go. He glared at her as he massaged his throat. "I will not forget that, Miss Trafalgar."

She didn't flinch. "You would do well to remember it, sir."

He grunted and motioned them forward, preceding them into the darkness. Trafalgar offered Dorothy a hand, pulling her away from the wall. Daniel and the twins brought up the rear.

"Brava," Dorothy said. "I shall have to think twice about crossing you in the future."

Trafalgar said, "A silver lining to this debacle, at long last."

Despite herself, Dorothy had to chuckle. "When we find this stone, he has to place it in your mouth in order for it to work. Right?"

"That seems to be how it worked last time."

"Then when the time comes, I will do my damnedest to make sure that doesn't happen."

Trafalgar said, "Hm. Does that mean we are no longer *reluctant* allies, Lady Boone?"

"It means..." She thought for a moment. "It means that when this is all said and done, I imagine you and I will have a markedly different relationship than we did before. And I'm not entirely certain that is a bad thing."

"Nor am I."

Ahead, Orville had stopped half in sun and half in shadow, bent forward slightly at the waist to examine a section of the wall. "Boone. Trafalgar. Look here." He stepped back and pointed. "There is something here."

Dorothy got closer and saw that there was indeed a seam in the brickwork. "Does anyone have a knife?" No one responded, and she rolled her eyes. "For heaven's sake, either you want me to do my job or you don't. I require the tools of my trade if I'm going to be the least bit successful. We don't have time for you to be paranoid about every little thing. If you would like, you could stand wa-ay over there and skip the knife to me across the floor."

Daniel stepped forward and held a knife out to her hilt-first.

"Thank you." She inserted the blade into the seam and worked it back and forth. "There's definitely some give here. Trafalgar, if you can try to find the other side?"

Trafalgar stepped forward and examined the wall. Within a minute she had found the other end of the blockade. Together they began muscling it free, grunting and straining against the stone. Sweat quickly began to drip down Dorothy's face, and she saw it beading on Trafalgar's brow and upper lip as well. She looked at the Weeks brothers and sighed.

"Would either of you gentlemen like to help?"

Orville gestured for her to get on with it. "Women's sufferage, and all that."

She smiled condescendingly at him, then grimaced as she returned her attention to moving the blockage. The slab finally came free, and Dorothy stepped out of the way so Trafalgar could slide it along the wall. Stale air flooded out and they all retreated a step. Dorothy and Trafalgar knew all too well the threat of dangerous spores that could be carried on that exhale. She untucked her ascot and shook it loose before bringing it up to wrap around the lower half of her face. When she saw Orville and Daniel watching her she sighed.

"I would suggest you take the same precautions, gentlemen."

Daniel said, "We'll be fine."

Trafalgar masked herself with a handkerchief and stepped into the opening. She was still breathing heavily from muscling the stone out of the way.

"Odd that there was nothing more than a stone to move. No riddle, no attempt to protect this stone from being moved. Most other precious sites took a bit more care in protecting their treasures."

Dorothy said, "An open door lets you stick your head in far enough for the blade to reach your neck. I suggest caution, Miss Trafalgar."

There was a wide concrete lip just inside the door with a series of rough-hewn steps leading down. Dorothy turned her torch back on and held her hand out to see how far down the light reached. She could see a landing fifty yards down where the stairs turned to the east.

"To be honest," Dorothy said to Trafalgar, "regardless of the circumstances, I can't help being a little excited. This is my favorite part."

Trafalgar smiled. "I think no less of you."

"Good. So... shall we, into the abyss?"

"Might as well."

Dorothy made sure her makeshift mask was securely in place, then held the torch out in front of her as she led the way down into the palace's depths. The walls of the hidden stairwell were uncomfortably close. Though there was enough clearance that the stone didn't scrape her shoulders Dorothy nonetheless felt the urge to turn sideways. Her feeling of claustrophobia, the sense of being completely enclosed, increased when they took the turn and could no longer see the entrance. The torchlight, which had been so brilliant up above, now seemed little better than a candle.

"How far down does it go?" Orville asked, and she thought she detected a touch of anxiety in his voice.

"Hard to say," Dorothy said. "There's another turn up ahead. It could go down for miles." She'd never heard of such a thing, but there was no reason to calm his nerves.

Trafalgar said, "There's a staircase in Lima with no end. It was built to entrap the king's enemies. They discovered a hidden passage and knew it must lead somewhere important. So they began to descend, and eventually began to fear there was no bottom. Their greed forced them to continue onward. They had already spent so much time climbing down that they knew there had to be some reward. Down they went... into the bowels of the earth. Some say they are still walking."

"Be silent," Orville growled.

Dorothy bit her bottom lip and glanced over her shoulder. Trafalgar winked at her and Dorothy smiled back.

Unfortunately Orville's discomfort was short-lived as they soon reached the base of the stairs. They were in a long and narrow room which stretched out to either side, one wall smooth limestone while the other was rough-hewn rock of the cavern. Dorothy approached the smooth wall and held the torch above her head to illuminate a carving directly ahead of the stairs. It depicted an axe with double blades standing above a Greek word.

"Labrys," Dorothy said. "The labyrinth. My god." She held the light out to the left, then to the right. "This is the labyrinth."

"Significance?" Orville asked. The terror had faded from his voice and was replaced once again by impatient boredom.

Dorothy scoffed. "You need me to tell you the significance of finding the labyrinth? You truly are a child playing with toys in his sandbox, aren't you?"

"Careful."

She sighed. "The myth claims that King Minos had the labyrinth built to imprison his disfigured child, the Minotaur. I've always believed differently. And now that you've come along with your information about powerful ancient artifacts being hidden here..." She moved to the right so she could see a little further along the wall. "I believe the Minotaur was here long before Minos. I believe the creature was the island's original ruler. Minos overthrew him and kept him in this prison. Or alternatively, the Minotaur anticipated his loss and retreated into the labyrinth with his riches so his opponent could not reach them." She was breathing heavily. "This could be the discovery of a lifetime."

"Take us to the center of the labyrinth," Orville said.

Dorothy laughed. "You can't be serious."

Daniel took out his gun and aimed it at her head. Dorothy looked down the barrel and held her hands out to the side.

"Either I die here or I starve to death in a few days inside that maze. I prefer quick and mostly painless. This is the labyrinth, Mr. Weeks. This is the oldest trap known to mankind. It was built as a prison but you can see that the door was left open. Why? Because the prisoner would never find his way out. Even if I could somehow make it to the center of the maze and get your precious stone, we would never escape. Not in this lifetime, not in five lifetimes."

Orville stepped closer to the wall. "But we're so close. There must be something we can do. Some way we can... we can..."

"This is not a puzzle that was intended to be solved."

Daniel grimaced and holstered his gun. "Perhaps not eight thousand years ago. But we have advantages King Minos did not." He swept his coat aside and reached into his pocket. He fished out a small block of clay and a jumble of small wires. He crouched and wedged the clay against the base of the labyrinth wall. "Whoever built this maze didn't anticipate the advent of gunpowder and explosives."

Dorothy lunged at him. "You madman! You mustn't..." Her legs shattered underneath her and she fell to the ground. She cried out in pain and surprise, then slapped her palm on the stone floor. "Call off your bloody psychic dogs! This imbecile is about to kill us all!"

"That man is my brother."

"Then he will be guilty of fratricide as well as simple murder." She pushed herself up, ignoring the psychic message that her legs were scattered around her in broken pieces. She stood and grabbed Daniel by the collar of his jacket and pulled him away from the wall. "Do you have any idea what an explosion in this confined space could do? Best case scenario, every wall remains standing but we are deafened if not obliterated by the blast. We are surrounded by stone on all sides, gentlemen, and our bodies are marshmallow compared to it."

Orville said, "So your alternative is to simply surrender? Give up and return to the surface?"

Dorothy sighed and turned her torch to the labyrinth wall.

"Theseus," Trafalgar said. "The king's daughter gave him a ball of string so he could find his way out. She also gave him instructions from Daedalus, the builder of the labyrinth." She tilted her head to the side thoughtfully. "Although if you're correct and the maze was already here when Minos took control of the island, then any advice given by its purported builder would be false."

"At this point I'm willing to take any advice, mythological or not."

"Always forward, never left. Always down, never right."

Dorothy looked at the wall again. "The only possible entrances are left or right."

Trafalgar said, "Perhaps the riddle indicates there is no way out. If you have to choose wrongly simply to enter the labyrinth..."

"Perhaps." Dorothy was emptying her pockets, noticing peripherally that her legs were miraculously once again intact. "We may not have a ball of string, but we certainly have the means to keep track of our progress. Coins, bullets, even knives so we can mark the walls as we pass."

"Bullets?" Orville said. "Are you sure your intention isn't simply to disarm us?"

Dorothy smiled sweetly. "I also said knives. If I try to get too clever you can always just stab me."

He said, "And as a precaution, I will leave the Petric sisters out here to watch the exit, just in case you intend to circle around and leave us behind." He looked at the bald women. "If either of them comes out of the labyrinth without me or Daniel with them, you know what to do."

Milena grinned, showing a row of small white teeth. Dorothy sneered at her before she turned back to Orville. "Now then. If we're all prepared, and if you're truly determined to continue this folly... Mr. Weeks, I suggest you lead the way. Left or right?"

He bounced his hand so that the coins cupped in his palm would jingle as he considered which route to take. Finally he walked to the right. Dorothy and Trafalgar followed him with Daniel bringing up the rear. The sisters remained behind them, obviously anxious about being left behind in the staging area. Dorothy turned the torch back on and shone it over Orville's shoulder to light the path ahead of him. The path was blocked by a door which he opened easily by placing his hands at shoulder-height and pushing.

A pungent smell greeted them as they stepped inside, standing in a cluster at the entrance. There was a light source somewhere, faint but bright enough that the torch was no longer an absolute necessity. Dorothy turned it off and stuck it into her belt to preserve the battery. The walls were a very pale blue, almost azure, and they seemed curiously inviting. She moved the light closer to the wall and watched as the beam bounced off thousands of small crystals that had grown embedded in the stone.

She had just opened her mouth to comment on how remarkable it was when the air was filled with a dull rumble. At first it sounded like a rockslide or underground thunder, more a feeling in their boots than a sound. Then it grew in texture, with an organic gurgling noise riding under the tremulous shudder. Dorothy saw the others scanning the path ahead of them, the narrow corridor that led into the labyrinth.

"What was that?" Orville spoke in a frightened whisper.

"I told you the myth," Dorothy whispered, well aware that her voice carried some fear as well. "The labyrinth, for whatever reason it was built, served as the prison for..."

Orville spun to face her. He tried to conceal his fear with anger. "I bloody well know what you said, but that was eight millennia ago! How could any creature still be alive?"

Dorothy stepped past him and aimed her light the way they would have to go. "Humans have such a narrow view of time. The creature could have been hibernating, or it could have reproduced asexually. It may simply have an extraordinarily long lifespan. Whatever the reason, I think we must accept one thing as fact." She swallowed as the roar diminished to a soft tremor in the stone. "I believe our presence here has woken the Minotaur."

Chapter Seventeen

Beatrice was sweating, both from exertion and the effort of keeping part of her mind on the airship slowly making its way to Knossos. Leola had driven past the ancient site to a remote location south of the palace to be sure they wouldn't run into any Society goons who had been left to stand guard. Now they were cutting through a field of overgrown weeds, the tall yellow stalks to her right seemingly collapsing of their own volition as Ivy made her way forward. Beatrice had a mental image of the *Skylarker* with the appropriate insignia on the side. She hoped it would be enough to convince the Society, however briefly, that they were being watched.

Ivy was walking ahead of them as a lookout. They were within a quarter mile of the site when Ivy whistled for them to stop. Beatrice and Leola both crouched as their invisible companion moved back to join them.

"Three guards standing watch, about thirty yards apart." She broke off a handful of grass so they could see where she was pointing. "There, there, and there. Plenty of room between them, but they'll have at least two pairs of eyes on you no matter where you try to go through."

"Can you take them out?"

Ivy said, "One, sure. But then the other two will know something peculiar is happening. They might just start firing blindly."

Leola said, "Beatrice and I can be in position when you make your move. It would offer them a false sense of security, to think their fellow soldier is far enough away to protect them if we make a move."

Beatrice said, "Or you could approach them alone. Feign wounded, then Ivy takes out one while I take out the other from afar."

Leola set her lips in a tight line and met Beatrice's eye. It was incredibly risky; to expose herself to the guards and trust that two women she'd never worked with before would protect her. A week earlier she would have considered Beatrice her enemy. She hadn't forgotten the fact that this entire misadventure had begun with the two of them brawling in the street. But Trafalgar needed her help, and Lady Boone was in similarly dire straits.

"I trust you. That plan would have the best chance to succeed. I will approach the guard in the center, Ivy will disable the eastern guard while Beatrice will take the one to the west."

Beatrice nodded. "We'll give Ivy time to get into position and then Leola, you can act. Five minutes?"

"Should be enough," Ivy said. "I'll wait until you're in position before I make a move."

"Then let's not delay any further."

Ivy took off at a slow trot, moving horizontally so the path she cut through the tall grass would be less obvious. Leola and Beatrice moved furtively to take position behind a tree with a tri-forked trunk. Beatrice pointed out the guard she would target, and Leola nodded her understanding. Beatrice held her hand by her side, clenching and unclenching a fist to build up the energy necessary for two simultaneous attacks. The ship needed its insignia to remain intact - she could envision it now, a gleaming icon emblazoned on both sides of the gondola, flashing just enough red and gold to make anyone on the ground question what they were seeing.

"Ready?" Leola asked.

"When you are."

Leola slipped out from behind cover. She had a baton tucked in the back of her belt, two blades up her sleeves, and had proven herself adept at self-defense even if she had been completely unarmed. If they hadn't been enemies she would have admitted she was starting to be a little attracted to the stoic woman. Although if she was completely honest, the fact they were enemies was actually sweetening the pot a little. She would have to see where things ended up once the Society had been dealt with.

"Excuse me," Leola called. "I was hoping you could help me."

The guard stepped forward. "You're not allowed to be here. Please turn around and go back the way you came."

"I was supposed to meet with my tour group at a parking lot near here. I stepped into the woods, you know... the call of nature... and I found myself turned around."

The guard hoisted his gun. "You can't be here, miss. Leave now or you'll be taken into custody."

Leola stopped and looked at him. "Are you police? What is this place?"

"I won't ask you again, ma'am."

The guard Ivy had chosen suddenly lifted both arms in the air and bent forward at the waist. He backpedaled as if he'd been kicked in the stomach, fumbling to keep hold of the gun as it was torn from his hands. Leola threw herself at the guard she'd been speaking to while the third man brought up his rifle to fire at her. Beatrice mimed throwing a baseball and sent a concentrated burst of energy at the shooter's head. The man reacted as if hit by lightning, throwing his gun and landing hard on his back. He twitched briefly but did not get back up. Leola dispatched her man with a final blow, stooping to relieve him of his weapons before she checked to make sure everyone else was safe.

"Miss Sever?"

"I'm in one piece," Ivy said, although a floating blossom of blood somewhere near her shoulder revealed that her victory hadn't been as complete as the others. "Come on. There will be others, and these three will be missed sooner rather than later."

Beatrice and Leola split their new weapons between themselves before they continued up the hill to the palace.

"What do you know about the Minotaur?" Dorothy asked. They were standing between the Weeks brothers and the interior of the labyrinth. The beast hadn't repeated its awakening grumble but they could sense it deep in the heart of its prison. Something was definitely awake and moving around somewhere in the warren of winding corridors.

Trafalgar shook her head. "Not nothing, but certainly not much more. You?"

"Bullish fellow, stands erect like a man. Unpleasant in every regard. I seem to remember the true difficulty in killing it was finding it. They sent children into the maze as an offering, and children couldn't very well stand against the beast. The only magical item Theseus required was the string that showed him how to get out again."

"I doubt we'll have trouble finding the Minotaur," Trafalgar said. "From the sound of things, he is looking for us."

"Lucky us," Dorothy muttered. She looked at Orville. "I don't suppose you'd be willing to let us have some weapons considering the threat we're likely to face."

Orville said, "When the time comes, if you need a weapon..."

She rolled her eyes. "This should be fun."

"Lead the way," Trafalgar said.

Dorothy glared at her.

"You have the flashlight."

"So I do." She took a breath and, against her better judgment, continued into the labyrinth.

The floor was indeed canted at a very subtle downward angle. When they reached the first branch she paused and shone the light inside. The ground seemed to rise and curve to the right. She passed the door and continued forward. "Always forward, always down." The path had a slight angle to it, and soon she became aware that they were skirting the outer edge of a wide circle. She could hear Orville's breathing even though he was bringing up the rear, and she looked back to see him running one hand along the wall.

"Everything all right back there, Mr. Weeks?"

"Just get us to the blasted stone," he snapped.

Dorothy said, "The instructions seem simple enough. We'll simply reverse them once we get to the bottom."

"Bottom...?"

"Oh, yes. Always down. Given the slight curve of the floor, I would say the labyrinth was originally constructed in a bowl of stone. We're descending even deeper. We must be half a kilometer underground by now. We're only going to go deeper."

Daniel said, "I know what you're doing, Lady Boone. You'd be well-advised to stop."

Trafalgar said, "There must be something more to the labyrinth than a simple memory device. Why would such a simple solution prevent the Minotaur's escape? Why would Theseus require a string to find his way out again?"

"Perhaps he got dizzy from walking around in circles." Trafalgar frowned at her and Dorothy shook her head. "I don't believe in borrowing stress. Either we'll discover further security measures or we won't. Whatever happens we probably can't predict it. No sense distracting ourselves before we have to."

As if to punctuate her point, the roar came again. This time it seemed closer, amplified by the curve of the walls until it echoed around them all. Orville seemed less concerned by the beast than by his awareness of how far under the earth they were. Daniel eyed his brother as he used the blade of his knife to score the wall. He used the tip to motion Dorothy onward.

"Go. We've waited long enough for this."

"Patience, Mr. Weeks. Treasures have been lost for sillier things than eagerness. We must do this properly." She continued forward. "We are the first human beings to set foot in this maze since pre-history. Empires have risen and collapsed since this air was last breathed. We have traveled back in time, gentlemen. Do you not understand how magnificent that is?"

Daniel said, "Forgotten kings in forgotten castles. Dust that our forefathers blew off the world before remaking it for themselves. We shall be the next to rule this world."

"'Look on my works, ye mighty, and despair'," Dorothy said. "'This mighty City shows the wonders of my hand.'"

Orville breathlessly laughed. "Yes. I quite like that. I like that very much."

Dorothy looked at Trafalgar in disbelief. "Yes. Perhaps instead of Felix Quintel you could name your ruler Ozymandias."

Daniel said, "I have the feeling you're mocking us, but I don't know why."

"Ozymandias." Orville exhaled sharply, puffing out his lips and wiping the sweat from his brow. "It is a damned good name."

Daniel snorted and shook his head. Trafalgar actually laughed, nudging Dorothy with her elbow to show she had gotten the joke. Dorothy shared the laugh with her as they took the next gentle curve and found themselves standing in front of a solid wall. The smiles faded as Orville and Daniel joined them in the alcove.

"Crumbs." Dorothy aimed the light up even though she didn't relish the idea of trying to climb over the obstacle. The wall had no gap before reaching the ceiling of the cavern. "We'll have to turn back."

"No! The rhyme said always down, never left or right."

"Then we must be at the treasure!" Dorothy said. She swept the light over the floor. "We shall be set for life with all of these riches."

Orville reached out and slapped her hard enough that she fell back against the wall. She dropped the torch and the light in the dead-end swirled. Dorothy remained where she had fallen for a moment, her hand flat against the stone with her face hidden in shadow. Her cheek was red and stinging when she finally turned to face Orville again. Her features were composed and her voice was calm, and no trace of emotion betrayed her voice as she said, "The next time you raise a hand to me, the fight won't end until one of us lies bleeding at the other's feet. Am I clear, Mr. Weeks?"

He started forward but his brother stopped him with a hand on his chest. "We still need her, Or."

"For now," Orville said.

Dorothy set her jaw and held his gaze until he turned to look back the way they'd come. "Now what do we do? Go back? Disregard the clue?"

"We have no other option. At this point we can only turn left, going into the labyrinth. We're still on the outside edge, which means this wall gives us no other option. But once we go through the door we'll be a level deeper and the chances for a fatal error will be even greater. I have to ask if you're certain this is the action you want to take. Is the prize honestly worth the risk that the four of us will die down here?"

"We're destined to have the stone," Orville said. "We've come this far. We cannot turn back."

Dorothy sighed. "Very well then." She stooped to pick up the torch and walked past their captors. The last door they'd passed was twenty yards back along the curve, and Dorothy stopped in the opening until Trafalgar could join her. She shone the light in both directions as another echoing roar filled the air. The sound had become like the rumble of a thunderstorm, obvious but easy to ignore after a few times. Dorothy said, "What say you?"

Trafalgar shrugged. "I believe your guess is as good as mine. I also believe we will all die down here."

Dorothy sniffed and reached up to brush a hair out of her face. "Optimistic. I like it. Gods, do I look as disheveled as I feel?"

"There's stone dust on your cheekbones, your hair is completely unkempt, and your clothing is filthy." She smiled. "It's the first time since we met that you've actually looked like you deserve your job. You look like an archaeologist, Dorothy."

"Ah, you called me Dorothy without prompting. You have changed."

"At the moment you certainly don't look worthy of the title 'Lady'."

Dorothy laughed. "I'll take that as a compliment." She turned and saw Daniel speaking quietly to Orville. The handsome Weeks brother was hugging himself, his head hanging low, his fingers trembling slightly. The man was obviously terrified. "Mr. Weeks. We should go forward now. We're going... left."

The Minotaur roared again, and Trafalgar touched Dorothy's elbow. "Wait." She lifted her head and listened. "What if the clue is part of the trap? If it was as simple as always forward, always down, why would Theseus require the extra cheat of the thread?"

"Okay. We've already determined it's impossible to follow the clues to the letter. Perhaps the thread was to prevent him from becoming disoriented."

Trafalgar said, "But he would still have to navigate to the center of the maze. He would have to know where to look for the Minotaur."

"Well, if this one is anything like his ancestors, that shouldn't have been too difficult. You can hear the blasted thing from the moment you..." She trailed off, realization widening her eyes. "Of course. We follow the sound of the Minotaur. It wouldn't leave its treasure unprotected. So we just have to follow the roars and we should be able to find our goal."

They waited in anxious anticipation until the Minotaur's rumble came again. Trafalgar and Dorothy both pointed to the right, smiling when they saw they were in sync, and Dorothy motioned with the torch.

"Come along, Mr. Weeks."

Daniel followed them into the secondary corridor, with Orville reluctantly trailing behind.

Milena and Mircea stood a few feet apart, arms behind their back and their feet planted shoulder-width apart. They still wore their glasses even though the tinted lenses made it nearly impossible to see now that the torch was gone. It didn't matter to them. When they were girls, the people in charge of the orphanage where they grew up often locked them in cupboards to keep them out of sight. After several days shivering in the dark together they learned to keep their mouths shut. No matter what they saw in someone else's head, no matter what hidden shame they knew about, they wouldn't speak it aloud. Standing in a wide, dark room was nothing new to them.

It helped that they were together. They turned their minds inward with tendrils sneaking out to meet their sister. The third Petric daughter, the unnamed, the one they had never met in person. When they reached out to her she always welcomed them in. To be together was to feel whole again. The Watershed Society had offered them the opportunity of searching the world and its hidden places. The possibility of finding their lost sister was too great. They would follow the Society to the ends of the world to find their missing third.

The perfect unity was disturbed by a sharp interruption. *If either of you bald freaks can hear this, you better get outside. Now. We have problems.*

Milena and Mircea looked at each other and decided without conferring. Mircea turned and ascended the stairs two at a time while her sister remained to await word from the Weeks.

The sun was painfully bright against her eyes as she returned to the surface, but she adjusted as she weaved back through the shattered rooms to the exterior of the palace. A shadow had fallen over the central courtyard and she knew what she would see as soon as she looked up. The massive airship was hanging heavily a few dozen yards above the stone slab, the wind from its engines kicking up dust in all directions. Eight of the guards who had taken up watch in a perimeter around the site were standing on the courtyard gazing up at the ship. She saw the insignia of the AAC on the gondola, but it had a glimmer on it that she couldn't quite trust.

Mircea reached out mentally to the ship. A small crew, which was curious for a Committee vessel. They were nervous, anxious, and... hopeful? They were hoping for success. That hardly made sense unless there was a reason they might fail. She cupped one hand over her eyes as a guard hurried over to stand beside her. She ignored the words coming out of his mouth. Everyone was so quick to voice their thoughts, unaware of the editing and obfuscation they did to themselves as soon as they opened their mouths. She instead listened to his thoughts and heard a less biased version of events.

He had been flirting with one of the other guards, a handsome but married man who had hinted at similar proclivities in the past, when the alarm went up. Three of their members had gone missing. They were discussing what to do about the errant members when word came from the other side of the perimeter that an AAC vessel was approaching. They had put down their weapons since even being armed in the presence of a Committee official was grounds to be considered guilty. But now the ship was simply hovering, and none of the men could figure out why.

Mircea dug deeper into the guard's mind and found a fantasy he harbored about himself and his fellow guard. As she crossed to stand under the ship she found the object of the first guard's affection and sent the image to him without context. She saw his face grow pale but forgot about him soon after he was out of her sight. She stopped beneath the wide gondola and looked up at the vessel. The insignia was wrong. It was draped like cloth against the side of the ship, or... perhaps it was...

She turned and looked into the woods. There was power out there, and she had a feeling it would account for the missing guards. She closed her eyes behind her glasses and focused on the illusion flying above her head. She imagined it as the end of a fuse, which she lit on fire. The flame traced back along its trail back to the source, and Mircea began walking before it had reached its destination.

Beatrice stopped in her tracks and swayed as if drunk. Leola stopped and looked back at her, and Ivy placed an invisible man on Beatrice's shoulder.

"Trix? Are you okay?"

"I..." Beatrice gasped. Her head flew back, blood gushing from both nostrils in a crimson cascade. Ivy grabbed her, preventing her from falling and making it look as if Beatrice was defying gravity. Leola cried out in anguish, unable to stop herself, momentarily thinking that Beatrice had just suffered the same fate as Adeline. She ran back to her new acquaintance and gestured for Leola to place her on the grass. Beatrice was shuddering and pale, but alive. The lower half of her face was slick with fresh blood, which had dripped down onto her neck and the collar of her shirt.

"What happened?"

Beatrice grabbed the chest of Leola's shirt. "Run."

Leola looked toward the palace and saw something utterly bizarre stalking toward them: a bald woman in a leather jacket, her eyes hidden behind glasses, her arms out to either side with her fingers spread wide. Blue light danced around her forearms and collected in spheres over her palms. They could hear the energy crackling even from thirty yards away.

"Run!" Beatrice said again.

This time Ivy and Leola heeded her warning and ran. Beatrice pushed herself up on bloody hands and watched the bald woman approaching.

"Let's see how good you are when you're not sucker punching me."

The bald woman only smiled and kept coming.

Chapter Eighteen

She could hear Orville and Dan whispering behind them, the homely Weeks reassuring the handsome one that they would be back on the surface soon. They had weaved through the maze with no regard for the initial clue. Occasionally they would go downhill for one curve and uphill for three. They took branches to the left, the right, and backward. Dorothy only rarely suffered from claustrophobia, but now even she was beginning to feel anxious about not knowing the way out. They all stuck their arms out to drag a bullet casing or a knife along the stone to mark their passage, and Dorothy used the torch to make sure the walls ahead of them were clear of any past marks.

Their only guide was the Minotaur's noises that were coming from... just ahead, around this bend, on the other side of this wall, or everywhere at once. Occasionally they could feel the ground trembling. Dorothy wondered just how massive this creature was. The heat was growing more oppressive the longer they walked. She had removed her jacket and unbuttoned her shirt as far as modesty would allow her. She didn't much care about the Weeks brothers seeing her underwear but there were lines she refused to cross. Trafalgar had removed her coat and had it draped over one shoulder, making her look strangely smaller as they moved through the twists and turns of the world's oldest and most diabolical maze.

"I'm beginning to see why this was an appropriate trap for the beast," Trafalgar said.

"So it would seem," Dorothy agreed as she scraped the bottom of the torch along the wall. She was feeling a bit queasy so she could only imagine how Orville was suffering. She refused to pity him, however; whatever he was suffering was a drop in the bucket against what he deserved.

They had almost reached a new branch when there was a roar so loud all four of them retreated a step. At the time Trafalgar happened to be in the lead and she dropped into a crouch with her shoulder tight against the wall. She craned her neck and looked through the doorway. Dorothy, pressed against the opposite wall, watched Trafalgar's eyes widen. She swallowed, looked at Dorothy, and nodded slowly.

Dorothy looked at the men. Orville seemed moments away from soiling himself, and even Daniel had a look of uncertainty on his face. No one seemed willing to breathe, let alone speak. Just through the opening they could hear feet sliding along stone, the quiet huff of the creature's breath. The air seemed disturbed by its presence, and after a moment Dorothy became very aware of a stench drifting through the gap in the wall.

Trafalgar stood up and walked to Daniel. She pushed her hands into his coat pockets and began searching, and he was so terrified of the Minotaur he did nothing to stop her. After a moment she withdrew her emei piercers and slid the ring onto her finger. Dorothy held out her hand. Without hesitation Trafalgar took the knife from Orville's sheath and handed it to her. Dorothy bent her fingers in a "more" gesture, and Daniel handed over his gun as well.

"Ready?" Dorothy mouthed.

Trafalgar shook her head, then gestured for Dorothy to lead the way. Dorothy stepped through the opening first and Trafalgar followed. The room they found themselves in was egg-shaped, with a narrow point across from the point they had entered. Identical doors marked the circumference of the room, a multitude of ways to escape. Arcane symbols marked the side of each entrance and Dorothy realized even the creature had tried to escape multiple times over its long life. Seven stone plinths formed a circle in the center of the room, and it was in this fenced-off area that the Minotaur stood.

The creature was at least eight feet tall, the muscles of its arms, chest, and thighs looking as if they had been carved from marble. Its skin was black as obsidian to match the fur of its bovine head. The Minotaur had two horns; on the right one twisted and curved so that it formed a widely-sloped S. On the left the horn was half the size and jagged at the end rather than pointed. It rose to its full height when they entered its den, its nostrils flaring in its wet snout. The creature stood naked and monstrous, swaying its weight from one foot to the other as it took the measure of the new offering.

Dorothy discovered her mouth was suddenly dry. She looked at Trafalgar and saw true fear in her eyes, her fist gripped tight against the double blades of her piercers. Dorothy cocked her weapon and looked at the Minotaur again. She didn't know what the next step would be, how they could proceed. She didn't want to antagonize the beast, didn't want to throw the first punch, but how could they hope to communicate? She decided the only option was to try.

"Hello," Dorothy said.

The Minotaur bellowed, a deafening cacophony in the confined space, and both Dorothy and Trafalgar cringed away from the sound instead of reacting logically. The Minotaur took advantage of their distraction and leapt. Trafalgar threw herself back, slid to the floor, and rolled away. Dorothy tried to evade on the side with the long and unbroken horn and discovered her error when the horn smacked her across the abdomen. She was carried with it as the Minotaur turned his head, then fell hard to the ground.

"You and your big mouth!" Trafalgar shouted.

Despite the agony in her stomach, Dorothy had to laugh. She rolled onto her hands and knees and, after checking that the skin hadn't been broken, got back onto her feet. The Minotaur had turned her back to her in order to focus on Trafalgar, and Dorothy smiled.

"All right, beastie. Let's dance."

Beatrice had an understanding of her mind that few people shared. To access her magical abilities, she envisioned a great wide room full of water. At the moment, lying on the grass while her adversary stormed toward her, she felt ripples in the surface of that water and knew the bald woman was trying to get inside. Beatrice built a whirlpool in the waters of her mind, swirling them rapidly to draw the invader toward the center. The centripetal force tugged the other woman's energy toward the center. Once it was trapped, Beatrice sent a bolt of her own energy back along its trail.

To dig into someone's mind, the attacker's mind needed to be open as well. Beatrice crashed into Mircea Petric's mind like a battering ram. Mircea had never needed to put up barricades to protect herself so she was utterly unprepared for the blow. Her advance stopped as if she had hit a brick wall, her lips parting in a surprised O. She brought both her hands up but they hovered at shoulder height as her knees began to give way.

Beatrice ignored the blood dripping from her nose, over her lips, and focused on making her counterattack as strong as possible. Another burst, and Mircea's head rocked on her shoulders. She hit one knee as Beatrice dug in her claws and refused to budge. She felt wrapped in a movie screen, images flashing all around her too large and obscure to make sense of. She saw blues: shoes in green grass, a face contorted in agony, horrible faces that took up the entire canvas. Beatrice smelled smoke but ignored it. She knew if she gave an inch the bald woman might recover and take her out. She couldn't risk it.

Mircea tore off her glasses to reveal eyes that glowed green so brightly that the light spread out underneath her skin. She opened her mouth and shouted incoherently, and Beatrice began to feel pushback on her assault. The burning smell intensified, and she felt another gush of blood flowing over her top lip, dripping from her chin.

There was a tremendously loud pop, and suddenly all the resistance disappeared. Beatrice stumbled forward with a gasp and watched Mircea fall forward, the light in her eyes dimming due to the bullet hole that had appeared above her right eye. Leola holstered her revolver and made her way to Beatrice's side, crouching next to her.

"Are you all right?"

Beatrice responded in Mandarin, English temporarily lost to her. She wiped the blood from her face and cleaned her hand on the grass. "Smoke?" she said when she could form the words. "Something. Burning."

"I believe it was this," Ivy said from behind her. "Your shirt..."

Leola looked. "My God. Has that ever happened before?"

Beatrice said, "What?"

"The back of your shirt is... burnt through." She touched the material. "But it seems as if it was burned by some sort of pattern. This tattoo on your back..."

"The tree."

"Yes. Apparently it burnt through your clothing."

Ivy said, "Must have been drawing from something pretty powerful for that to happen."

Beatrice said, "Yes. I must have..."

Milena's entire body shuddered, her hands twitching like someone who had just woken from a bad dream. She looked to her left and right. She had been alone since Mircea went to the surface, but now the loneliness surrounded her completely. "Mercy?" she whispered, the first word she had spoken aloud in years. "Mercy?" She sent the plea out with everything she had. For the first time since they were children, there was no response. She turned and started up the stairs, her assignment forgotten. She was struck dumb by confusion and fear, crawling up the stairs when she stumbled because standing would take too much effort.

Into the sunshine, not even squinting against its glare as she moved from dark to light in the shattered palace. "Mircea," she whispered. "Milly needs you. Please. Mercy, please." She walked into the courtyard and saw Dummies running around underneath a large airship. She reached out to all of their minds, watched them slow down as she sought information about her sister.

Where is my Mercy?

Where is my Mercy?

WHERE IS MY SISTER?

Everyone in the courtyard stopped where they were, stricken by a strange and incapacitating headache. None of them had the answer, however. Milena looked around and then began walking, her legs as uncertain as a newborn colt. She walked through the tall grass near the palace grounds, weaving around trees even as she seemed unaware of their existence. She reached a clearing and saw a body lying in front of her. Its head was destroyed and shattered by bits of blood and brain and bone. Milena stared at the thing that had been her sister and dropped to her knees with a keening cry of loss.

Three Dummies were crouching nearby, the black one, the tan one, and the one without any skin but an unsilent mind. Milena ignored them as she dropped to her knees and lifted her sister's impossibly light body off the ground. Mircea's face was intact, but her body was empty. Her mind was silent. Milena held the body against her chest and rocked it back and forth, sobbing silently as she stared at her sister's slack features. She heard the Dummies at the back of her mind.

Look at her. It would be kind to take her out of her misery.

She's not a threat. Killing her would simply be cruel.

Milena ignored the Dummies and lifted her sister. She found the strength she had lost a moment earlier, cradling Mircea in her arms before she began to walk away. The Dummies moved out of her way and watched her go. She didn't know where she was going or what lay ahead. She had no plans. All she knew was that she had to take her sister and leave. Nothing else mattered to her.

Trafalgar skirted the wall to the Minotaur's right, while Dorothy stayed to its left. It pivoted at the waist to track their movements, unable to attack either of them without exposing itself to the other. It made quiet chuffing sounds, revealing plank-like yellow teeth and a thick gray tongue. Everything about its body was human, the hands and trunk of its body, but it had grown in proportion to the bovine head. Occasionally Dorothy spotted Daniel Weeks peering through the door to check their progress, but the cowardly brothers made no attempt to join in the fight themselves.

"Any clever ideas?" Dorothy asked.

"Yes. I shall now begin an ingeniously clever series of actions which lead to victory."

Dorothy said, "I like the last step. Any chance of clarifying a few points?"

"Unfortunately everything but the final step is a bit hazy at the moment."

The Minotaur apparently tired of waiting. It chose Trafalgar, lowering its head to charge her. She pulled her coat from her shoulder and hurled it at him. The material ballooned out and draped across the Minotaur's face, temporarily blinding him as Trafalgar rushed forward. She placed her hands on his head and pushed down, leapfrogging over him and landing on his back. He was knocked to his knees as he tossed the coat aside and twisted to grab her. She ducked his arm as the act of twisting caused him to lose his balance. Trafalgar skipped away from him and smiled.

"Great big head, awkward center of gravity." She ducked as he spun around. "We have to stay inside the range of his horns. If he can't gore us–"

"Then he can grab us with his human arms," Dorothy said as she ducked the point of his unbroken horn. "We can't hope to overpower him. Even if you stabbed him with those piercers of yours, I doubt it would do much more than slow him down. I'll distract him while you make a run for the treasure."

"I..."

"Damn it, Trafalgar, just do it!" She dropped into a crouch and threw herself at his midsection. The Minotaur threw a punch that caught her in the head, then swept her legs out from under her. Dorothy went down but bounced back up quickly. She reached into her pocket and swung up something long and brass. The Minotaur expected a knife so he recoiled just enough that Dorothy could aim the beam of her torch directly into its eye. The Minotaur screeched and backed away blindly.

Trafalgar was most of the way across the room, eyeing the possible exits that would lead to the treasure. The Minotaur swiped at her, and Dorothy stomped the back of his leg so that he fell to his knees. The beast let loose a fearsome bawl and turned its attention fully on her. She tried to retreat but the Minotaur snagged her foot, pulling it out from under her. She yelped as she fell, and the beast gathered her up in its arms.

"Come now, fellow," Dorothy said with panicked breathlessness. "Don't take it personally..."

The Minotaur threw her. Dorothy had never been thrown before, had never felt the utter weightless, helpless feeling of being hurled by another living creature, and she had to say she did not approve of the sensation. Even worse was the landing, hitting hard enough that her entire body flashed white before the pain was localized to her arms and hip. The Minotaur had crossed the space between them while she was in the air, and when she rolled onto her back it loomed over her. It raised one leg and brought its foot down as hard at it could on her chest.

Dorothy wailed in pain as she felt the bone fracture. The Minotaur tried to step on her again, but she raised her left hand to block him. His foot slapped against her hand and she pushed sideways. He was thrown off-balance and crashed to the ground hard enough to aggravate Dorothy's injury. She used her feet to push herself away from the Minotaur and it grabbed her foot, squeezing her ankle through the boot. Tears filled her eyes as she felt the bones shifting in his grip.

Trafalgar descended like an avenging angel, pouncing on the beast and stabbing her piercer through its bicep. It let go of Dorothy and clawed at Trafalgar, who clung to its back. The Minotaur shook its head, knocking its horn against the wall. A piece of it broke off and fell near Dorothy's hand, and she grabbed hold of it. For a moment she considered jamming it into the creature's eye, but then she had another thought. She looked at the Minotaur, then began using the shard of its horn to scratch on the ground next to her.

The Minotaur rolled and tossed Trafalgar away, her blade still embedded in his arm. She managed to land well, getting onto her hands and knees within seconds of landing. The Minotaur lowed as it pulled the blade from its muscle and dropped it onto the ground. It turned to look at Dorothy, arms bracketing its sides as it rose up and took a step forward.

"Look!" Dorothy barked. She slapped her hand on the double-bladed axe she had drawn, then slapped her chest. She pointed at the Minotaur and then slapped the axe drawing again. The Minotaur stopped and watched her odd display, following her hand from it, to the drawing, to herself. "Labrys. Female goddesses, female power. Protection. Maternity." She slapped the axe again. "This is your symbol. This is on the outside of the labyrinth. You are here not as a prisoner but to protect the treasure. Help us. Help us protect the treasures."

The Minotaur snorted and looked hard at her. It took a deep breath and turned slowly to look at Trafalgar. She swallowed hard and made a point of taking off the remaining blade of her emei piercers, and she tossed it aside. The clink of metal hitting stone echoed in the sudden silence of the chamber.

"Help us," Dorothy whispered. She pointed toward the door, then drew an X over the axe with her finger. "They are bad men. They will stop at nothing to get your treasure. If they were gone, my friend and I would leave as well. We would do you no more harm."

The Minotaur looked at Dorothy's arm, apparently indicating she was the only one who had come to any real harm in their assault.

"Your horn has seen better days as well." She looked at the shard she was still holding and she let it drop from her fingers. "You could kill me, and then Trafalgar could cripple you. I think we should focus our attention on the men who only want to use your treasure for their own gain."

The Minotaur dropped to one knee and collapsed forward, face-down on the floor. One large, almost human eye stared directly at Dorothy and then looked toward the door. It let out one long wail and let its arms fall limply to either side. It looked for all the world as if the thing was dead.

Trafalgar swallowed the lump in her throat. "Lady Boone has slain the beast. Good lord." She sagged against the wall and put a hand to her forehead.

"Slain, or tamed..." Dorothy raised her voice. "Mr. Weeks!"

Daniel was the first through the door, taking a step back to give the beast a wide berth. He blinked rapidly at the massive body as his brother joined them.

"Good Lord," Daniel said. "Look at the size of it."

Dorothy clutched her shattered shoulder. "I hope your study has a particularly large wall."

"Pardon?"

"You are standing next to one of the most impressive beasts to ever walk this earth. It was killed so you could profit. You're not even going to take a trophy? This magnificent creature at least deserves awe and respect after death, even if it is hanging over your mantle."

Daniel nodded slowly. "Yes. Right... y-yes." He stepped forward and drew a knife. "It's going to take hours just sawing through the sinew and muscle..."

The Minotaur reared up and swung its head toward Daniel's voice. The newly-broken horn pierced Daniel just below the sternum and lifted him up off the ground before coming through his back. His face was twisted in a mixture of shock and pain as he was dropped, blood pouring from his wound as he crumpled to the ground. The Minotaur pushed itself up and turned toward Orville. The handsome Weeks brother shook his head, babbling as he nearly tripped over his feet running toward one of the many exits in the chamber. He disappeared into the darkness already running. The Minotaur looked at Dorothy and Trafalgar, then took off in pursuit.

Trafalgar listened to the beast howl as it began pursuing its enemy. "Good lord. Do you think it will catch him?"

Dorothy winced and remembered the mental anguish she'd been subjected to aboard his airship. "I hope not. I hope the bastard runs this maze the rest of his life." She tried to sit up and cried out in pain, drawing Trafalgar to her side. "Crumbs."

"I would say this is much worse than crumbs." She helped Dorothy up, propping her against the wall. "Is it just your shoulder?"

"No. When he grabbed my ankle, I believe he twisted it."

Trafalgar sighed and shook her head. "You are a mess, Lady Boone."

"I thought we had moved on to Dorothy."

"When one wishes to express disappointment, one must resort to titles."

"Or middle names," Dorothy said with a pained groan. She looked around the chamber. "I don't suppose there's a lift hidden around somewhere..."

Trafalgar shook her head. "Not that I saw. Dorothy... thank you. These injuries were inflicted because you gave me an opportunity to reach the treasure."

"You found it?"

"And the stone." She took it out of her pocket. It was infuriatingly plain, save for a few indecipherable carvings on its face. "Of course, that was before I knew you would achieve solidarity with our tormentor."

"The chalcedony. Are you going to keep it?"

"No. It's far too dangerous to keep anywhere in London, and I would say we've proven this is an adequate hiding place. Stay here and I'll replace it."

She stood up and went through one of the archways. Dorothy reached up to touch her shoulder and hissed in pain. She looked at the ceiling, hoping there was some kind of secret written there. She had a feeling that if there was a way out, it would require walking or at least being mobile. The corridors of the labyrinth were far too narrow for Trafalgar to support her; they couldn't walk side-by-side through the twists and turns, and they certainly wouldn't be able to ascend the stairs. Not to mention the twins... if by some miracle they escaped the labyrinth Trafalgar would be weary and encumbered when she came back upon Milena and Mircea.

Dorothy took out her revolver and checked the load. Trafalgar would never leave her behind, and there was no point in both of them rotting there. Her left arm was the one injured, so she used her right hand to raise the gun to the soft part of her chin. She rested her head against the stone wall and braced herself for the blow. She squeezed her eyes shut and fought back the wave of terror and sorrow that threatened to overtake her. She had to do it. Trafalgar might survive long enough on her own to find a way out, but with a broken woman weighing her down~

"Absolutely fucking not."

Dorothy looked at Trafalgar, who was stalking toward her. "It's my decision, Trafalgar."

"The hell it is." She took the gun from Dorothy and tucked it into her belt. "We'll find another way out of here. Both of us. You saved us from a damned Minotaur. I won't have you surrendering after victory has already been achieved."

"Quite a Phyrric victory. We defeat our enemies and wind up trapped forever in the Minotaur's chamber. Not that it should take long to succumb to hunger or dehydration. Of course, the Minotaur may change his mind after a week or two. He could decide to simply eat us to put us out of our misery."

"You are a very nihilistic person, are you aware of that?"

"I prefer the term realist. That way I'm either right or pleasantly surprised. It works out well for me more often than blind optimism."

"Well, look at me. I was born to a world where I wasn't given a name just in case I died as a child. I could have lived out my days getting water from a well, caring for my father and sisters, having fat little babies that I couldn't get too attached to because of disease and environmental dangers... I was kidnapped by evil men, brought to a world where I barely spoke the language." She sighed. "Nothing in my life has been the optimistic choice. And yet, here I am. Trapped in a pit with a ferocious half-man, half-bull. Just another day in my life."

Dorothy laughed. "Well, thank you for including me."

"Of course."

"We can't walk out of here. Even if I tried leaning on you, the corridors are too narrow..."

Trafalgar stood up and went to her discarded jacket. "We can use this as a sled. Tie the arms around my waist, you sit on the end, and I drag you out of here following the marks we made in the stone on our way in."

"Hardly dignified."

"Would you rather have dignity or your life?"

Dorothy sighed. "Fine. String yourself up. Let's get this over with before our beastly friend comes back."

Chapter Nineteen

THE SIGHT of Beatrice walking into the courtyard with her face and clothes smeared with blood was enough to convince the majority of Watershed goons to put down their weapons. They didn't know what had happened with their leader's pet psychics, but the fact the bloody woman was still moving forward was proof that fighting wouldn't do any good. They had seen those creepy sisters win fights without even throwing a punch, so anyone who walked away from a fight with them had to be unimaginably formidable. They got onto their knees and laced their hands behind their heads. One man brought up his gun only to have the weapon ripped from his hands by an unseen force and used to pistol-whip him before it was tossed into the woods. That display was enough to make the rest of them surrender.

Once the ground forces had been subdued, Araminta carefully landed the airship on a clear piece of ground north of the palace ruins. Her crew helped secure the prisoners, while the medic tended to Beatrice and Ivy's wounds. He had a little trouble treating Ivy's arm seeing as the wound was the only part of her that was visible, but he eventually managed to get a bandage wrapped around her upper arm. When he was finished the circle of gauze hovered in midair like a persistent smoke ring.

Araminta looked into Beatrice's eyes to check for a concussion. "She must have hit you pretty hard if you're still dazed."

"It was my own fault. I used too much energy." She brushed off the medic's attempts to check her out. "I'll be fine. We should concentrate our efforts on finding Dorothy and Trafalgar."

"They're still inside somewhere?" Araminta asked, turning to look at the palace ruins.

"Under," Beatrice said. "When I was... when that woman and I were grappling, I was inside her head. She had just come up to the surface after being underground." She looked at Leola. "I was hoping you could connect the dots. Trafalgar said you were good at putting the pieces together, making leaps. How should we go about finding them?"

Leola took a deep breath and looked at the area. "Underground. A vast treasure of immeasurable power, somewhere underground." She narrowed her eyes and tilted her head to one side. "It would be very dark."

Beatrice raised an eyebrow and looked at Araminta.

"Unless," Leola said, brushing between them to point at three large pits cut into the courtyard. "Unless there was a method of providing light to the underground network."

The women approached the center opening and peered down into the darkness.

"It seems to be a very long way down."

Beatrice had already slipped out of her jacket. "Work up a harness, find some rope. A hundred yards should do it, if you have one that long."

Araminta snapped her fingers at the nearest crewmember and gave him the assignment. She looked at Beatrice and said, "You're not thinking of going down there alone, are you?"

"It has to be me. I have the best defense."

Ivy cleared her throat. "Excuse me, hello."

"Fine, the second-best. But the difference is that if I fall or if the rope is too short, I can float."

"You can fly?" Leola said.

"I can hover. I can cushion a fall."

Leola shrugged as if it didn't make a difference. "Sounds like flight to me."

Beatrice smirked and let Araminta help her into the harness.

"We'll stay up here in case there's any trouble. What else do you need before you go down?"

"Weapons."

Araminta gave her a pistol, a knife, a flashlight, and after a moment of consideration a first-aid kit. Beatrice put it all in a satchel and slung it over her shoulder. They checked to make sure the rope was secure and then Beatrice moved to stand next to the lip of the opening.

"If it's too far down for me to shout back up, I'll tug on the rope three times as a signal to you to reel me in. Try not to get pulled over the side. It'll be dangerous enough without one of you falling on me."

Leola rolled her eyes. "We'll try to be careful. Ready?"

Beatrice turned her back and braced her feet on the lip of the opening. She tested the rope, took a few steadying breaths, and then began walking down into the pit. The walls had been lined with claw bricks, which were sturdy enough to provide a grip for her boots as she descended. The opening was wide enough that she couldn't reach the opposite side without pushing off and swinging. She was very aware of gravity trying to pull her down, and grateful for the women fighting to keep it from succeeding on the lip of the hole.

"Trix!" Araminta called down. Beatrice looked up and saw the silhouette of her head outlined against the sky. "You have about twenty yards of rope remaining!"

Beatrice looked down and saw the tunnel was about to start narrowing drastically. "It should be enough!" Her voice bounced back to her several times before she saw Araminta nod. Beatrice untied the rope and let herself fall the rest of the way, her feet slipping on the sloped bricks. Instead of forming a cup, there was a narrow opening just wide enough for a person to slip through. She crouched down and saw that it led into a narrow corridor of blue stone.

She slipped out of her harness, dropped the satchel of supplies through the opening, and then got onto her stomach to shimmy through.

"I wonder if there's any connection... labrys being associated with female empowerment and the word labia. Although the axe symbolism is unusual. I should do some reading on that when we get out of here."

Trafalgar blew a puff of air through her lips. "Yes. You. Should do that."

"Hm." Dorothy was seated on the tail of Trafalgar's jacket while Trafalgar held the arms around her waist to form a sled. She had dragged Dorothy through several twists and turns of the labyrinth, pausing occasionally to shine the torch on the walls to see if there were any directional markings to be found. So far they seemed to be in an entirely different section of the labyrinth than before. Trafalgar shone the light on both sides of the wall, saw nothing, and sighed as she shoved forward.

"Labia is Latin for lip, I believe. But labrys is... Lydian? It's difficult to say for certain without checking my references. Odd, though, that two civilizations would use the same root for such different ideas. Although a weapon and a maze could be said to describe a vagina as well."

"Lady Boone!" Trafalgar snapped. "Despite... what you seem to believe. This. Is not easy. And your. Incessant prattling on about genitalia is not. Exactly. Helping the situation."

Dorothy winced. "My apologies, Miss Trafalgar. Talking helped take my mind off the pain." Her injured arm was up across her chest, gripping the uninjured shoulder to keep the arm immobile. "I didn't mean to distract you."

Trafalgar breathed out sharply and took them around another curve. They could hear noises echoing down the corridor, shouts of alarm or maybe just fear.

The Minotaur bellowed from time to time; it was still hunting for the remaining Weeks brother. Dorothy listened for any hint they had gotten closer, but each time she heard evidence of the chase they were farther away.

"It's ironic," Dorothy said a moment later. "We're counting on the fact Orville Weeks won't be able to escape this maze while at the same time expecting to find a way out of here ourselves."

"We have the Minotaur on our side."

"Hmph. I would say–"

"Shush."

"Sorry. I know you said no talking. The pain..."

Trafalgar dropped the arms of her coat and drew her knife. Her voice dropped to a whisper and she shuttered the torch. "No, shut up. Someone is coming." She moved to the side of the corridor. A moment later Dorothy could hear footsteps coming from the other direction.

Dorothy whispered, "You can't just leave me in the middle of the corridor like this!"

"Sh, shut up!"

"I'm a sitting duck!" She began to fumble for her weapon, grunting at the pain that shot through her arm as she did.

Beatrice spoke before she appeared around the corner. "If I were looking to kill you, you've both made more than enough noise already." She turned on her torch and shone it into her face as she stepped into view. "Fortunately, I am here to rescue you."

Dorothy beamed. "Trix!"

"Miss Sek." Trafalgar sheathed her knife. "It is very good to see you."

"And you, Miss Trafalgar. I'm glad to see you well. And the Lady Boone." She crouched next to Dorothy and cupped her face. "Hello, mum. I've missed you terribly."

Dorothy was surprised to find herself teary-eyed. "I've missed you as well, Miss Sek. What... what happened? There's blood all over you."

"You're one to talk. What happened to you?"

"I was stepped on by the Minotaur."

Beatrice smiled. "You have all the luck."

Trafalgar said, "Can you fix it? You seem rather adept at conjuring."

"Conjuring is one thing. I can't and won't use it to fix a bone. It wouldn't heal properly and lead to trouble down the line. But I can offer you palliative respite from the pain until we have a chance to properly treat the injury. You might feel a little lightheaded and discombobulated, but at least it won't hurt anymore."

"Yes, please."

Beatrice leaned in and kissed Dorothy's lips. Trafalgar looked away, ostensibly to check for Weeks or the Minotaur. When she looked back Dorothy's body language was more relaxed. Beatrice opened the first-aid kit she had brought with her and found a sling. She carefully helped Dorothy into it, resting her arm comfortably in the folded cloth before wrapping her ankle with gauze.

"Thank you, Trix."

"Any time." She looked up as the air was shaken by another scream, quickly followed by another low roar. "I suppose you're ready to get out of here."

Trafalgar said, "Faster would be better, yes."

Beatrice stood up. "Lucky for you, I know a way." She held her hand out, fingers splayed, and the corridor ahead of them light up bright blue. "I left a trail of breadcrumbs."

Trafalgar helped Beatrice get Dorothy onto her feet. She was still favoring her injured ankle, but for the moment Beatrice's magic would help her stand. Trafalgar inspected the damage to her coat and slung it over her shoulder.

"It will be a slow trip back to the surface. We'll have to go one at a time. But I don't think you'll complain much as long as it gets you out of here."

Trafalgar shook her head. "Beggars can't be choosers. Lead the way, Miss Sek."

It was decided that Dorothy would be hoisted up first, followed by Trafalgar, with Beatrice coming last. They called up that Dorothy was injured, so the women on the surface took their time to ensure a slow and steady ascension for her. Once she was safely out, Beatrice helped Trafalgar into the harness and tugged on the rope to let Araminta know she was ready. They pulled her up, and Beatrice kept an eye on the tunnel in case anyone wandered by before the harness was sent back down for her. The corridor remained empty, although she could hear quiet sobbing from somewhere far away. Finally the harness was dropped a third time, and she hooked herself up to be lifted back to safety.

When she reached the surface, Dorothy was already being examined by the *Skylarker*'s medic. "Fractured clavicle, sprained ankle, various bumps and bruises. Scrapes on her hands and knees."

Dorothy said, "You should see the other fellow."

Araminta smiled and looked at Trafalgar. "What should our next move be?"

"A pair of psychic twins are still in the palace somewhere."

"Handled," Beatrice said.

"Ah. Well done. Then we should conceal the entrance to the labyrinth again. It's not as if it was particularly difficult to find, but better to be safe than sloppy." Trafalgar looked at the restrained society members seated in a row on the opposite side of the courtyard. "It would appear you've been busy while we were wandering around in circles."

"Araminta Crook," Dorothy said, "never one to rest on her laurels." Her eyes were half-lidded from the mystical pain remedy Beatrice had applied. Araminta told Trafalgar to show her troops where the labyrinth door was so they could block it, and Beatrice helped the medic prepare Dorothy for transfer to the airship.

"I assume everything worked out down there," Beatrice said. "With the stone..."

Dorothy nodded. "I'll fill you in once we're in the air."

"It killed me to leave you in Rome. You know that, don't you?" Dorothy nodded and gripped Beatrice's hand. Beatrice turned and watched Trafalgar leading Araminta's crew into the palace. "But you swear she had your back?"

"And then some. I owe her my life."

Beatrice chuckled. "Bit hard to believe, given your history together."

"Hm. But that's history for you. Always in the past, while the future is always changing. It can surprise you in the most unexpected ways. I doubt our interactions with Miss Trafalgar will be the same after this little adventure."

They were delayed in Knossos for most of the day, dealing with the local authorities and the true Archaeological Advisory Committee. The Watershed Society faced official sanctions for their unauthorized activity and taken into custody. Trafalgar informed the supervisor that Orville Weeks was still alive inside the labyrinth when they left, though she doubted that was still the case. When she started to warn him that his men should be cautious if they chose to go looking for him, the man stopped her with an upraised hand and shook his head.

"We've had incidents like this in the past. You are hardly the first to discover the entrance to the labyrinth, and Mr. Weeks is hardly the first to not make the return trip."

Trafalgar frowned. "So why do you not block the entrance or post warnings?"

He smiled and lifted his shoulders in a shrug, already turning to walk away. "You presume it is our decision. He was here first, after all."

Trafalgar was stunned at the man's cavalier attitude, but she supposed he had a point. If someone went through the proper channels to access the labyrinth they would receive warnings. Surely people like the Weeks, who thought they could slip around the rules, deserved to suffer the consequences. Still, the idea of Orville Weeks wandering the maze until he starved or was brutally murdered like his brother didn't sit well with her. It seemed barbaric. Then again she was wholly unmotivated to lead a rescue team back down to drag her kidnapper to safety, if he was even still alive, so perhaps there was a little savagery in her after all.

The Weeks brothers would have killed her without hesitation, would have made her Felix or Felina Quintel, and they would have used her to start a second

Great War. Thousands, perhaps millions would have fallen in their bid for world domination. The more she thought about it, the less concerned she was about leaving him behind. He would only be put into another concrete box with no hope of escape. At least this prison had the benefit of being just.

Trafalgar touched two fingers to her eyebrow, a sign of respect for the beast that existed below the ruins of the palace, and turned to board the airship so Araminta could begin takeoff procedures. The sun was beginning to set, casting long shadows and painting the ruins in shades of red and gold that hinted at the splendor it had once boasted. With a good headwind they could be in Paris by morning and home in London by the following afternoon.

Araminta insisted on having a celebratory dinner once they were in the air. Dorothy ate a bit before begging off to get some sleep. The pain had started to come back in her shoulder and she wanted to be sure she got enough rest. Trafalgar and Leola spent some time on their own since their final mission together was over, and their return to London would mean parting ways once and for all. Ivy borrowed some makeup and a uniform so she could join the festivities without controversy - "Have you ever watched an invisible woman eat? Even if the food isn't visible for the whole process, thank God, it's still not the most attractive sight." - and Araminta commented on how attractive she was. It was no surprise to Beatrice, then, when the captain offered the invisible assassin a tour of the ship that somehow lasted the entire evening.

Beatrice went alone to her room, locking the door behind her. For most of the trip she had put disturbing questions out of her mind but with the quiet of the ship she could avoid her mind no longer. She unbuttoned her blouse as she crossed to the en-suite. There was a trifold mirror above a water basin, and she twisted at the waist so she could see her tattoo. The bathroom had electric lights but she left them off as she cupped her hands in front of her chest and formed a simple ball of light. The pale blue energy coursed up her arms, thin glowing lines in the subcutaneous tissue of her forearm and wrist. It glowed through her fingers and formed a perfect sphere in the space between her palms.

The tattoo remained the same, so she focused and pushed more energy out. Her muscles burned, and the glow increased exponentially until the whole room was bathed blue. She felt moisture on her upper lip and saw in the mirror that she had a nosebleed. She ignored it and focused on the tattoo. Her shirt had been burnt in a perfect outline of the tree, and she was certain--

There. The branches of the tree were illuminated. It was subtle but there, difficult to make out given the lighting in the rest of the room. As she watched the glow became brighter. More blood trickled from her other nostril but she ignored it as the light spread downward into the trunk of the tree. The tattoo pulsed with light from the tip of its highest branch to the roots. The blood reached her lip and spread out. She tasted copper as she watched as the tree took on a steady burning brightness.

She wanted to see how far she could go, but a sudden pressure behind her left eye frightened her enough to stop. She slapped her hands together and sent the energy out in a sloppy wave, causing the entire ship to rock violently for a moment. She knew that the crew would blame turbulence and she was prepared to let them. It would be easier than trying to explain something she herself didn't understand.

Beatrice ran some cold water and washed away the blood from her lips. When she was finished she pinched the bridge of her nose and leaned forward, unable to look away from her own reflection as she tried to staunch the bleeding. She thought back to the old man from her earliest memories, the man who had dragged her to Paris and left her there with no way of finding a trail back to her past.

What did you do to me, old man? Or where did you find me? What am I? What did you make me into?

Answers, as always, weren't forthcoming. She checked to make sure the bleeding had stopped, rinsed out the towel, and took herself to bed where she could hopefully find some peaceful slumber.

Araminta plotted a more leisurely and far more scenic route back to England since there was no longer a timetable on their journey. It was sunset by the time the city was in view, and Dorothy went to one of the large windows along the gallery to watch as it unfolded before her. She was aware of Trafalgar joining her at the glass but she didn't acknowledge her arrival until she broke the silence.

"Not one of them knows how close they came," Trafalgar said. "If the Weeks had gotten their stone, I would be coming back here with another creature in my head. They would attempt a coup, and this world would be once again thrown into bloody conflict. You and I saved them from all of that but no one down there has a clue."

Dorothy said, "Well, I'm certain a few of them suspect. But you're right. They don't know. It's better that they don't know. All the foiled plots, all the schemes that never come to fruition. It would drive them mad if they knew how often we existed on the edge of destruction."

"I don't agree. I think if they knew how often their lives were at risk, they might appreciate them more. They might appreciate those they love more."

"Hm. You may have a point there, Miss Trafalgar." She turned to face her. "I would have died multiple times on this excursion without your help. It's not easy for me to admit that, but I would be cross with myself if it went unsaid. I owe you my life. Thank you."

Trafalgar said, "I wouldn't have been able to stand against the Weeks brothers without you there. I may not have died, per se, but... you saved me from a fate far worse."

Dorothy turned back to face the window. "It will be hard to consider you a rival after this."

"But you shall try?"

"No. It's a waste of time. We're not enemies any longer, Miss Trafalgar. From now on I shall gladly call you a friend."

"That would be acceptable to me, Lady Boone." Dorothy glared at her. "Force of habit. I would be happy to call you friend, Dorothy."

The Rookery was devoid of cheering celebrants and confetti, their lone receiver being Desmond Tindall. He greeted Dorothy with a kiss on either cheek and shook hands with both Trafalgar and Beatrice. He looked at Dorothy's bruises and sling with true alarm.

"What on earth happened to you?"

"We won." Dorothy linked her other arm with his. "For now, that's the only thing that matters."

Ivy came down the gangplank and touched the brim of her hat to Dorothy. "It was a pleasure, Lady Boone. Hopefully the next time we meet we won't be enemies."

"Good day to you, Miss Sever."

Leola and Trafalgar had arranged for their own transportation, and Beatrice followed Dorothy to the car Desmond had rented for them. She helped Dorothy get settled in the backseat so she wouldn't aggravate her arm, then got behind the wheel and waited for Desmond to climb in beside her before she started the engine. She paused before setting out and looked over her shoulder.

"Any stops you want to make?"

"No," Dorothy said with a sleepy smile. "Take us home, Trix."

"Yes, ma'am."

Dorothy reclined against the seat with her hand in her lap, the other held tight against her stomach by the sling, and looked out the window at the airships buzzing back and forth across the Thames. The muddy waters reflected their bumblebee shapes against the golden sunset. People hurried across their paths, and others walked alongside them on the street, blissfully unaware of the madness the Weeks brothers had planned to unleash on the world. Dorothy smiled and closed her eyes, thinking about what Trafalgar had said. Maybe it was good to know the world lived on the brink, maybe being so close to the potential tragedy had turned her into a woman who didn't let an opportunity slip through her fingers.

Though the ride from the Rookery to Threadneedle Street took less than twenty minutes, Dorothy was already asleep by the time Beatrice pulled up to their front door.

Epilogue

Six weeks later

Dorothy swung her blade, grimacing as she missed the mark and left herself open for a counterattack. She retreated by shifting her weight to her opposite foot, but she was too slow. Her opponent took advantage of the mistake and thrust her weapon forward. The blade pressed into Dorothy's blouse just above her heart. Her shoulders slumped and she reached up to push her mask out of the way. "This doesn't count toward your overall average. I'm fighting with my weak arm."

"The hell it doesn't," Beatrice said as she unmasked herself. She walked to the table under the window and poured them each a glass. "You have to learn how to fight even if your dominant hand is out of commission. You never know when it might be necessary."

Dorothy swung her epee a few times, still getting used to the weight in her left hand. "I'll be out of this sling in two more weeks."

"This is for the next time."

"I don't plan on letting any more minotaurs step on me."

Beatrice said, "So this time it was part of your plan?"

Dorothy grinned. "It's all part of a plan, my dear Trix."

Beatrice put down her glass and peered out the window. Her attention was drawn to the street and her demeanor changed. "I believe we're about to have company. A carriage just pulled up."

"Desmond?"

"Doesn't look like."

"Hm." She took Beatrice's epee. "I'll put these away. Let them in and see what they want. Perhaps a commission."

Beatrice said, "In your condition?"

"I can handle myself. Go." She swatted Beatrice's rear end with the sword and went to put them away. She quickly changed out of her gear and daubed at her sweaty forehead with a towel. She was just putting up her hair when Beatrice returned.

"Miss Trafalgar would like an audience."

Dorothy blinked. "Trafalgar. Here? How unusual. Did you ask her to wait in the parlor?"

"Yes, ma'am."

"Thank you."

Dorothy went downstairs and found Trafalgar standing by the fireplace to examine the books lining her shelves. She was still wearing her jacket, but the parts where the leather was ruined by dragging her through the labyrinth were expertly repaired. She had a bowler hat tucked under one arm and her hair was tied back in a single braid.

"Miss Trafalgar." She turned and Dorothy smiled. "Welcome to my home."

"Thank you. It's nice to be here under less dire circumstances."

Dorothy indicated the sitting area and they moved toward it. "I heard you were out of London for the past few weeks."

"Yes, Leola and I went to the Red Sea to give Adeline a proper farewell. Then I escorted her to Egypt so she could get set up in a new life in Port Said."

"Oh? And what will she be doing?"

"She wanted to work in a museum. She always said the best part of working with me was seeing everything I would bring back, so..." She made a casual gesture. "I had a friend who is curator, and he arranged something for her. I believe she'll be a docent."

Dorothy nodded. "I'm sure she'll be fantastic at it."

Trafalgar smiled and looked toward the window. "I came here today to make you an offer. I want to give you my contacts and the artifacts I've been holding on to for safekeeping."

Dorothy was completely thrown. "You're closing up shop? Whatever for?"

"It was difficult enough in this business when I had Leola and Adeline providing support. Now I'm alone. I can't possibly continue. Working with you has convinced me that you're a worthy successor. If you want, I could arrange for the movers to bring everything this weekend. Or if you would prefer, they could wait until your arm has completely healed."

"No."

Trafalgar said, "This weekend won't work...?"

"No. I don't... I don't want your things."

"Ah. Well, there are others who will be eager. I thought I owed you the right to first refusal." She stood and put on her hat. "I can show myself out. No reason to bother Beatrice."

Dorothy stood as well. "Wait! I don't want your things because it would be a huge folly for you to just... to just walk away. Working with you has proven to me that you're one of the... smartest, most resilient people in this business. You can't simply take down your shingle and walk away."

"I can't do my job alone."

"Then we can be partners."

Trafalgar stared at her. "I beg your pardon?"

Dorothy shrugged and moved toward the fireplace. "I've grown weary of constantly seeking patrons and working with students and weekend adventurers. In a perfect world I would fund my own expeditions, but I can't afford to bankroll ten or twelve people. I could, however, bankroll one other person who was worth ten or twelve people all by herself. We've proven we can work well together, even if we don't always agree."

"You're serious."

Dorothy smiled. "Of course I'm serious. I just think it would be a tremendous waste if you simply packed up and found new work." She furrowed her brow. "Ah. Unless you already had something else arranged, in which case–"

"No, nothing else." Trafalgar was looking at the carpet. "I must say this is entirely unexpected, Lady Boone. I would feel marginally safer if I was around to make sure you stayed out of trouble."

Dorothy laughed. "Whatever lies you need to tell yourself. You could of course keep your own clients, your contacts and collections would be your own. We would simply collaborate when necessary." She walked closer. "The simple truth is that we are both very good at what we do, but we're even better together. We faced the Minotaur together and we won! What can't we do if we put our minds to it?"

Trafalgar raised an eyebrow and nodded slowly. "Necessity often creates strange bedfellows. Very well. Perhaps on a trial basis, we could see if we can refrain from murdering one another for a few weeks."

"There's actually a case you could help me with. I put the client off until I was fully healed, but if you're willing to operate in my stead...?"

Trafalgar considered the offer. "Yes. I would be willing to take a look at it."

"Excellent. Stay here. I'll be right back."

Dorothy went upstairs, wondering what she had just done while finding herself excited at the prospect of working with Trafalgar. She went into her private office where she had left details of the prospective assignment, a job that could take them as far away as Chile if Trafalgar was willing to literally lend her a hand. A half-finished map of Knossos was sitting on the desk awaiting her return, but it would have to wait even longer now.

As she crossed the room she paused and went to the bookshelf where her latest memento was displayed. The piece of the Minotaur's horn that had broken off, which had then served as the means through which she negotiated their truce, had been sanded, waxed, and mounted on a piece of marble. She touched the smooth curve of the horn and remembered the pain and fear she'd been in when she first picked it up.

Strange bedfellows indeed, she thought. She took her notes from the desk and switched off the lamp as she left the office, trotting downstairs to share the information with her new partner.

About the Author

The author is (Geonn Cannon/some guy with a weird name/being lazy). He was born (in Oklahoma/in a cross-fire hurricane/under a bad sign). He has written (way too much/almost nonstop for 15 years/24 novels and counting). He was the first (male/lazy/bald) author to win the GCLS for Best Novel. When he's not writing he's (trying to come up with an interesting bio/actually never not writing/watching TV with various snackfoods). He is the author of (the Underdogs series/the Riley Parra series/the Claire Lance series/an official Stargate SG-1 novel/War & Peace/All but one of the above). This is his twenty-fifth (novel/break with reality/book/child).

You can find the correct answers to this Mad Lib, along with over 200 free stories, on his website geonncannon.com.

www.ingramcontent.com/pod-product-compliance
Lightning Source LLC
Chambersburg PA
CBHW060558310726
48982CB00008B/1166/J
* 9 7 8 1 9 3 8 1 0 8 7 8 5 *